Priscilla Masters

A Fatal Cut

PAN BOOKS

First published 2000 by Macmillan

This edition published 2001 by Pan Books
an imprint of Macmillan Publishers Ltd
25 Eccleston Place, London SW1W 9NF
Basingstoke and Oxford
Associated companies throughout the world
www.macmillan.com

ISBN 0 330 39353 7

1 3 5 7 9 8 6 4 2

A CIP catalogue record for this book is available from
the British Library.

Typeset by Intype London Ltd
Printed and bound in Great Britain by
Mackays of Chatham plc, Chatham, Kent

This book is dedicated to my son and his flatmates, due to qualify as doctors this year. May they never make such mistakes as some of the characters in this book.

I would also like to point out that neither of the surgeons in this book is based on any surgeon I have ever known – least of all my father!

Also to Kerith and Catrin, two truly good friends.

26 June 1987

It was supposed to have been a joke. Something said in jest when they were stiff and sticky from sitting too long in a hot examination room. It had not been meant to be taken seriously.

But he had taken it seriously.

His question. 'What will you do if you fail your A levels?'

Her answer. Flippant. 'Shoot myself. I will. I'll shoot myself. I'll feel such a failure. I won't know what else to do. Not to get in to do the right degree would be worse than death. There wouldn't be any point them offering me another course. There isn't anything else I want to do with my life.'

His eyes, opened as wide as they could go. Fringed by dark, girlish lashes. 'Would you really? I mean, shoot yourself.' A pause. 'How would you get hold of a gun?'

And so easily it had progressed further than she had meant it to. Much further. 'Easy. My uncle's got a gun. He doesn't even keep it locked up like you're supposed to. He's ever so careless.'

His interest, feigned she knew afterwards. 'What does he use it for?'

'Clay pigeons.'

'Does he keep it loaded?'

1

'No. Even he's not that negligent. He keeps the pellets in a special box at the bottom of the gun cabinet.'

So she had spread the noose on the floor in a perfect circle, and watched him step inside it without understanding. Anything.

'Who is your uncle?' Asked without deliberation, casually.

'My mum's brother. Lives a couple of doors away from us.' She echoed his question back at him. 'What would you do, Sam? If you failed? If you didn't get in?'

It was the question that had dominated that whole summer. What they would do if . . .?

'The same.' His answer had been said with enough empty bravado for her to believe she could safely disregard it.

'You wouldn't.' She'd said it scornfully, with derision. 'I bet you wouldn't.'

He'd held out his hand. 'I bet I would.'

She'd stood up then, brushed the newly mown grass from her skirt. 'I don't know why we're having this stupid conversation. We'll both pass.'

But he'd fallen silent and looked away from her, beyond the playing fields of the King Edward the VI School – which hated losers – towards the skyline and the university across the road. Students' Union block, tall clock tower, gracious Victorian buildings, waiting for the successful.

If not earlier, she should have known then.

23 July 1991

The surgeon was sweating. His paper cap and face-mask were already damp. Dewdrops of sweat shone on

his forehead, picked out by the operating lights over-
head.

The theatre sister watched him. She glanced over
his shoulder at the list of names written on the whiteboard, all cases set for this afternoon. He *couldn't* be
ill. There were six more patients lined up, the next
probably already in the anaesthetic room, nervously
preparing to sink into oblivion. The others would even
now be having their pre-med on the ward. The operations *must* go on. But not without the surgeon.

He was still sweating.

Opposite, and to his left, stood the registrar, new the
week before. A Greek. In his luminous eyes she saw he
had noted the surgeon's condition and she read his
own misgivings: that he wouldn't be able to handle the
remaining cases. Not alone. She guessed – whatever his
references said – that he'd performed only minor solo
ops before moving to England. He didn't have the skill
of the operating consultant.

She took another surreptitious look at the surgeon.
Sweat was trickling towards his eye. Unable to wipe it
himself he was blinking rapidly, his gaze drifting away
from the open wound. She sensed it was a struggle
for him to concentrate on the operation. He was even
having difficulty holding the scalpel handle accurately.
Instead of holding it delicately, like a fine fountain
pen, he was grasping it in his hand like a ham-fisted
amateur, his face flushed with effort. The theatre
sister glanced round for some explanation. Maybe the
problem was the heating. It was always kept warm in
here in deference to the still figure on the operating
table. She called the theatre porter across and asked
him to turn the air-conditioning dial down by three

degrees. Then, using a pair of long, angled forceps, she dropped a sterile gauze swab into the student-nurse's hand and asked her to wipe the sweat from the surgeon's brow.

He couldn't do it himself without contaminating his gloves. And that would mean abandoning the entire operation and having to rescrub, while the patient waited and bled.

Silently the student nurse moved behind the green-gowned figure and wiped the sweat away with the gauze. The surgeon should have been grateful for this courtesy. Normally he would have been.

But today the act seemed to annoy him. He half turned from his patient and snarled at the nurse, so violently that she dropped the swab onto the sterile green towels. There was a horrified silence, broken only by the rhythmic rise and fall of the ventilator. Everyone knew. The swab, touched by the nurse's ungloved hands, was contaminated. And now the green towels were too. And the green towels surrounded the gaping open wound; flesh unprotected by skin. True, only a hernia repair but nevertheless a deep slice through the skin, muscle and blood vessels of a living person. A living person now exposed to infection through the clumsiness of a member of staff. The silence emanating from the surgeon was both tense and angry. Breathing heavily, his hands remained poised a few inches above the 'dirty' swab as though the air around it was also infected.

The theatre sister rescued the situation. Muttering a swift, 'Sorry, sir,' she placed a spare pair of artery forceps into the nurse's shaking hand so she could retrieve the gauze swab without crossing the invisible barrier of sterility. Then, using another pair of long artery forceps, she draped a fresh green towel across the suspect patch before shooting the unfortunate nurse a comrade's look of sympathy. They'd all gone through the same experience at least once before. A tetchy surgeon, a hot day, a stuffy theatre, complicated surgery.

Only this was none of those things. 'Pinky' Sutcliffe had a reputation throughout the hospital for being calm and even tempered, a cool professional who tended to limit his conversation to demands for instruments and spasmodic explanations to teach the medical students. A snarl from him was out of character. For him to sweat he must be hot – or ill. The theatre sister frowned. The case on the table was not complicated, bread and butter work in a healthy subject. So far.

The entire theatre suddenly fell quiet as though all the staff sensed something was not quite right. For a couple of seconds even the ventilator seemed to be holding its breath. Over her mask the sister's black eyes scanned the operating room, trying to hunt down the cause of the surgeon's poor humour. Her gaze rested first on the registrar. An incompetent import, but with a steady hand for holding retractors. No more was demanded of him. The problem was not here. She glanced across the room at the two medical students. Fourth years. One a plump male, the other a small female. Both were dressed appropriately in theatre greens and white leather clogs, and that was as far as their involvement in the proceedings went. They were leaning against the far wall, sharing some private joke. Mentally she tut-tutted. A perfect chance to study the anatomy of the rectus sheath and they were more interested in the gossip of the day. She watched them giggling, for a fleeting second almost envious of their lack of responsibility in the proceedings. She took in the male student's arm lightly resting round the girl's shoulders. *They* seemed to have no worries. Her eyes moved back to check the surgeon's face and her alarm intensified. He was staring down into the wound as though struggling to focus. Oblivious to the medical students. His distress was nothing to do with them.

She shifted her attention to her side. A thin, shy figure in white cotton, hands subserviently tucked behind his back – like a member of the royal family – or someone who did not know quite what to do with them. The theatre porter. Quiet and unobtrusive as a ghost. Earnest, new, inoffensive. However seriously the porter took his job no one really took much notice of him, least of all the surgeon. She smiled at the thought that the theatre porter could possibly be responsible for Pinky Sutcliffe's uncharacteristic behaviour. She was still smiling as her eyes rested speculatively on Bill Amison. Tall, muscular, blond, the anaesthetist was, as usual, struggling with *The Times* crossword, paying the patient the very minimum of attention. He looked up for an instant and caught her gaze. She gave him a broad wink which he returned before glancing mean-ingfully across at the surgeon. His message was clear, what's up with him today?

She shrugged an 'I don't know' and continued pon-dering. But there was only one more person in the theatre. The unfortunate student nurse who had dropped the swab and whose face was still flushed with embarrassment. As flushed as . . . her eyes swivelled back to the surgeon with alarm. As flushed as the surgeon.

The theatre sister continued handing him the instruments but her unease mounted. She was mechanically going through the motions of something so routine she hardly needed to think about it: assisting at a hernia repair; automatically passing instruments – sutures, scissors and forceps – most of the time without the surgeon even needing to ask for them. Something she did five days a week. But not like this.

Today something was very wrong. He was fumbling, awkwardly holding instruments that were as familiar to him as his own fingers as though they were foreign. He kept staring at them as though he had never seen them before. Twice he grabbed hold of forceps by the blades. Once he requested a stitch when there was nothing to stitch. She handed it to him and watched him drop it in confusion. As she retrieved it she peered at his face and saw someone unfamiliar to her.

It was a few moments more before she knew exactly why she could not relax. It wasn't just his clumsy hold of surgical instruments. There was a fine tremor in his hand which was making him dangerously inaccurate. Hardly noticable if you only watched the fingers. But when you studied the pointed end of the scalpel blade you could see it vibrate like a tuning fork which has been struck against a hard surface. Dumbly she watched the surgeon's fingers, pale and dehumanized, encased in sterile latex as they fumbled the scalpel through bleeding tissue. The blade, meant to peel away a band of muscle, hacking through it instead, like a butcher.

Truly alarmed now she looked again at the

surgeon's face, at his two visible features, blank eyes
and furrowed forehead. His nose and mouth were
shrouded by the paper mask, which was saturated with
his sweat. The sister's discomfort turned to panic. She
didn't know what to do. Pinky Sutcliffe was a respected
senior surgeon; she was only a junior theatre sister. She
was aware that her primary responsibility was to her
patient, the man who lay beneath all their hands,
unconscious of the drama being played out above
him. So she stood between her two obligations, her
professional duty and the invisible hierarchy that per-
meated the medical profession. It was not done to
question the competence of a senior surgeon.

Once again she cast a desperate glance at Bill
Amison. He had stopped struggling with the crossword.
The paper lay discarded on the floor and he was
holding the respirator tube hard against the patient's
mouth, his other hand checking the radial pulse. As
she watched he registered the patient's blood pressure
before looking straight at her.

They were both watching the surgeon now. His
head was swaying, his eyes glazed unaware. He was
ill. He *must* be ill. And he was getting worse. Sutcliffe
glanced up. He seemed unable to focus on her. Concern
forced her to say, 'Sir, are you all right to carry on?'

The surgeon giggled.

Both medical students stared across at him, startled.
The student nurse opened her mouth to speak, met the
sister's warning glance and shut it again. The Greek
registrar picked up a large artery clamp and held it like
a defensive weapon, ready – if needed. Bill Amison
looked at the cardiorator and pressed his fingers even
harder against the radial pulse. He muttered some-

thing. No one knew what, but no one asked him to repeat the words. The theatre porter backed against the wall, as though he wanted to disassociate himself from the proceedings. They all watched as the scalpel slipped and severed a minor blood vessel. The theatre sister mopped the oozing blood away. The registrar touched it with the diathermy. There was an acrid scent of scorching flesh. Blue smoke hung over the body and turned hazy under the operating lights.

The bleeding stopped. The registrar used a swab on some sponge forceps to mop around the wound.

Bill Amison checked the patient's blood pressure yet again and speeded up the IV drip. He sat, upright on his stool at the patient's head. The crossword was forgotten. They were all tense. All except the patient. Oblivious to it all.

The surgeon giggled again, blood smearing the forefinger of his glove. He moved the finger in front of his eyes and gazed at it, fascinated.

The theatre sister peered into the abdominal cavity with a mounting sense of alarm. Less than a centimetre away from the surgeon's blade pulsated the femoral artery, a major blood supply to the lower part of the body. She watched the rhythmic beat with a feeling of absolute dread. As the scalpel descended towards it she involuntarily closed her eyes.

Chapter One

They took the short cut which led them towards the
back of Queen's Medical School, through an ever-open
fire door and straight into the side entrance of the
lecture theatre. If you were late, and lucky, you could
slide into your seat halfway through and no one would
notice your arrival, including the lecturer, because of
curtains draped loosely at the side of the seats. Easy
then to shuffle up one – or two – or three. The four
flatmates often used the side door to give them a way in
for a lecture almost missed. Another party, another late
night, another skinful. But, late and hasty though they
were, a block of colour drew them away from their
usual hurried path, towards a patch of waste ground,
and the bottom of a shallow ditch.

Something yellow. A plastic bag.

Six months into their clinical years they were
already aware that objects in hospitals are colour coded.
Reds and yellows stood for danger; radiation; contami-
nation. Yellow plastic bags were used to contain clinical
waste, a fact that was printed in large black letters on
both sides of them. They were meant to be heaped
straight away into the hospital incinerator – not left out
here in the open. The object of their attention was a
double-sized clinical waste bag. Two taped together.

Body-long, bright as a canary, particularly on this dull, late November day when earth, sky and hospital all seemed to blend into the uniform grey of 1930's concrete. Shapes were blunt and ill-defined, outlines blurred in damp, insubstantial fog, indeterminate and shadowy. Not this shape though.

Medical students are curious creatures. Late as they were for the third lecture of the day all four took a few steps forward to peer at the bright parcel in its gaudy, plastic shroud. Tom stretched out a tentative hand.

'I think it's a stiff,' he said incredulously.

Their eyes scanned the patch of scrub, and returned to the bright plastic. And yet, because bodies are not an unusual object on a hospital site they stood around and discussed it.

Michael was the joker. 'I suppose,' he said, laughing uneasily, 'that someone's committed a murder and wants the hospital porters to dispose of the body for them. In the incinerator.' As though the joke had been made by a consultant on a ward round, the other three gave a polite, forced chuckle.

'Or a surgeon made a bodge of an operation, and just had to dispose of the evidence.' This was Jake's contribution.

Used to laughing at the macabre they stood and joked with something like bravado. It was Ben who brought them to heel. 'I think,' he said seriously, 'that we'd better let someone know.' His three friends nodded in agreement. All four of them knew the implications. They wouldn't be at lectures for the rest of the day.

*

Dr Karys Harper had taken the morning off after a night on call and was padding round the flat in a white, towelling dressing gown, yawning, brushing her hair out of her eyes and taking long sips from her mug of black coffee. Following on-call duties there usually was a certain amount of weariness. When the telephone rang she muttered a soft curse. Always uncomfortably aware that a summons could arrive at any minute, it didn't even occur to her that it might be a social call. No friend would expect her to be at home at eleven o'clock on a weekday morning.

She took the call calmly, scribbling down the directions on a pad she kept near the telephone. By the time she had showered and pulled on some trousers and a thick sweater she had shaken off the yawns and tiredness, but she felt a heaviness that was never there when she was completely off-duty. She blamed it on an awareness of impending responsibility. A readiness for action.

She drove to the scene in her black Mercedes convertible, accelerating along the Bristol Road, using the bus lane more than once to undertake drivers turning right. She couldn't justify her driving with the usual doctor's excuse – that she might save a life with the few minutes bought – she merely enjoyed the speed, for its own sake. She found the site easily. The area was familiar to her, no more than a few hundred yards away from her own slicing ground, the hospital mortuary. She turned into Edgbaston Park Road, left into Metchley Lane, and parked just beyond a crowd of rapidly gathering voyeurs clustered round a couple of police cars. It was strange how flashing blue police lights drew the spectators. She did her best to ignore the ripple of excitement that followed her. Having noticed her black scene-of-crime bag someone was helpfully informing the others who she was. She wasn't ready to talk to anyone, yet. Not before she knew the facts.

She kept her gaze on the ground, ducked beneath the police tape and slid down the short bank towards the white canopy erected over the corpse. There were two figures mounting guard over the body, a Detective Inspector in his thirties, casually dressed, slim with fair hair thinning on top, and a stout Detective Sergeant. Karys greeted both of them with a smile. They were old acquaintances.

She set her bag down by the side of the body. 'New experience for me, this.'

Sensing what was coming, the two police officers shifted uncomfortably. They were familiar with Karys's strange sense of humour.

She indicated the yellow plastic bag with its descriptive black lettering along the side, CLINICAL WASTE. 'Having the corpse gift wrapped and labelled.'

There was a strained smile in return from DS Fielding. DI Forrest remained stony faced. Karys shrugged and opened her bag. 'When was the body discovered?'

'About an hour ago. By some medical students.'

She looked up. 'Skipping lectures?'

Forrest shrugged. 'Let the university sort that bit out. We've got enough to worry about.'

'Hmm.' She slipped on a pair of examining gloves before picking out a hunting knife, sharp with a serrated edge used to sever ties or nooses, cut bonds, preserve knots. 'Any objections, Inspector Forrest?'

'No.'

13

'You've checked for prints then?'

His face was already tinged with a sickly green. 'I don't know why we bother. They all use gloves these days.'

'Right then. Here goes.'

She made a slit in the thick, yellow PVC and all three peered in. Inside was a thin, bony man, lying on his back with a bloated, dead-fish face, his eyes bulging, arms folded across his chest, chin dropped down. He wore a blue-checked open-necked shirt and black ankle socks. No shoes. Otherwise he was naked – apart from a wristwatch and a tie, knotted but not tidily arranged around the collar. It had been pulled lethally tight around the neck.

Karys stared at the victim for a few moments to absorb as much detail as she could. She wanted to forget nothing. When she had imprinted the picture on her mind she allowed herself to touch him. He felt cold. Ice cold. She tried to move his arms. They were stiff. Rigor mortis was still present. She peered closer. There was no discernible bruising but some lividity on his lower buttocks, shoulders and heels. Karys moved the tie to reveal a line of bruising, noticing it was a 'fun' tie sporting the Disney characters Mickey and Minnie Mouse – waltzing by the look of things. The only other visible injury was a narrow line of congealed blood in his right groin. Karys studied it closely before touching it with her gloved index finger. It was a neat, regular wound, quite straight and about four inches long. And it had been clumsily drawn together with five untidy silk sutures, their ends long enough to prickle her fingers. Karys pondered over the wound, trying to piece together the sequence of events.

14

When she looked up she could see that both the DI and the DS were staring at the same scar. Neither of them spoke. They were waiting for her.

'Interesting,' she said.

'Yeah,' they chorused.

'And what exactly do you think, Inspector Forrest?'

'Well, it looks as if he's had an operation.'

'Possibly.'

'What else could it be?'

'I don't know,' she said. 'Maybe it'll all come clear during the PM.' Her gaze went over and beyond the DI's shoulder to the huge, grey hospital looming against the sky. 'Are there any reports of missing patients?'

'Not so far.'

'Hmm,' she said again. Her attention returned to the groin wound. Then she palpated the face, tested the knees for depth of rigor mortis and used a rectal thermometer to gain a core-body temperature. 12°C. Her thoughts galloped through the textbook graph. He'd been dead for more than twelve hours. Could be as long as twenty-four. A quick glance at her watch. Eleven forty-five a.m. He'd died sometime yesterday afternoon to evening and the body presumably dumped under cover of darkness. Not this morning. The hospital site was too busy for the killer to have risked dumping a body in daylight. Knowing DI Forrest would press her for a more precise time of death she tried to work it out. The victim was a thin man, only partly clothed, so he would have lost body heat relatively quickly, add to that the fact that it was a chilly, damp day and the plastic would have formed poor insulation.

Forrest must have guessed what she was thinking about. 'Eight degrees centigrade,' he supplied gruffly.

She smiled her thanks.

His temperature had almost reached that of his surroundings, so probably the man had died sometime yesterday afternoon, late-ish. This was all straightforward textbook stuff. But her mind was working furiously to try to piece together the sequence of events. What *could* have led to this man being strangled, then dumped on the hospital site? A recent operation? A patient who had wandered away from the ward? Certainly he had had the recent attentions of a medic blessed with only tolerable competence. The stitches weren't *that* neat. And why had he been wrapped in a clinical waste bag? It was puzzling. Incredible.

She was curious to know what other findings would be uncovered at the post-mortem.

While Karys rang the coroner from her carphone, Forrest was already initiating primary investigations. By that afternoon the corpse was shelled of its PVC wrap and lay naked on the mortuary slab. More importantly, he was no longer anonymous. He had an identity and personal details. The pale Caucasian man was Colin Wilson, aged thirty-five, coincidentally the same age as DI David Forrest himself. They had an address for him too: 8, Jasmine Place, Erdington. Colin Wilson had had a wife, named Laura, and a ten-month-old daughter named Heather. He was now much more than a murder victim to the investigating team, he was a family man.

As soon as Karys entered the PM room she noted the tension in the waiting team of police which comprised Forrest, DS Fielding and a couple of SOCOs. As was her habit, she ignored them and busied herself with observing the primary details of Colin Wilson's body. Thin and bony; undernourished rather than simply slim.

Like most pathologists, Karys had her own unique way of conducting a post-mortem. A mixture of traditional methods plus personal foibles. Those who had worked with her before knew the drill inside out; she would frown all the time she tied the bows at the back of her surgical gown; she would push her heavy glasses hard up her nose as though daring them to slip once her hands were sheathed inside the surgical gloves. Those gloves which often tore because she pulled them on too hard, as she frequently did in cases of suspected murder. She had once confessed to Paget, the mortuary attendant, in an unprecedented burst of candour, that murder upset her more than it should a pathologist. It had been a frank apology for her weakness. She knew that murder should not upset her at all, it should not penetrate her shell. That shell was her protection against emotional involvement in the case. It was her job to be a scientific observer, detached, impartial and above all, accurate. That was the theory.

Those who knew her well were perfectly aware of her involvement with murder cases.

Paget stood by silently. He had been embarrassed by her admission and had done little more than grunt. But he had never forgotten her confession. The memory of her disclosure returned today as he watched her psych herself up to deal with the case, standing at the foot of the mortuary slab with her gloved hands clasped together, as though praying. He remembered something else she had said at the same time, in the same burst of candour – that she felt she should spend this silent time communing with victims of violence because it helped her to piece together the full sequence of events, each blow, which, in its turn, had finally led to the victim's death. The evidence would all be there, waiting for her in the tissues, to be laid bare by her knife. And it was this sequence of blows, of defensive injuries and trauma, that would give her the truest of clues into the killer's mind. She must not miss things. She owed it to her 'patients' to glean every cell of evidence a corpse could possibly yield and help point the finger. Towards innocence. Towards guilt. Towards accident. Towards manslaughter. Towards murder. Even, she believed, occasionally, towards the murderer.

At last, to the relief of the waiting police officers, she sucked in a long, deep breath, as though preparing to dive from a high board. She unclasped her hands and finally broke the silence to begin a superficial examination of the head and the back of the neck, talking to the waiting police officers as well as into a small dictaphone.

'Cause of death', she began, 'almost certainly strangulation. With this tie.' She severed the dark blue tie with its bright Disney motif and passed it to the Scene of Crimes Officer. Underneath, the livid red line stretched almost all the way around the neck. She turned the head to the side and fingered a swelling at the nape the size and colour of a Victoria plum. 'I think this probably happened first.' She paused, then continued decisively, 'Yes. That's it. He was stunned first.'

Forrest looked up. 'Any idea what with?'

'A blunt instrument. Could have been a baseball bat. Something like that. Hard and blunt. Wielded with some force. As for this . . .' She jabbed her finger at the neat, straight wound in the corpse's groin. 'I'm intrigued.' She addressed DS Fielding. 'You're sure his wife said he *hadn't* recently been an in-patient for an operation on his groin, for example the repair of a hernia?'

'No. He'd been to work today as normal. She said he hadn't had an operation since he had his tonsils out when he was a kid.'

Karys couldn't resist another prod at gallows humour. 'Well no one got his tonsils out through this wound.'

A few of the waiting officers, unused to her medical jokes, shifted uncomfortably.

'And if he hasn't had recent surgery I can only think he must have cut himself accidentally during the course of his work. What does he do?'

Again, it was the stout DS who answered. 'He was a plumber, Doctor.'

'Unlikely, then, that he gave himself this. But possible. Have you started enquiries at hospital A&E departments? The wound looks recent.' Forrest shook his head and she continued, 'Well somebody must have put these sutures in.' She bent over to peer even closer at the wound. 'They aren't very neat. Maybe a medical student. Or a GP. They don't get a lot of practice at suturing.'

David Forrest gave a shrug. 'We did wonder,' he ventured, 'if it was an attempted suicide?'

Karys gave a low, considering sigh. 'It's possible,' she said. 'He could have self-inflicted the groin injury although I've *never* heard of a suicide using the femoral artery to bleed himself to death. But he didn't sew

19

himself up, did he? And he definitely didn't inflict his own head injury – from behind – or strangle himself with the tie, or wrap himself up in a clinical waste bag, or dump his own body on the hospital site. No. Something must have happened. Some very peculiar events. But goodness knows what they were.'

Unabashed, Forrest tried again. 'Then what about this scenario?' He glanced helplessly at DS Caroline Fielding, appealing for back-up. 'I mean, people do slash their wrists. He could have done *that*,' his eyes lingered on the groin wound, 'as a variation. And then a friend, maybe a doctor or a nurse or someone with a bit of medical training, tried to save his life by sewing him up.' Again an apologetic, tight laugh and a glance around the room for support. 'And then when that didn't work the friend panicked, killed him and ended up dumping the body at the hospital. It's just an idea.' He ended limply.

'And what about the blow to the back of Wilson's head?'

Forrest started chewing his lip. 'Anaesthetic?' he ventured lamely.

'It could have happened that way, I suppose,' Karys said kindly as her gloved fingers probed the sutures again. 'All I can tell you at this stage with certainty is that Colin Wilson was murdered. He didn't die from natural causes. And the only other comment I can make, for all that it'll help you, is that the wound is in exactly the position where you'd cut if you wanted to repair an inguinal hernia.'

David Forrest spoke again. 'You don't think it was a doctor, or someone from the hospital, do you? That this is botched surgery and that the head injury was caused by his falling off the operating table?'

Through Karys's glasses her grey eyes looked enormous. 'Inspector Forrest,' she said gravely. 'What *are* you suggesting? That one of our surgeons is making such a mess of his work he's reduced to dumping the body of his patient in clinical waste bags on a patch of ground at the back of the hospital?'

Forrest looked ill at ease. 'Well you did say . . .'

Karys fingered the sutures once more. 'I have asked for full toxicology studies on the serum samples but I don't really think that's the answer,' she said quietly.

But the words 'botched surgery' had conjured uncomfortable visions in front of her eyes. No dreams this time. Reality. Cruel, stark reality. For the first time in months she suffered the familiar tight chest, rapid over-breathing, nausea.

Her eyes moved across to the police specimen bag. Plumbers didn't normally wear ties to work. Wilson's shirt was blue denim, casual wear. She knew that the tie was another part of the killer's debris, his personal signature, as individual as handwriting. And as handwriting scrawled a person's character across a blank page so the killer had autographed his corpse with his own warped joke. Karys stood very still, chilled at the sudden insight she had gained into the killer's mind.

It took a movement from David Forrest at her side to force her back to the job. She shook herself and concentrated again on the surgical part of the postmortem, first by standing back while the police photographer shot his pictures from all angles, until even Inspector Forrest's exacting standards had been met.

Then it was time to start, beginning with the head.

They always started there; it was, as often as not, the source of fatal injury and she worked deftly, making decisive comments on her tape recorder as she proceeded. Head injury not fatal. She continued in greater detail. She might be glad of it during question time at the inquest. Not conceivably fatal, but enough to stun. Cause of death – she fingered the livid line, touched the petechial haemorrhages above the bulging eyes – strangulation. No doubt about it. Quick, simple. Equipment ready to hand, a cheap, funny tie, looped beneath the chin, pulled tightly from behind. Clear marks around the ears as the victim had dropped and the tie had been pulled upwards. A fractured hyoid. Then on to the thorax and finally the abdomen. But throughout the entire procedure her eyes kept straying down to the victim's groin as she set herself the inevitable question. What had been the *exact* sequence of events?

She was in for a surprise. Naturally she had assumed the groin injury had been inflicted before death, but as she worked she began to realize that the evidence was pointing in a different direction. The groin wound had been made *after* death. The evidence was all too clear. Indisputable. There was little to no tissue reaction round the suture line, virtually no bleeding at all into the surrounding cells. The edges of the wound showed no sign of even early union. As she worked she became even more convinced: *dead* pieces of skin had been drawn together by the black silk. The murderer had killed his victim before he had attempted surgery. So if not real surgery or the union of a traumatic cut, what had been the *point* of the wound? Quickly she ran through one of her many forensic psychiatry lectures. Mutilation usually indicated a sadistic killer, some gratification had to have been gained from witnessing the victim's suffering, and it was usually mixed with sexual perversion. But there had been no sexual interference at all. She had examined Wilson's body very carefully. He had not been sexually assaulted, and he would have felt no pain from the mutilation. He had already been dead. A sadist could have derived no pleasure from his act. So why had the wound been inflicted? She glanced across the mortuary table at David Forrest, knowing he would be able to read the puzzlement on her face. 'You can forget about A&E departments,' she said very quietly, hearing a quiver of shock in her voice, 'and GPs. They don't suture corpses.'

'What?' The watching police officers stiffened.

'Wilson was already dead when this was done. I should know,' she added, 'I've reopened enough recent suture lines on people who have died on the operating table to know the difference between injuries inflicted pre- and post-mortem. I'm sure of my facts, Inspector.'

David Forrest kept his eyes on her but there was nothing more she could add. So she bent over the corpse again to search for an explanation. By the time she had removed the six stitches and probed the wound itself she was no nearer an answer. The post-mortem had merely compounded the questions, made them more confused. What was more, the surgery had been only skin deep. Nothing but a token slash, superficial mimicry of a surgeon's work. There was one curious fact that might or might not be relevant. Although the incision had not been deep it had severed the femoral artery. Had the victim not already been dead – or as good as – he would have bled to death quickly with this one, sure incision.

Still puzzled she mopped the sponge around the back of the abdomen and squeezed the blood out into the sink. No more or less bleeding than normal and that further underlined her conclusion that strangulation had been the cause of death. She knew at some point she would be standing up and stating this in a court of law, and that her opinion would be challenged. It didn't bother her. She knew she was right. But her questions were still unanswered.

She pressed her lips together and left the table to study the whiteboard and reappraise what she knew – her own observations plus the facts the police had fed her. At the top of the board, printed in Paget's irregular block capitals, was Wilson's name, gleaned from a wallet found buttoned into his shirt pocket, as though the killer had wanted his victim identified quickly. DS Caroline Fielding had filled her in on the relevant details: Wilson had been a jobbing plumber who had lived, apparently blamelessly, with his wife and baby daughter in a Victorian terraced house in Erdington, four miles from the hospital. Fielding had given Karys a graphic description of her visit to the house. When she had knocked on the door it had been flung open by a frantic woman with a baby on her hip who had said, 'Colin—' before she had seen who it was. Then, 'car accident', before Caroline had had a chance to say anything else. Seconds later Wilson's wife had been staring at her, disbelieving.

But Caroline Fielding had been sent to see Wilson's widow for another reason, to tease out of Laura Wilson some important facts as a starting point for their investigations. Laura Wilson had last seen her husband on Monday morning when he had set off to fit an en suite bathroom. When he had failed to return that night she had been worried. Yes, of course she had been worried. But she had imagined he had been delayed somehow. She had rung the customer. Colin had been called away to repair a leak and had failed to return. They weren't too impressed. But as a plumber's wife she knew leaks could be tricky things, and he could not abandon a customer with such a problem. There would be a rational explanation. And then she had fallen asleep on the sofa. When she woke her husband had still not returned.

But the wife's story did not help Karys. She moved away from the board to stare again at the corpse on the slab. She gave a long sigh, peeled her gloves off and left the post-mortem room without adding anything.

Forrest followed her into her office. 'Well?'

She met his eyes with a tired frustration. 'Well what?'

'Come on, Karys.' He was always hesitant about using her first name. Over the years of dealing with her she had never once encouraged any sort of personal friendship. At first he had recognized, then respected her distance, and the fact that she seemed to need to hide behind barriers. Lately he had found them an irritant, a hindrance even. 'Help me.'

'What do you expect from me?' She ran her fingers through her lank hair. 'I'm just a pathologist. I've told you everything I can about Colin Wilson's death. Someone bopped our little plumber on the head. While he was – at the very least – unconscious, probably stunned and confused, it wasn't a very bad head injury, they strangled him.'

'Ye-e-es?'

'And then, for some completely unknown and incomprehensible reason, either the murderer or someone else slashed his groin and then stitched him up. Those, Inspector Forrest, are the facts.'

Uninvited, he sat down opposite her and locked his blue eyes onto hers. The time had come for him to break down some of those barriers. They *must* work together, without this uncomfortable distance. 'I know you've given me all the *facts*,' he said patiently. 'What I'm asking for are *ideas*. Tell me what's in your head. Tell me what you *think*, Karys.'

Her lips tightened at the second use of her first name. 'Inspector Forrest,' she said very formally, 'I am a pathologist. I deal in the evidence of the tissues. That's my job. I might try to understand what's happened, but in this case I might lead you horribly astray because I don't really know. At the PM I tried to reconstruct the events. At first I thought you might be right.' She smiled. 'Even the falling-off-the-operating-table theory. But I couldn't work out any scenario that fitted all the forensic evidence. I just couldn't. It's far too weird,' she finished helplessly.

Forrest cleared his throat. How many cases had they worked on together? Sixteen? Seventeen? And she couldn't bring herself to call him David? Once he would neither have noticed nor have cared. Now he did both. And it annoyed him. He stood up.

She tried to mollify him. 'Maybe what you could do with is a forensic psychiatrist. It's their job to understand the warped and sick mind.'

Almost at the door Forrest turned. 'And you believe that's what this is the result of? A warped and sick mind?'

She didn't even bother to answer. *It had to be.*

Forrest ploughed on, still attempting to draw her out. 'Any idea what weapon was used?'

Karys shook her head. 'As I said, maybe a baseball bat, an iron bar. Something like that to the back of the head. And you saw the tie for yourself.' She knew she was deliberately not answering his question.

'And . . .?' He was suddenly understandably squeamish. 'And the, umm, the other wound?'

Karys took her glasses off to rub her tired eyes. 'He was a plumber,' she said. 'A Stanley knife is sharp, isn't it?'

But the vision that appeared in front of her eyes was provoked not by Colin Wilson's profession but by the suggestion of the person who had drawn together the edges of the wound. 'Or a scalpel,' she said in a voice not much more distinct than a whisper. 'He could have used a scalpel. Like a . . .' She suddenly found she couldn't go on. She felt sickened by it all.

But the concept of a 'surgeon' had been born.

Chapter Two

David Forrest had spent hours puzzling over Colin Wilson's murder. Day and night it lodged in his mind. But a week later he was still no nearer to understanding the sequence of events. Everything about the case baffled him: from the seemingly motiveless killing itself, through the post-mortem mutilation and the pointless suturing, the wrapping of the body in a hospital disposal sack and the dumping of the corpse on the hospital site itself. The murder seemed inexplicable.

In the early hours of Tuesday morning after the discovery of Wilson's body he had a particularly vicious nightmare. Wilson's corpse was central to the dream, floating in front of his eyes, a white shape that dangled in a black void, bleached skin stretched taut over the bones – ribs, hips, knees, legs, all clearly marked as though for an anatomy class. But it was the groin wound that held his attention, the black slash contrasting with the whiteness of the skin, the line constantly changing shape, as though it was a mouth – speaking. In front of Forrest's horrified gaze the thin line curved upwards in a mocking grin. Forrest woke up, sweating. It was time to get up.

He had been assigned a large and efficient team of

workers headed by DS Rupert Shaw and DS Caroline Fielding. Fielding he was happy with. Plump, sensible, married to a copper, she was above all dependable, a characteristic Forrest liked in his colleagues. But DS Rupert Shaw was a different matter. Since Shaw had joined the local force eighteen months ago Forrest had made no secret of his dislike for him. Young, too intelligent for his own good, fast-tracking through the ranks at a rate of knots after gaining a degree in sports science and business studies. What the hell did either of *them* have to do with being a good copper? It didn't help that Shaw was black-haired, blue-eyed and six foot three, with looks maidens would willingly be deflowered for. Shaw had enough attributes to make many men resent him and Forrest was no exception. He could feel the sourness well up every time the young DS bounced in with his bright ideas.

Shaw and Fielding had been given two different approaches to the case. Shaw had been dispatched, with a team of junior officers, to dig around the hospital, speak to staff, patients, the medical students and patients' visitors. DS Fielding, on the other hand, had spent the last few days interviewing Wilson's family, neighbours, friends, anyone who might conceivably have some clue as to why Wilson had been murdered. So far, neither investigation had unearthed anything.

As Forrest's car crawled along the Bristol Road towards the police station in Edgbaston he ran over the statements in his mind. They told him nothing. Like many statements they were crammed with irrelevant detail. Once they had weeded out irrelevancies there was nothing left – nothing of substance, nothing that seemed to have any bearing on the case.

He parked his car in the closest vacant spot to the front door. Shaw was ready for him inside his office and handed him the medical students' statements.

'The first thing any of them knew about a murder was finding the body. I'd stake my reputation on that.'

Forrest narrowed his eyes. 'Well, *someone* at that bloody hospital must know something. The plastic bags almost certainly came from there, and the sutures. Someone slashed at Wilson's groin. And Doctor Harper thinks the cut *could* have been done with a scalpel. So get talking.'

'Who to?'

Forrest eyed the young detective with hostility. 'How about the hospital manager?'

Shaw shrugged. 'If you think . . .'

'I do.'

Shaw slammed the incident-room door behind him.

It took Forrest a couple of minutes to calm down. Shaw invariably had this effect on him: made him angry, resentful, doubtful that his own ideas were valid. He always had the sneaking suspicion that, with his sharp intelligence, Shaw could handle a case better himself. That was why he never invited comment from him. Never asked him what he thought. What *his* opinion was. Dammit. Shaw made him feel inferior. Why hadn't he been assigned Leven, or Tideswell, or any one of the other competent members of the team?

It took him another five minutes to forget Shaw and start thinking again about the person who had strangled Wilson only to perform mock surgery on him.

He fished a piece of paper out of the drawer. At the top he wrote the headings to two columns: *Who? Why?*

As always, he started with family. The trouble was

he couldn't think of a why. According to DS Fielding, Wilson had been a happily married man and she had been insistent that there was nothing of the flirt about Laura Wilson. Forrest stared into space. Not like his wife, Maggie. Everyone had known what she was. Everyone except him. With his experience maybe he should check Laura Wilson out himself.

So who else?

A member or ex-member of the hospital staff? But there again the why was a little tricky. A grudge against the hospital rather than against Wilson personally? Was the dumping of the body on the hospital site meant to discredit its public image? Why would someone do that? Forrest scratched the top of his head. He couldn't think of a reason, not for murder. Besides, balanced against this hypothesis was the fact that the hospital ran rigorous checks on all their staff. The merest hint of mental instability and they would not employ.

Forrest dropped his chin into his hand and stared at the piece of paper.

Who else? A member of the public? The trouble again was the why. Some grudge against the hospital? Forrest made a face. Plenty of people might bear a grudge against a hospital. Bereaved relatives, sacked employees, people left maimed or disabled by their brush with the health service. He found this hard to swallow. People would have options open to them other than murder.

His thoughts began to turn to other possibilities. Had Wilson's killer watched an operation, witnessed suturing, and decided to mimic the procedure? He must have done at some time to have displayed even that amount of skill. There were plenty of television programmes that showed surgery in graphic detail. However, at some point the killer had stepped away from the world of the television documentary towards reality. And he must have prepared by acquiring the tools of his chosen trade. The instruments must have come from somewhere.

It *must* be someone connected with the hospital.

Forrest was not the only one whose thoughts seemed glued to Wilson's murder. The work of the 'surgeon' had had its effect on Karys too. The day after the PM on Colin Wilson she had found herself staring out of the window in her flat, paralysed by unwelcome memories. Memories she had managed to convince herself had been buried so deep they could *never* be unearthed. It was a shock to find they had only had a handful of sand scattered over them, that it had taken the softest of winds to blow the grains away and leave them raw and exposed. For the second time in her life she was weighed down with a need to confess. Had she been a Catholic she could have off-loaded her guilt onto a priest and then gained absolution followed, maybe, by permanent peace of mind.

But not being a Catholic she had no priest to turn to. She had told Tonya, of course, soon after they had first met.

Tonya had listened with her head on one side and tried to soothe her. 'Karys, it wasn't your fault. It was just something that went wrong. An accident.'

But Tonya had not understood. And she had been forced to tell her more: that she believed it had been no accident; that it had been designed. Cleverly. And she had been the trigger, again, by a careless joke, a flippant statement. Again.

She had watched as Tonya pulled a face of disbelief, incredulity, then of disgust, 'Drop it, Karys. Just drop it.' She had advised sharply. 'It was a long time ago. Put it right out of your mind. Get on with living, your career. The damage is done, it's forgotten. I bet no one even thinks about it any more.'

How could Tonya be so wrong? She had thought about it frequently. And, since she had dissected Colin Wilson's body, constantly.

It had taken a few more days before Karys felt prepared to assemble her thoughts and analyse them during a quiet period at the mortuary. Why had the murder of Colin Wilson evoked such uncomfortable memories? His was not the first post-mortem she had performed on a murder victim. She had done many. Too many. Each one a simple or a complex tragedy, but they had not disturbed her buried memories. So why now? What was it about Wilson's murder that had left her feeling so exposed?

Was it the cheap, common humour of a cartoon tie? Or the clumsy attempt to link murder with the normal workings of a hospital? The obvious and deliberate disposal of the body in a clinical waste bag, as bright and yellow as a child's gaudy toy, guaranteed to catch the eye? The careless dumping of the body right on the hospital grounds, in a place so obvious it had been meant to be found? On the killer's part there had been no attempt to conceal his work. But of course, Karys sucked a square of chocolate absent-mindedly, a real surgeon had no need to hide his mistakes. They could be dealt with as this pseudo-surgeon had dealt with his, by laying them out in the open. Karys hugged her arms round herself and tried to force her mind to move on. But it refused to budge. It was stuck. Stubbornly determined to compare the present with the past. Karys allowed it to wander.

So, maybe, it was another aspect of the murder that was causing her to feel so unsettled, perhaps the fake operation itself? Or, to be more specific, the groin wound. It was a common enough incision, she had seen hundreds during the course of her work, same side, same wound.

It wasn't that.

It was only by pondering each point in turn that she knew with a sudden flash of clarity exactly what was disturbing her. It was only partly the sheer pointlessness of Wilson's abduction, murder and mutilation, the careless, cheap wasting of life. It was something more. Something deeper.

Although she had protested to Forrest that she had no insight into the mind of the killer it was impossible to perform a post-mortem without gaining some understanding of both his methods and his nature: bruises indicated violence; superficial slashes a lack of purpose. Without particularly wanting to, she knew things about the 'surgeon'. She had recognized in both the tie and the clinical waste bag a macabre touch of humour. She knew he had laughed as he had killed. Laughed as he had cut. Laughed as he had slipped the body into the bags and taped them together. And the final and loudest laugh had been retained for the moment when he had rolled the body down the bank, dumping it back on the hospital site. He had found the entire incident, its investigation and repercussions *funny*. That had been the point of it.

Dammit. Was he laughing now?

'Shit.' She looked at the foil wrapper in her hand. Crumpled. Empty. A whole bar of chocolate gone, when she had promised Tonya to limit herself to one bar a day, for the sake of her health and her waistline. A resolution she really had meant to stick to. And it was still early. Hours before the end of the day. And there were more bars of chocolate in her desk drawer. She must stop thinking like this.

DS Rupert Shaw leapt up the hospital steps two at a time. He really hated these places. The smell of disinfectant, the doctors, nurses, the clinical whiteness only partially relieved by the Hospital Trust's pathetic attempts to turn the place into a luxury hotel – probably at the expense of it being an efficient working hospital, he thought cynically. He was stopped just inside the door by a heavily made-up blonde who sat behind a wide desk, repeating the phrase, 'May I help you?' like a talking Barbie doll. He took malicious delight in flashing his ID card and watching her blue eyes turn big and round and impressed. She leant forward intimately. 'Is it about the murder?'

Shaw nodded solemnly. The girl was curious. Of course. Curious but not frightened. She wanted to talk. He didn't. At least, not to her. Brusquely he asked her to direct him towards the hospital manager's office. She half stood in her eagerness. 'I'll get someone to show you the way.'

Shaw lounged against the desk as he waited for her

to use the telephone, delighting in a sense of poetic justice.

His gran had come here to Queen's Hospital six months ago, for a 'few tests', her GP had said. Shaw winced. He was a policeman, not a doctor. He knew absolutely nothing about illness and disease, but he could have told the lot of them his gran would die. It did not matter what of. She had looked like death already.

'Make her comfortable. Don't let her suffer.' That was what he had wanted to say then, to this blonde who had been sitting at the same reception desk. But he hadn't had an ID card then. He had been brushed aside – merely an anxious relative. His lip curled as he recalled all his emotions of the time, all the things he wished he had said, not simply thought.

The doctors had crowded round, murmured something about a rare condition. New treatments. He had grown to mistrust them all, sensed accolade via medical articles and observations. Not one of them had shown a spark of humanity. Especially that pompous surgeon. The one who always wore a navy-blue suit with flashy ties, and had sat, patronizingly, on the bed, embarrassing his gran. Spoke to her as though she was a two-year-old, holding her hand as though they were old friends. But they weren't. He was her doctor, and he had bad news to break to her. The old lady had wanted to preserve her dignity, had stared straight ahead, proudly, waiting for this man to get off her bed. Then they had talked, the old lady and her grandson, her claw-hand patting his as though he was the one with the terminal illness. Despite himself Shaw smiled. Funny phrase, he'd always thought it, terminal illness.

Reminded him of bus routes. But then that was what it had been for his gran. The end of the line.

Someone was walking towards him. Grey-suited. With a red tie. Thick brown hair and a wide, wolfish smile. The wolf held out his hand. 'Detective Sergeant Shaw?' A heavy, confident shake. 'I'm Jonathan Deanfield, the hospital manager here at Queen's. Sorry, I've been in a meeting.' He wafted a hand along the corridor. 'Shall we talk in my office? Along here.'

Feeling as though he was being shuffled away from the public view, Shaw followed him along corridors of pale grey lino, round a corner past a spiralling staircase and through a set of double doors.

Deanfield said little until the door was closed behind them and they were sitting in a large, light room scattered with tall pot plants, padded green chairs and a low wooden coffee table. Shaw sat facing a high, arched window, which overlooked the medical school. Kingfisher-blue curtains completed the colourful, luxurious ambience of the room. It had an atmosphere at variance with the teeming hospital outside.

Deanfield sat opposite him, crossed his legs and frowned. 'I don't see how on earth we can help you. I am *sure* this unfortunate man's murder has absolutely nothing whatsoever to do with Queen's Hospital.' When Shaw made no comment he added quickly, 'I mean it has to be pure chance that the man's body was dumped here, actually on the hospital site.'

Shaw could have responded to this statement with the indisputable facts: the wound, the sutures, the clinical waste bag, but he didn't bother. He had a warrant which gave him the power to spend as much time as he wanted in Deanfield's office, rifling through

staff records and asking questions. Whatever Deanfield's objections he had no choice.

Shaw smiled.

'What are you looking for?'

Shaw decided to be honest. 'We don't really know.
At the moment we're pursuing the line of questioning
that the killer could be an ex-member of staff.'

Deanfield gave a sickly smile. 'That's ridiculous. I
mean . . .'

Shaw could read his mind, 'The publicity,' was what
he meant.

He felt he should placate Deanfield. 'We do have
our reasons. And it shouldn't take long.' A swift,
friendly grin. 'You don't know how many blind alleys of
enquiry we're forced to pursue.'

Deanfield looked slightly mollified.

'I'm sure you're right and Wilson's murder will
prove to have nothing whatsoever to do with the hospital.' He jerked his head towards a side door. 'Would it
be OK if I worked in there?'

Deanfield nodded. 'It's where we keep the old staff
records anyway. Paper files for more than five years
ago, since then on disk.' He followed Shaw through into
a small room packed with filing cabinets, a desk, and a
computer terminal which he switched on and logged
into. 'Can I get you some coffee?'

Shaw settled in front of the blank screen. It was
going to be a long job.

1 December 1999

It was the next day before Forrest had time to work on
an idea that had been going round his head. He took

some coffee and sandwiches into the main office and linked into HOLMES, the Home Office Large Major Enquiry System, the police database on serious crime. It was possible that the 'surgeon' had operated before. There was something organized about the murder, and he didn't want to find that Wilson was the eighth victim of some potty serial killer who'd been hacking people about up and down the country. It would make bad headlines, lose him some useful facts, and delay chummy collaboration between forces. Besides, it was easy, and quick. Simply run through a list of major incidents in, say, the last couple of years. Start in January 1997. He munched his way through two slices of brown bread wrapped around a wedge of the strongest cheddar cheese the local deli supplied and stared at the screen.

The first fact he gleaned surprised him. There hadn't been as many killings as he would have thought. On average fifty-three a year. He homed in on the last year. Forty-seven had been solved quickly, within a day or two. Hand on the collar of the obvious suspect. Never mind the crime writers' favourite ploy of the *least* obvious suspect, the little parlourmaid who'd served up sandwiches in chapter one. Forrest grinned and chewed his food at the same time. Killers were so bloody obvious, for goodness' sake. Fake alibis: 'Down the pub with a couple of mates – can't remember their names', or 'my husband went out. He didn't say where, or with whom'. It was all so naive. What wife would fail to ask such questions unless she already knew the answers? Killers. They all thought they were the only one, didn't realize the police had seen it all before. Forrest almost yawned. They were all so very unsubtle.

Unsubtle in a way that the 'surgeon' was not.

Out of these killings not one shared any similarities to the 'surgeon's' work. True, there were eight stunnings with a blunt instrument, but six of these had been gangland bashings, crude bludgeonings, quarrels over the two necessities of life: women and drugs. Never any witnesses, of course. Like Wilson's killing. But that was where the similarity stopped. Forrest was sure Wilson's murder had not been witnessed by folk too frightened to talk. It had no hallmarks of a gangland execution. And the other two blunt-instrument killings had also been crude, not followed by throttling with hands – or a tie.

Forrest turned back to the computer. There had been stranglings in the last year. Husband of wife almost exclusively. One wife of husband. With a tie. But Wilson's wife was not even a suspect.

Forrest did the same research into the two previous years before turning away from the screen. The 'surgeon's' absence was unmistakable in the killers' gallery. There was nothing in any previous murder that bore even the vaguest suggestion of surgical mutilation. No murder weapon had ever been listed as a scalpel, let alone any mention of that distinctive line of subsequent stitching. The other indicators were also absent – no clinical waste bag, no dumping of a body on a hospital site – anywhere in the UK.

Interesting.

Forrest switched the computer off. He knew now that Colin Wilson, plumber, had been the 'surgeon's' first victim. What he was worried about was that he would not be his last.

*

Half an hour later he was in conference with Chief Superintendent Farley Waterman, facing his superior with the usual feeling of inadequacy. Waterman was a perfectionist, an exacting man. Six feet four inches tall with piercing blue eyes, a luxurious head of steel-grey hair and a brisk, military manner, his was an imposing presence. Forrest stood smartly to attention without speaking or moving as Waterman slowly read through his preliminary notes. At last he looked up and Forrest felt the full force of his gaze. 'You have a problem here, Forrest,' Waterman said crisply.

Forrest shifted his numbing leg. 'Yes, sir.' He wished he had been invited to sit down. The man was a sadist to keep him on his feet.

Waterman stared straight ahead. 'I see no motive.'

'No, sir.'

'Not the usual one, anyway. No robbery?' He looked up for confirmation.

Forrest gave it. 'No, sir. His wallet was found in his shirt pocket, credit cards and ten pounds cash.'

'No sexual attack?'

'No, sir.'

'And I take it the victim's wife wasn't having an affair?'

'She appears devoted, sir. And there is a baby a few months old. We've gone into both his personal and his professional life.' A pause. 'As far as we can tell, sir, this was an assault by a stranger.'

The statement earned him a hard stare from beneath the bushy eyebrows and Forrest felt his face flush. But he was not being naive. The description DS Fielding had given of Colin Wilson's home life had been one of simple domestic harmony. She certainly had not cast Mrs Wilson in the role of femme fatale, responsible for her husband's murder – even indirectly. And Colin Wilson had worked alone – there had been no envious colleagues. Neither had there been any complaints from the customers they had so far tracked down.

Waterman folded his arms and continued to stare straight ahead. 'So we're left with the ugliest motive of all. Someone who kills because they like to.'

'It would seem so,' Forrest said cautiously.

'And what did the pathologist think of the groin wound?'

'She was puzzled by it, sir.'

'Did she think it could have been accidental?'

'It could have been.'

Waterman's eyes swivelled round to meet his. 'And the stitches?'

'Again, sir, she was puzzled by them.'

'So . . .' Waterman stroked his chin. 'No motive and the pathologist is – puzzled.'

'Yes, sir.'

Waterman was silent for a moment. When he spoke again it was with the vaguest hint of embarrassment. 'Forrest,' he barked. 'I've been approached by someone who claims to be able to help us.'

'Sir?' Forrest was curious.

'I heard about this man a while ago at one of these . . .' Waterman cleared his throat ' . . . police conferences.'

He pulled a card from the top pocket of his jacket and flipped it on to the desk. Forrest picked it up. It was white, boldly printed in black letters: Doctor Barney Lewisham Consultant Forensic Psychiatrist. And below, a mobile phone number. There was no address.

Not even the geographical clue of a direct-dial code. It made the psychiatrist appear curiously insubstantial, disembodied even, which in turn made Forrest feel disadvantaged. 'We haven't used one before,' he said.

Waterman lifted his hand. 'I think you will agree, Forrest,' he said in his clipped voice, 'that this is an unusual, if not unique, case.' He cleared his throat again. 'Dangerous too. I don't want unsolved murders on my patch.' He leant across the desk. 'The man might strike again.'

He stood up and Forrest suppressed the temptation to salute. Waterman moved towards the door and held it open. For a brief moment their eyes met, then Waterman focused, as usual at a point above Forrest's shoulder. 'Other forces seem impressed by this process. Man's a doctor,' he finished unnecessarily and closed the door.

Forrest glanced again at the card. He had read about many cases where a forensic psychiatrist had helped towards a solution. He had also read in the police journals, of cases where the intervention of a psychiatrist had hampered proceedings. Misdirected them even. Cases had been thrown out of court through the efforts of forensic psychiatrists. He wondered into which category Dr Barney Lewisham would fall.

There was one sure way to find out.

As soon as he was back in his own office he dialled the mobile phone number. It was answered after one ring as though Lewisham had been poised, waiting for the call. Still wondering where in the country he was phoning Forrest gave his name and a brief introduction. Lewisham listened without comment until he had stopped speaking.

'An interesting case,' he said. 'That's why I came forward. I heard something of it on the radio. Only the bare bones of the facts, of course, but I suspected there was more. Much more. Huh.' He gave a dry croak of a laugh. 'Dumping the body on hospital grounds for a start. And wasn't there mention of a yellow plastic bag? Wouldn't happen to have been a clinical waste bag, would it?' he asked shrewdly.

'Yes.'

'I see.' Lewisham was silent for a moment. 'Even I hadn't guessed all this. And what exactly do you want me to do?'

'Work with us.' Forrest knew he sounded humble. 'Just point us in the right direction so we don't waste too much time.'

'Of course.'

Forrest was trying to form a mental impression of the man. He sounded an intelligent eccentric. There was an energy about him, a sort of vibrant dominance. Each word was measured and careful, decisive yet at the same time defensive. The thought wormed its way into Forrest's brain that it was almost as though the psychiatrist expected the psychoanalysis to be turned on himself. On the other end of the phone Forrest felt himself grow increasingly self-conscious. He had little experience of forensic psychiatrists. The title alone had an effect on him and plenty of his colleagues. Worried about the impression he might be giving he found himself considering and rejecting words to answer Lewisham's questions.

'Umm . . . we found the umm . . .'

'Corpse?'

It sounded too cold, lacked involvement. 'Body . . .

down a small bank between the medical school and the—'

He was relieved when Lewisham's voice cut in. 'And the victim? What sort of man was he?'

'A plumber.' And even in that simple description Forrest found himself criticizing his choice of words, as though describing Colin Wilson merely as 'a plumber' was a condescension, categorizing the dead man without any appreciation of who and what he had really been. So he added quickly, 'A family man with a young—'

Lewisham's voice interrupted again. 'And the post-mortem findings?'

Forrest outlined Wilson's injuries with an equal amount of discomfort. 'Hacked, sewn up, gift wrapped.' Would this Lewisham man decide he was taking sadistic delight in the victim's suffering?

'A stunning blow to the back of the head, strangulation, a groin wound.'

As he had expected, Lewisham gave a long, 'Aha,' and homed in on the groin wound.

'The pathologist was of the opinion that it had been done with something very sharp. Possibly a Stanley knife or a scalpel. It had been inflicted and sewn up after death.'

Another 'Aha?' To his surprise Forrest could even hear brisk enthusiasm behind it. Maybe he had a lot to learn about the preoccupations of a forensic psychiatrist.

'Sewn up, you say?'

'With silk.' Self-consciousness made Forrest fumble for words. 'The kind a surgeon would use. But more untidy.'

'Really?'

Forrest gained the impression that the psychiatrist was smiling as he said the next sentence. 'And you say the stitches were . . .' a pause ' . . . untidily inserted?'

Forrest frowned. 'Yes.'

Lewisham went silent. Forrest restrained the temptation to ask him if he was still there or if the phone had suddenly gone out of range, he could hear the man breathing, hard. Had Lewisham not been a psychiatrist Forrest might have wondered about his reaction to a murder case. Was it normal to get so turned on by detail? Or was this healthy, professional curiosity? Forrest shrugged. Everyone knew psychiatrists were – unusual people.

'So.' Lewisham finally spoke again. 'We need to know what moved this man to commit his crime.'

'You think it was a man?'

Lewisham's voice came back hard and precise. 'Statistically it's more likely. Violent crime is, even today, less likely to be committed by a female.' There was a half-crazy chuckle. 'Despite growing aggression in the fair sex.'

Forrest said nothing. What could he say?

'And there are questions, aren't there? Interesting questions. Such as, why perform such an unnecessary procedure? From what you say, not for purposes of torture or sadism. You tell me the victim was already dead before the incision?' Lewisham didn't even wait for confirmation of the statement but hurried on, excitedly. 'Why waste time sewing him up? Risking discovery. A dead man's wounds will never heal, Detective Inspector Forrest.' The enthusiasm in the doctor's voice was making him speak quickly. 'This case smacks of some deep, psychological obsession with the workings of an operating theatre. More precisely with the skill of a surgeon. I have to say, Detective Inspector, that I am *extremely* interested in the killer of Colin Wilson. He promises to reveal a fascinating psychological profile. Besides which he will – I believe – kill again. You realize he has the hallmarks of a serial killer.'

'He hasn't killed before, sir. I've checked.'

'Well, I believe he will kill again, Inspector, and for that reason alone I could not refuse this case. I owe my services both to you and to future, intended victims,' he said grandly. 'I shall solve it, you know.'

For the first time, Forrest felt a prickling of unease. Was it sensible to call in a clinical psychiatrist who had such a monumental ego? Or might it prove a weak point in the solution to the case? To put it bluntly, and in police jargon, might Lewisham trip over his own head?

He waited a long time for Lewisham to speak again. He heard pages being flipped. A filofax?

'I need to address your officers,' Lewisham said finally. 'Collectively. How about tomorrow? Morning? Ten o'clock?'

'Thank you.' Forrest was not quite sure what to call him, Doctor? Sir? Even Barney in these days of first-name informality? He finally settled on a resentfully muttered, 'Doctor,' and listened to the click of disconnection before he, too, hung up.

After the phone call Forrest sat for a while and stared through his fourth-floor window at the chilly November day outside. The police station was a bare mile from the university and the teaching hospital; the campus was on a small hill so it was visible from his office. He crossed the room towards the window. Through the dusk he could still make out the square grey outlines of the hospital buildings and the prominent spike of Big Joe, the clock tower. He could hear the hospital too. In the distance an ambulance was droning along the top road towards the maternity hospital. A new life about to begin, as had the life of Colin and Laura Wilson's baby a few months ago. Forrest felt a surge of fiercely protective anger. Hospitals were vulnerable places, easy to walk into, full of folk unable to defend themselves: weak, ill, tired and suffering people. It should have been the safest of environments yet it wasn't. It was horribly open, with strangers hurrying in and out of the buildings and numerous unguarded entrances, no one could possibly check them all. The site was visited by hundreds of people in the course of one day. Not all of them could be identified. It was a logistical nightmare. Especially now, with a murderer possibly loose on campus. Someone who might appear normal, who might look and act like everyone else wandering round the hospital complex. Busy, preoccupied, professional. But underneath . . . Sudden concern made Forrest press his face to the blackening glass and peer out. Lampposts threw hazy orange light into the night joined by blue lightning flashes as an ambulance pulled up outside the yawning doors of the A&E Department. Forrest's eyes drifted upwards, towards long, uncurtained windows. Nurses would be working. Four p.m. and it was pitch dark. Early rush-hour traffic was choking the streets. Headlights furred with mist silhouetted people hurrying along shining pavements.

Forrest felt a sudden, blinding panic. Among all these people where would they start searching? How the hell did he expect to find the man? Or, if Lewisham was right, the next victim?

He needed to think intelligently, logically, as had the psychiatrist. Forrest dropped back into his chair, found a sheet of blank paper and a pencil and started doodling. It helped him think. Always the same depressing yet strangely comforting picture. Stair-rods of heavy, leaden rain that dropped on a row of identical roofs over identical houses. It was only by peering closer that you realized the rain was not rain at all but stiff bowler-hatted men in identical dark overcoats, the terrible sameness merely implied by skilful artistry. It was a copy of a picture he had firstly hated, then understood, and lastly admired just before it had been removed – the picture that had once hung over the fireplace in his own sitting room. Maggie's picture.

And as he drew he began to think. Where had the killer got his equipment from? The needle and silk that had been used to sew up the wound. Was it definitely surgical silk? Had he used a real scalpel? Had he stolen the clinical waste bag? From Queen's?

Again and again Forrest asked himself the same old question. Why had that unnecessary cut been made? What had been the point of it? Why had Wilson died at all? Had he been an intended or just a random victim?

He heard a crunch. His pencil had scored a line right through the paper and the lead had snapped. It stopped him doodling. Not knowing where to find a pencil sharpener, he rolled the stump to and fro between his fingers and repeated a question he had asked himself before. Had Colin Wilson any connection with the hospital? Answer – as far as they knew – none, apart from the birth of his daughter.

Surely that could have no connection with his death? But he couldn't rule it out. In fact he couldn't rule anything out – yet.

He glanced at his watch. Twenty past five. He still had ten minutes before the briefing. He began rubbing the top of his head then stopped. If he carried on doing that he would soon have a bald spot. Just like his father. Just like my father.

Thinking about his father never failed to depress him. And the depression made him feel lonely. The loneliness, in its turn, left him with an overwhelming impulse to talk to someone. Not just anyone – someone who might bounce back some suggestions of their own. Not Lewisham. Certainly not Fleming or Shaw or Waterman. Shaw only irritated him. The Chief Superintendent did not invite confidences, neither did Fleming. In fact, he did not want to talk to another policeman. What he yearned for was a quiet voice speaking slow, careful words, a clear, logical brain, someone who already knew all the facts, someone who could help him put his own thoughts in order before adding to them. He knew exactly who he was thinking of, but nervous of a rebuff, he eyed the telephone on his desk for a few seconds before finally tapping out her number.

It only took two rings to be connected.

'Karys, it's David Forrest here,' he said. 'I wondered if I could talk to you about the case. It's sort of – preying on my mind. It would help to talk it over.'

She listened without comment to his ramblings

about the need to make an early arrest. Then chipped in. 'You don't have much to go on, do you?'

Forrest was gloomily silent.

Karys spoke again. 'You could really do with talking to a forensic psychiatrist.'

'One's been called in. He'll be talking to us in the morning.'

'I think he'll be of more help than me.'

'But you did the post-mortem.'

Karys gave a dry laugh. 'That's right,' she said. 'I can tell you all you need to know about haemorrhage and bruising, fractures and tissues. I try to work out what happened. Even sometimes why. But I'm stumped here, Inspector. I don't really know much about distorted minds.' She followed the comment with a heartfelt, 'Thank goodness.'

'But you must pick up things while you're doing the PM.'

'Ye-es. I try. Sometimes I come up with ideas. Sometimes not. This was one of the occasions when I didn't. I couldn't think why he'd added that cut.' She fell silent.

Forrest wanted to say so much more, that he simply wanted to talk – to her – that having no wife or close colleagues he needed to air his own ideas as much as hear hers. But maybe Karys did understand what he was really asking because she said briskly, 'OK, why don't you come over tomorrow? Late morning. After the shrink has run through his ideas with you. You can tell me what he said. I've a quiet morning ahead, so far. We can run through the points together over lunch.'

He left the room with a buoyant step, irrationally feeling that he was inching closer to an understanding, a solution even. Stupidly he believed that Karys' help would lead him straight to his quarry.

An hour later Forrest was congratulating himself that the briefing was going well. Although at this point it was really nothing more than a simple swap of information, and a careful deployment of available manpower towards a cost-effective arrest. Most of the revealed facts had already been fed to him. He sat on the desk, affecting a casualness he did not feel, swinging one leg, and listening. It was DS Caroline Fielding, the brave, middle-aged officer with strong, shapeless legs and gravelly voice who stopped him short. 'Do we have a motive yet, sir?'

And the words of a Scottish senior officer from years before crawled, unwelcome, like an ant, through his brain. 'Every so often, Davie, we get a murderer and we don't have a clue why he killed.' The officer had paused to allow his next words to take full effect. 'And then we've got a ree-a-l problem.'

'No.' Forrest gave DS Fielding a sour smile. That was exactly what he had now, a real problem. He turned his attention back to the room. 'Did we have any luck with the tie?' Again it was Fielding who answered the question.

'It wasn't Wilson's. I asked his wife. He didn't go in for joke ties.' She sat down abruptly, ignoring the looks of sympathy directed towards her. No one liked reporting violent death, especially to the wife, particularly one with a new baby. Fielding's description had been graphic enough to touch their feelings.

They ran over the few known facts yet again. Colin

Wilson had been putting in an en suite bathroom in one of the large, Edwardian houses in Metchley Park Road for a family named Bristam. At about three in the afternoon his mobile phone had rung. Someone had reported a leak. Wilson had said they sounded in a panic and he had responded.

DS Rupert Shaw spoke from the back of the room. 'I did a check on the mobile. Caller was anonymous. Came in at three o four.'

DS Fielding stood up. 'The Bristams said Wilson was laughing when he took the call. Thought the caller a bit of a wimp. Made some sort of comment that most guys should be able to cope with a leak. Anyway, he went, promising to be back within the half hour.'

The room fell quiet.

Other officers had further contributions. They had put up notices at all the entrances to the hospital.

A body was discovered here on the morning of Tuesday, 23 November. Did anyone see anything?

Judging by the response no one had.

Preliminary enquiries had drawn a complete blank. On the surface, at least, Colin Wilson had been an innocent tradesman, who put in long hours to keep his family in a modest home. There appeared no rational explanation for his death.

'Did any of you uncover any connection with the hospital?' Forrest threw the question into the room with some desperation.

Blank faces.

He tried again. 'Or a doctor? Any doctor? Not necessarily a hospital doctor. Even a GP?'

Caroline Fielding was the only one even to attempt an answer. 'Just the baby.' It was old ground and they all knew it.

Worst of all Forrest knew he was clutching at straws. 'There was no problem with the birth?'

She gave him a sharp look. 'No,' she said flatly. 'I asked Mrs Wilson.'

David Forrest frowned. 'So nothing there?'

She shook her head. 'No, sir.'

Forrest's forehead was criss-crossed with lines. His earlier optimism was swiftly fading. The reality was that, as Karys had said, they had so little to go on.

Shaw piped up again from the back. 'I've been thinking, sir.'

Forrest bit back a dozen sarcastic replies. 'Are we sure the stitches were surgical sutures?'

Forrest waited.

'Because if the cut was done with a Stanley knife, apart from the plastic bags the only real connection we've got with the hospital is that the body was dumped there. And there aren't a lot of patches of waste ground so near the city centre, are there?'

'So what are you saying?' Forrest challenged sweetly.

'Just that I might be . . .'

'Wasting your time focusing your enquiries on the hospital?'

A lesser man might have backed down. Not Shaw. 'Yes, sir,' he said boldly.

'Got any better ideas, have you, Sergeant?'

Shaw shook his head. 'Not yet.' He sat, tapping his biro into the palm of his hand.

Forrest ignored him and continued discussing the

statements from Wilson's neighbours, but ten minutes later Rupert Shaw piped up again. 'Did the pathologist feel the suturing needed much medical knowledge?'

Forrest glared at him. Persistent, arrogant sod. 'No,' he said rudely. 'That good enough for you?'

Rupert Shaw shut up.

Forrest turned back to the whiteboard. 'Right. The question now is where do we go from here? Personally, I think we might get a little further in this case if we investigate Colin Wilson's background. I want to know everything he did since he left school, especially any- thing – ' he emphasized the point by tapping his knuckles on the desk with one hard rap – 'any connec- tion he had with Queen's.'

Caroline Fielding was watching him carefully. 'You think . . .?' She hesitated. Forrest was well known for making you appear an idiot if you said something just a bit weak.

But all Forrest's aggression had been vented on the unfortunate DS Shaw. Now he was feeling benevolent. 'Go on,' he prompted.

'What about if he did some work as a plumber, maybe for a doctor, and got it wrong?'

Forrest stared at her without speaking. 'It's a possi- bility,' he said. 'Before I saw Wilson's corpse I wouldn't have believed murder could possibly be revenge for bad plumbing.' He gave a rueful grin. 'Let's just say I'm revising my opinions. I'm open to suggestions. However, let me remind you of the pathologist's opinion. *If* a doctor inflicted the post-mortem wound on Colin Wilson he wasn't a particularly competent one.' A flash of inspiration provided him with his next

statement. 'It *could*, of course, have been a newly qualified doctor, or a nurse.'

The officers fell silent. They had all seen numbers
of nurses milling around the hospital site. Hundreds.
Typically it was Shaw who broke the spell.

'There is another possibility. Perhaps the murder
was done to discredit the place, sir. The hospital trust.
There must be plenty of people not too happy with
their treatment. I mean there's always, always someone trying to sue hospitals.'

David Forrest's eyes grew storm-grey and hard.
'Then, when you've finished reading through the staff
records, Shaw, perhaps you'd like to follow up that lead.
Look at all cases of litigation against the hospital over
the last five years.'

The tall detective seemed to shrink. 'But there must
be hundreds—'

'Start with the really serious grudges,' Forrest interrupted, 'and concentrate on recent cases where the
plaintiff lost his case against the Hospital Trust.' Rupert
Shaw opened his mouth to speak only for Forrest to
interrupt him again, but more kindly this time. 'We've
got to keep this investigation going, Shaw. That seems
as good a place for you to work as any. It'll keep you
near the hospital site. If you should find that one of the
plaintiffs not only lost his case but had a history of
violent crime against the person, all the better.' He fore-
stalled the DS's objections. 'And anyway you may as
well work on that lead because apart from researching
Wilson's background and sticking to the hospital site, I
don't have any better ideas myself.'

Rapidly he moved on. 'DS Fielding . . .' The DS stood
smartly to attention. 'I'd like you to continue inter-

viewing staff at the hospital. And you might pop up to the maternity ward while you're at it. Have a chat with the midwives, and others who might have helped the Wilsons through their happy event.' He was aware he sounded sour and cynical. It was a side of himself he would like to shed. Maybe he would, one day.

Fielding allowed herself one quick glance at any colleagues sympathetic enough to smile. 'What line of investigation should I pursue, sir? Loony surgeon?'

'I don't know, Fielding,' David Forrest said, irritated at her flippancy. 'I don't know. Just speak to them. Concentrate on the surgical wards and theatres. Come straight back to me if you unearth anything – however trivial it seems.'

As she heaved a deep sigh, Forrest addressed DC Murray Lowen, a Brummy with a thick accent. 'Speak to the four medical students again. They aren't really under suspicion, but I would lay a bet they're observant young men. Just check whether they saw anything they haven't already told us about.'

DS Steven Long was next in his line of fire. 'Apart from the plastic bags the only real link we have with our killer is the tie. He must have bought it from somewhere. Get a list of stockists. You know the drill. Follow them all up. It might be our only solid clue.' He shifted uncomfortably. 'Before you disperse I have to tell you that Chief Superintendent Waterman, in his wisdom,' he added, under his breath, 'has decided to accept the services of a forensic psychiatrist to help us find Wilson's killer. It's just possible that our briefing in the morning, with him, will alter our lines of enquiry.' He shrugged. 'We'll see.'

He watched the officers file past him until the room

was empty. They all had their orders, what should he do? Maybe it was time he spoke to Wilson's wife himself. DS Fielding was a competent professional, but he had years of experience. There was no substitute for talking to someone in person. He started to feel slightly happier. This was old policeman's textbook stuff. Talk to the next of kin then spiral outwards, a satellite circling the sun in an ever-increasing arc until you hit Planet Solution.

Chapter Three

2 December 1999

It was almost exactly ten o'clock the following morning when Forrest answered the knock on his door with a curt, 'Come in.' He looked up curiously as a thin rookie held the door open and ushered Barney Lewisham in.

Forrest had already formed a picture of a long-haired eccentric. He was partly right. Lewisham had almost black hair, not long but greasy and badly cut in a crude pudding-basin style. He was about thirty, short – barely five feet four – with very pale skin emphasized by a nine o'clock shadow already showing. He was casually dressed in an open-necked check shirt and a misshapen sweater. Both were olive green, the sweater more faded than the shirt. His trousers were brown, baggy and flopping round his ankles. Forrest judged him a strange man even before he met the curious marmalade-coloured eyes peering over his gold-rimmed, half-moon glasses, which, to the policeman, seemed an affectation.

He stood up to shake the proffered broad hand.

Lewisham got his introduction in first. 'Barney Lewisham,' he said. 'Consultant forensic psychiatrist.' He grinned. His teeth were stained nicotine-yellow although the scent of smoke around him was only faint.

The two men sat down and surveyed each other warily.

Lewisham leant back in the chair, pressed his fingertips together and peered over his glasses. 'I felt compelled to offer my services,' he said. 'This is the devil of a case. And now I must have all the facts. Please be accurate and concise.'

Forrest began with ground he was sure of, Wilson's details: age, marital state, physical appearance.

Lewisham soon interrupted him. 'I don't think much of this is relevant at the moment.' The strange marmalade-coloured eyes gleamed. 'Tell me exactly how his body was found.'

So Forrest began again, with the story of the four medical students, the clinical waste bag that had drawn them from the short cut to the university.

Again Lewisham interrupted him. 'Did they move the body?'

'No.'

'So it was found as your killer had placed it?'

'We got the impression it had been rolled down the bank.'

'Aha.' Lewisham looked pleased with himself and leant forward, hands pressing on his chunky thighs. 'Dumped, you say. Not laid with care. Significant. And how securely was the body fastened inside the bags?'

Forrest quickly had to think back. 'Very,' he said. 'It was taped up. The pathologist had to slit the side of the bag open with a knife.'

'Good.' Lewisham really did look pleased.

Gaining confidence, Forrest continued to describe Wilson's injuries but Lewisham interrupted him yet again, rudely. 'I don't think *your* observations will be of much value. What I need is a copy of the pathologist's post-mortem report.'

Forrest felt deflated. He fumbled through the pile of papers; a couple slipped to the floor. Without moving Lewisham watched Forrest pick them up and waited for him to find the PM report. He didn't even lean forward to take them from Forrest's grasp. Forrest handed them to him with a touch of resentment.

Lewisham seemed able to read and absorb quickly, flipping through both text and photographs with barely a glance. Moments later he grunted and looked up. 'This is a dangerous man, Inspector.'

Forrest found his resentment mounting. Stretching out his arm he shortened his shirt sleeve and peeped at his watch. It had taken him less than ten minutes to dislike Dr Lewisham. It would take him weeks to know how that dislike could grow.

Lewisham leant back and closed his eyes without speaking. Forrest suffered the silence. He felt a certain impotence in the presence of the psychiatrist. He had only ever met this sort of purposeful dominance in one person before – his junior-school headmistress. He had hated her for all the years he had attended primary school, for the way she had belittled him on the first day when he had accidentally wet his grey shorts. He didn't mind that Lewisham was a control freak except for one aspect. It would be picked up by the junior officers – especially Shaw – and that would rob him of the authority necessary for the senior investigating officer on such a serious case. He was already on his guard and was relieved when Lewisham finally broke the silence, stood up and asked where the briefing room was.

*

The thirty or more officers who sat, stood, or lounged against the wall, all gave Lewisham a fair hearing. Glancing around at their faces Forrest couldn't read a trace of scepticism either for the psychiatrist's message or the man himself. And yet Lewisham was talking down to them, addressing them like a maths teacher explaining a difficult concept to a class of remedials.

'My name is Doctor Lewisham. I am a forensic psychiatrist. That is, I specialize in the study of the diseased and criminal mind.' He scanned each face in the room to make sure they had understood and were being attentive. This further irritated Forrest. 'My role in this particular case is to help you understand the type of person who would have committed this crime, what was in his mind as he mutilated the corpse, his undoubted pleasure at the activity and the motives for it. During your investigations I should be able to eliminate certain character types and illuminate groups of people you *should* be concentrating your attention on. Later, when you have a suspect, I will direct you in your choice of questions in order that you will have the best chance of obtaining a secure conviction.'

He paused before carrying on, in his over-loud, slightly nasal voice, which Forrest also found irritating. 'What I *cannot* do is to walk the streets of Birmingham, put a hand on a man's collar and tell you – this is your killer. This is not possible,' he paused for a reaction to this statement before adding, 'even for me.' Another pause. 'When I know more about the case I shall be able to fill in the details, narrowing the field of suspects considerably. But for the moment I want you to bear this in mind: the perpetrator of this heinous crime against Colin Wilson is aged between twenty-five and fifty. He is in good health, in fact relatively strong. He has a driving licence. He works alone, probably unsupervised, possibly as a self-employed person – if he works at all. He lacks close friends and he has *some* connection with the hospital, however tenuous. This man has studied a true surgeon work.' Again Lewisham paused as though he expected someone in the room to challenge something he had said. Forrest watched him carefully, puzzled. Most of what the psychiatrist had said seemed logical enough. There wasn't really anything to challenge. Surely? But someone did.

'If he's playing doctors, sir . . .'

Forrest craned his neck to see who had spoken. Shaw. Of course. Only he would have the arrogance to interrupt the psychiatrist.

But Lewisham seemed not to mind. In fact he gave Shaw an encouraging smile and prompted him. 'Go on.'

'Why does he *kill* his victims? I mean, doctors usually try to *cure* their patients. Not kill them.'

Lewisham's strange, marmalade-coloured eyes peered over the gold-rimmed glasses and seemed to lock onto the young policeman's face. 'I'm not positive,' he said, 'but I think that without the benefit of modern anaesthetics it might be the only way he could be absolutely sure his patients would stay still.'

There was a ripple of distaste around the room.

Still Shaw persisted. 'But if he's got a doctor complex . . .?'

Lewisham glared at him. 'He hasn't got a *doctor* complex,' he spat out, 'he's got a *surgeon* complex.'

'I don't understand.' Shaw wasn't the only one.

'Look at the patients surgeons relate to,' Lewisham said. 'They lie passive, awaiting the knife, like lambs to the slaughter . . . and of course,' Lewisham had waited for his words to take full effect, 'he could *never* afford for his patients to speak.'

Now the entire room was silent. Senior officers, junior officers, CID and uniformed, male and female, were mesmerized by Lewisham's words. Forrest watched from the side of the room with a growing sense of unease. They trusted him. Implicitly. Even Shaw.

Everyone except Forrest, whose dislike for the man was deepening into something much stronger. When the psychiatrist's eyes searched him out he flushed. Lewisham had noticed his antagonism, but Forrest saw that it did not upset him, rather he seemed to revel in it. It pleased him. He *wanted* there to be antipathy between himself and the senior investigating officer on the case.

Why? A love of conflict?

Lewisham was still talking. 'So how can we prevent another fatality? What groups of people are most at risk from him? We can best learn this by asking ourselves the question: why did our killer select Colin Wilson, a plumber with no obvious connection with the hospital?' He looked up to address the officers almost severely. 'Although I do have to say I am of the conviction that Wilson *did* have something to do with the hospital at some time, it is simply that your investigations have failed to unearth the connection.' Again Forrest picked up a hint of the headmistress in his manner, of the hand being slapped by the ruler, of punishment. Forrest stared at the man. As a psychiatrist did he have no insight into the impression he made on people? Didn't he realize how quickly he provoked dislike? Or was it all deliberate? Some people did provoke such a reaction purely to stimulate results. Forrest himself had worked with such people. But a swift glance round the room confirmed his earlier observation. He was the only one to feel this. The others were listening intently. Taken in. Lewisham carried on. 'I believe our surgeon will attack again. Why do I believe this?' He peered around the room, staring at each face for a second or two. When he had completed the circuit he smiled, in satisfaction. He was the only one with the answer. He spent a couple of seconds savouring this personal knowledge before throwing it before them. 'Because this was a ritual killing. Each facet of Colin Wilson's murder satisfied some deep need in the killer: the stunning, the killing, the maiming. This *need* will compound, become stronger. Have to be satisfied, again, and again, until he is stopped.'

Inappropriately he smiled. No one smiled back.

Lewisham continued. 'So who should we be protecting? Doctors, nurses, ancillary staff? Or vagrants? Men? Women? Children? The easy targets?' A shudder rippled round the room as though a window had been opened letting in a draught. The thought of a child being subjected to . . . Lewisham pursed his lips and lowered the half-moon glasses down his nose. 'So let's look closer at Colin Wilson. He is our only clue – so far. Was he an easy target? What do we know about him? That he was a family man, not a vagrant, and his connection with the hospital must be tenuous or you would have unearthed it by now. So, did the murderer select Wilson for a specific reason? If so what? Or was the killer driving along when he saw Wilson's van in front of him displaying, of course, the mobile phone number. Was it painted on the side?' There were a few nods.

A common enough practice. This was how tradesmen advertised. Lewisham waited for them to work this out for themselves before putting further questions to them. 'How was his killing planned? These are the questions we must ask ourselves. Constantly.' Again Lewisham waited before dropping his next stone into the pond. 'Have you thought anything about the "surgeon's" premises?'

Judging from the blank faces no one had.

'I have. Our killer is a neat man. Methodical. He likes to line things up, have rows of instruments in order. And his instruments are laid out – somewhere. He has some sort of a makeshift operating theatre, somewhere he won't be disturbed, somewhere no one will ask questions about blood on the floor, strange comings and goings, the accumulation of hospital stores, suturing material, clinical waste bags, scissors, scalpels, forceps.' Lewisham's voice rose as the list grew longer. 'He has all these things. Do you think he only intends to use them once?'

Forrest stared at him. How could he know this?

Surely *someone* would challenge his assumption. But no one answered. Not even Forrest himself. Even the usual mutterings were absent.

'Think about it,' Lewisham said. 'Just keep thinking.'

He waited for the first person in the room to move before giving Forrest's hand a firm shake. 'I'll be in touch, Inspector. In the meantime, keep me informed. You can reach me at any time on my mobile.'

Brenda Watlow had got a lift to work in Terry's van.

She glanced across at her son-in-law's fleshy profile.

He was a good lad, was Terry. She didn't really deserve him. And Shani definitely didn't. Her mouth twisted. Idle little cow, doing nothing all day except eat, smoke and get fat. Not like her mum. Brenda glanced down at a pair of shapely, plump thighs nicely exposed, she fondly thought, by the new bright red mini-skirt. She gave Terry another sly glance. *He* certainly appreciated the way she dressed. As they pulled up in front of the main doors of the hospital she smiled at him. He grinned back. 'All right, Ma?' It was a bit of a joke between them, the 'Ma' bit.

She leaned right back in her seat and stretched her arms above her head, yawning, knowing it showed her breasts off. Firm for a woman of forty. Again she mentally compared herself to her daughter's generous form. Obese. That's what Shani was. Slyly she answered Terry's questions. 'Yeah, yeah. I'm all right.' She crossed her legs and flashed him a warm smile. 'Just wondering what Pinky's got in store for me this afternoon, that's all. Always tries to sneak in a couple of extra cases on the end of the list. He's a crafty one. And half the time they're private, people he's doing for a backhander. You do have to watch these surgeons.' She gave Terry's shoulder a playful tap. 'Not all they're cracked up to be. Stories I've heard would make your hair curl.'

'Huh. I'll bet.'

She glanced reluctantly at her watch. 'Well no time for gossiping now. I'd better be off. First patient'll be having his pre-med by now and I've got plenty to do. Pinky doesn't enjoy being kept waiting and there's all them trolleys to set up. Still.' She gave Terry another of the flirtatious smiles she fondly believed set his heart racing. 'I'll be scrubbed up before you can say . . .'

'Intestine,' Terry supplied.

Brenda giggled. 'Well, intestinal obstruction any- way. Know that job so well I could do it blindfold with my hands tied behind my back.'

Terry leaned towards her. 'Don't tempt me, Ma.'

For answer Brenda uncrossed her legs and swung them towards the passenger door, keeping her knees firmly clamped together. She flicked the handle open. Terry leant back in his seat, closing his eyes. Some- times – only sometimes – Brenda's teasing really got to him. Needled him.

She climbed out of the car and slammed the door behind her, and had crossed to his side by the time he opened them again. He caught a waft of cloying, rich perfume as she leant in at the window to give him an affectionate kiss. 'Ta Ta, my darling.' But she was not fool enough to rumple his curly hair. Terry didn't always like it. She had learnt to read the signs early on in their relationship when her daughter had first brought home the taciturn young man and Brenda had signalled her attraction to him – a signal she believed had been returned. But with Terry one could never be quite sure. Sometimes she knew she had overstepped the mark. His eyes would change, his forehead pucker. She read the signs very quickly. Terry had a nasty temper. More than once Shani had fallen prey to it and earned herself a black eye. But Brenda was older, wiser, a professional woman. She had no intention of mis- reading the auguries, and as fast as she read them she made excuses for Terry's sudden bursts of temper. Dif- ficult fancying his mother-in-law more than his wife. Brenda had decided, early on, that she could be both lover and mother-in-law to him, if that was what he wanted.

She shot him a swift glance and was reassured. There was no hint of that deeper, more complicated person as Terry returned her smile. 'You be all right getting home tonight, Ma?' He allowed his eyes to rove around her shapely form and she in turn allowed her mind to wander. There weren't so many years between them. She'd had Shani when she was only sixteen, had brought her up virtually alone, thanks to Stuart, managed all her nurse training with the help of reliable friends to look after Shani all hours.

Her eyes darkened at the memory of Shani's dad. A waster. That's where her daughter had got all her obesity, laziness and slovenliness from. She shook herself free from the uncomfortable memory and returned to Terry. He was six years older than his wife. And Brenda consoled herself that she was only just forty – and didn't look anything like it. More like twenty-five – or so she fondly thought without realizing that the student nurses, all under twenty-one, mocked her behind her back. Whereas Shani . . . Her face grew tight, hard, competitive, selfish. Shani deserved all she got, or didn't get. And one of these days she would lose her Terry to an older woman. Brenda looked deep into her son-in-law's melting brown eyes. That daughter of hers couldn't appreciate a sexy, attractive man even when she slept beside him every night. Shani was blind whereas she was not. Still, she stopped leaning in at the window and stood up, there was no point pushing her luck, rushing things. Terry would speak – when he was ready.

So she weighed up very carefully whether to accept his offer of a lift after work and in the end declined it.

'It's OK, Terry, love. I'll get a taxi. Don't you worry about me.'

But Wilson's murder had made him more assertive than usual. He put his hand on her arm. 'Hang around for a taxi, after that bloke was murdered? Risk him getting hold of you next? You must be joking. I'll be here. Now, what time?'

'But, Terry, I don't know when we'll be finished. The list can go on. And then there's the emergencies.' Brenda loved to maximize the number of emergencies they had to deal with. One a week – if that – but she'd never told Terry it was anything but 'lots and lots' or 'snowed under'. The drama excited her and elevated her status in her son-in-law's eyes.

Simply saying the word 'emergencies' made her feel important. 'Emergencies', she said again.

Terry took his hand off her arm and slipped the car into gear. 'If you can't give me a time then ring me,' he said. 'Just ring me. Otherwise I'll come and sit in that ruddy operating theatre and wait for you there. I can't risk anything happening to my best girl.'

'But what about your work, Terry? I can't have you losing . . .' She hesitated, not quite sure whether to say time or money.

'Look,' he said. 'The man's body was dumped not two hundred yards from here. The newspaper said something about insider knowledge. They think someone from the hospital did it.'

Brenda watched him uneasily, vaguely aware of white-coated medics and nurses wrapped in navy capes going past them. From the centre of the campus Big Joe struck one. It shook Brenda out of her reverie. 'I shall have to go, Terry,' she said, her face whiter now than it had been. 'Now I *will* be late. And Pinky likes to start dead on one thirty. I've got loads to do. Sterilize the instuments, set the trolleys.'

But Terry had that vacant look in his eyes again. 'Funny isn't it,' he said, 'the way we say things. And they get twisted.'

'What sort of things?'

Terry gave a short, explosive laugh. 'Dead on one thirty. I hope not.'

Brenda joined him in a weak, nervous giggle.

'Right then,' Terry said abruptly. 'I'll be seeing you later. All right? Ring me.' He put his forefinger underneath her chin. 'Promise? Your little boy'll be cross and sulky if you don't.'

Brenda was suddenly enormously *fond* of her son-in-law. The feeling of affection made her reckless. She leant in at the window and gave him a hard, uncompromizing kiss on the mouth. The first ever.

'Thanks, Terry,' she said. 'See you later.'

Terry kept his eyes on Brenda until she was swallowed up by the giant swing doors of the hospital before pulling away in his van.

Chapter Four

As Karys opened the mortuary door to him Forrest was
glad to see that although she was still wearing her green
cotton gown she had taken off the rubber apron and
surgical gloves. He didn't think he could get used to the
idea of a woman who wore post-mortem garb while she
ate. She gave him a shy, twisted smile.

'Paget got us some sandwiches in,' she said.

Her discomfort transmitted itself to Forrest, he felt
acutely awkward. He held out his white paper bag. 'So
did I.'

The action went some way towards melting the
tension.

'Tuna,' Karys said.

Forrest opened his bag. 'And more tuna.'

Karys giggled. 'Then I hope you're hungrier than I
am, and fond of tuna.'

'Not particularly,' Forrest said. 'Too fishy.'

The ice was broken.

Karys chattered easily as she walked back down the
corridor. 'There's no one else here. Paget's gone home
early. Time owing. There really isn't much to do today.'
She laughed and half turned round. 'Quiet. No bodies.
Someone's good fortune.'

'Yeah, well, long may it last,' Forrest said soberly.

Karys nodded her head. 'Absolutely. Look', she said, suddenly awkward again. 'I don't know what you think I can do . . . I just guess, you know.'

'But your guesses are founded on the PM, aren't they?'

'Yes, I suppose they are.'

'Then why don't you put the kettle on and we'll start by eating these sandwiches.' Forrest said as they moved along the corridor. 'I realize all this psychiatry business isn't your scene but you must have done some psychiatry in your training.'

'A couple of months, no more. A few forensics lectures.'

'I've always thought . . .' they'd reached the kitchen ' . . . that doctors have to be psychiatrists.'

Karys laughed. 'You mean to read what's really going on in patients' minds?'

'Yes.'

'I suppose we are – to an extent.'

'Anyway, as I told you yesterday, Waterman's insisted we rope in a forensic psychiatrist because of the mutilation on Wilson's body.'

She half turned. 'Who is it?'

'A guy called Lewisham.'

Karys stopped abruptly. '*Barney* Lewisham?'

'That's the one. Though how much help he's going to be I'm not sure. He seems a bit of a pompous git to me.'

'He is that.'

'You know him?'

'We were medical students together. An experience I'd much rather forget. Well, it's a small world, as they say.'

The mortuary kitchen was a tiny, clinical place, white tiled and tidy with only a Belling cooker, an electric kettle and a fridge. Karys filled the kettle and switched it on.

Forrest said bluntly, 'Do you think the killer is likely to be someone from the hospital?'

'Oh, come on. You can't expect me to commit myself.'

'Well, it would narrow the field considerably.'

'I know that but – '

Forrest frowned. 'I've been trying to work it out. Was it just chance that the body was dumped there in a clinical waste bag after what looked very much like botched surgery? All these medical connections.' He was about to scratch the thinning part at the top of his head then, remembering his father, resisted the urge. 'They have to mean something. Even you must admit it seems to point to an inside job.'

Karys stiffered for a moment before answering. 'Inspector Forrest,' she said formally.

'Call me David – for goodness' sake, Karys. We've worked together for more than five years.'

Karys jerked her head. 'OK then – David,' she said uncomfortably. 'We've called it botched surgery because the stitches weren't very neatly done. But I've been thinking about it. A lot. It wasn't botched at all.'

'What do you mean?'

'There was nothing botched about it, apart from the suturing. No vague attempts at cutting. Just one sure slash. Like a surgeon would make. Careful and straight. The sutures were clumsy – but not that clumsy. They're a bit of a knack. Look. I'll show you.' She vanished from the room and returned carrying a small foil pack and some surgical instruments plus a couple of gauze swabs. She lay them out on the work surface, tore open the foil pack and a length of silk attached to a curved needle dropped out. She anchored the needle between the jaws of some forceps, the kind Forrest had often seen her use routinely during post-mortem, then she threaded the needle through the swabs, pulling the silk behind it. Releasing the needle she wound the thread around the blades of the forceps and tugged the free end through, pulling it tight to make a suture. She snipped with the scissors. Only then did she look up at Forrest. 'See what I mean?' she asked. 'It's a knack. And our "surgeon" appears to have had it, albeit clumsily. I don't think he's had much practice. It was superficial surgery, fake surgery, but it wasn't botched surgery.'

'Are you saying that – '

'I'm saying nothing,' Karys said, 'but let's begin by getting our facts right at the very least.'

Forrest persisted. 'Are you saying then that this was a trained hand?'

'Let's just say, that if this was a lay person it was a very sure cut. Coldly done. And what lay person could manage a suture like that – even clumsily? Could you? Just after killing someone?'

Forrest shook his head. If he was impressed with the way Karys had analysed the evidence he was also a little uncomfortable at the unemotional way she dealt with this killing. A necessary part of being a pathologist, maybe, but an unsettling trait, this detachment. It made him wonder about her.

Fearing a rebuttal Forrest was hesitant about asking

his next question. 'So what sort of person—' He got no further.

Karys interrupted him. 'That is the psychiatrist's field.'

'Well, you've done some psychiatry. You just said so.'

'As a medical student. And that was dealing with the odd schizophrenic, personality disorders, manic depressives. Not *forensic* psychiatry. I've sat in at lectures but I haven't worked with criminal minds, David. It isn't the same as actually meeting them, talking to them, asking them questions about what they do and why they do it. If I had worked among these people I would know more – for certain. Barney,' she used the name, Forrest was pleased to observe, with some reluctance, 'for all his conceit and . . . unpleasant personality. Barney will *know*. I don't understand the criminal mind or what makes someone kill. Especially the mutilation bit. I want you to understand, I'm just guessing.' She thought for a minute. 'But I can't believe this is the work of someone medically qualified. I mean – why would he?'

'So you're saying it *wasn't* a medic?'

'Well, I don't think so. For one thing it's the very opposite of our training.'

'You use cadavers to practice on.'

Karys was stung. 'We don't kill them to get our practice in.'

'I'm sorry. I'm sorry, Karys. But this isn't an ordinary killing.' Forrest said the words in a low, unhappy voice. 'I've led murder investigations before, but this is more abnormal than anything I've ever encountered. I've *never* dealt with post-mortem mutilation before. I'm worried, and I'm puzzled. There seems so much medical jargon that I don't understand.' He handed her a couple of forensic reports.

Karys was a tiny bit mollified. 'Well,' she said grudgingly, 'even a House Officer would do neater stitches than that.' She read through the top page and smiled. 'At least I can help you with this. It's about the sutures themselves. They're 5/0 silk. That's quite fine stuff, normally used in delicate surgery although there is the odd general surgeon who prefers to use fine silk as it leaves less of a scar.' She scanned a couple more lines. 'The needle it was attached to was what's known as a reverse cutting needle. That means a curved needle with a sharpened edge on the inside of the curve. They could tell by looking at some of the excised skin under the microscope.'

'Knowing this must narrow the field considerably.'

Karys agreed. 'It should help.'

'Anything more?'

She met his eyes. 'It *was* a scalpel blade that made the incision.'

'They're sure?'

'Ninety-nine per cent.' Karys said. 'They think the blade was probably large, with a curved edge. You realize that rules out a Stanley knife? I've got a chart in my drawer showing various blades. I'll show you.'

The kettle started boiling. Temporarily it distracted them. 'Tea or coffee?'

'Coffee please. White, no sugar.'

Karys allowed herself a quick smile at the policeman. 'Dieting?'

Forrest shrugged his shoulders. 'My wife used to nag . . .'

The tense struck her. 'But she's stopped?'

Forrest shrugged again. 'She's stopped nagging about my weight because she doesn't care any more. She's gone off with someone else. She can nag him instead.'

It was nothing more than a touch of masculine bravado, which Karys recognized. 'Oh, I'm sorry.'

Forrest's face froze. 'So was I,' he said, 'at first.'

'And now?' She watched the steam billow from the automatic kettle and reflected that they always boiled for a little too long, switched off a little too late.

But Forrest said nothing and Karys dropped the subject.

She poured the boiling water onto the teaspoonful of Nescafé in each mug before adding the milk. Then she put them on a tray together with the sandwiches, still in their bags and carried them into her office, Forrest close behind her.

It was a light, clean room, if a little small, with plain grey carpeting, two scarlet-coloured armchairs, a teak desk, and frosted glass windows. An organizer cork board held a couple of notices about medical lectures and a calendar with appointments scribbled on most lines. The coffee table and filing cabinets both held toppling piles of magazines. All, it seemed to Forrest's curious glance, on forensic medicine. In fact, he observed, the room contained nothing else except a mirror on the wall over the filing cabinet, and even that was half obscured by the leaning pile of journals. Vanity here, it seemed, played second fiddle to knowledge and practicality. There were no photographs: no husband, lover, boyfriend or children. That made him thoughtful. In fact, now he wondered about it, in the five years he had worked with Karys he had never once heard her talk about her family. Yet she must have someone. Everyone had someone. Everyone except him. The old emotion of bitter self-pity threatened to swamp him. He hadn't been a bad husband. He'd worked long hours, but that was surely part of his job, she'd known that when she'd married him. No, the problem had been that after marriage Maggie had changed and he hadn't. She had matured, become sophisticated, interested in art and painting, music, ballet – he grimaced – culture with a capital 'C'. He watched Karys settle into her seat and put the sandwiches on a plate, laying them out as neatly as his mother used to.

But he asked the question too soon in the embryonic relationship. 'You married?'

Instantly Karys looked up with a fierce, guarded look. 'No,' she said shortly and handed him a sandwich. 'Tuna?' And then, as though it would help regain the easy, comfortable mood she asked, 'Or tuna?'

'Tuna,' he said.

Karys crossed her legs and leant back in her chair, without knowing it mirroring the gesture with which Brenda Watlow had attempted to attract her son-in-law. Forrest caught a vague waft of a soapy, sweet scent, a strange contrast to the green cotton surgical gown that enveloped her short figure. But despite the gown, the attitude had overtones of sexuality of which Karys, unlike the theatre sister, was unconscious. For an instant Forrest had a flash of perception. If she had felt anything for him she would have changed into something a little more flattering. The realization depressed him.

'Well go on,' she prompted, speaking seriously. 'Ask

away, although I really don't know what I can do to help.'

Forrest took a mammoth bite out of the sandwich and spoke with his mouth full. 'I know it's going over old ground but let's start with the killing. There was no medical knowledge needed for that, was there?'

'The killing itself? The blow to the head? No,' she said decisively. 'There was no specialized medical knowledge in that at all. It was the same old clumsy thing, the bash with a blunt instrument. Favourite thugs' greeting.'

Forrest pursued the point. 'So anyone could have done it?'

Karys nodded. 'Anyone.'

'And the strangulation?'

'Anyone.' The answer was the same but the question diverted her thoughts back to the tie, the funny, Disney cartoon tie and she felt a shudder of recognition as though she knew the mind that had used it.

Forrest took another large bite out of his sandwich before proceeding.

'The sutures and scalpels and things like that – it seems to me that anyone can get hold of them. We rang the surgical suppliers. They don't make any checks. You simply order.'

'I've run some checks myself,' Karys said. 'Unofficially. On the sutures. The suppliers have told me they deliver around 200 boxes every month just to this hospital. A box contains 20 packs.'

'What sort of accounting is there?'

Karys just stared. 'In the hospital? You must be joking. *Boxes* of them could go missing every single day and no one would be the wiser.'

'So they could have come from Queen's.'

'That's not all,' Karys said. 'They also supply veter-
inary surgeries, GP surgeries, some dentists, you name
it, David.' She was a little more comfortable using his
first name second time around. 'And not being classed
as a drug or anything there are no tight controls.
Anyone could steal them. From anywhere. They're not
even locked up. They're just lying around. And that's
ignoring the fact that, as you said, the suppliers deliver
to virtually anyone who orders from them.'

'So the list is thrown wide again?' Karys nodded.
'But the bags are marked with the hospital code.'

'Yes.' Karys's answer was reluctant.

Forrest leant in close, hoping to catch another waft
of her scent. He was disappointed. 'What other equipment would he have needed? Something to hold the
skin?'

'Maybe. He'd definitely have needed a pair of
forceps to grip the silk. Scissors. Any old scissors. But
anyone can buy a pair of forceps or some scissors. Boots
sell them as well as all the other chemists. They don't
have to have come from the hospital at all.'

'Could the lab tell us anything about the scalpel?'

'A bit. The same sort of sources as the sutures.
Chemists don't normally supply scalpels. Particularly
specialized ones.'

Forrest was appalled. 'But it's potentially a lethal
weapon.'

'How many murders have you heard of using a
scalpel?'

'None – illegally.' It was a sick joke.

Karys ignored it.

'The actual blade?'

She drew a small chart from the top drawer of the desk. It was a catalogue of scalpel blades, twenty-eight in all. Different shapes and sizes. 'Each one is used by a surgeon for a different part of the body or a different procedure,' she explained, before pointing out a large, curved blade with a number 22 etched on it. 'This is the one that carved through Wilson's groin,' she said. 'The lab could afford to be ninety-nine per cent sure because at one point our "surgeon" had missed his mark. Then he retracked to his original, planned line. By looking at the layers of skin under the microscope the lab could be quite sure.'

'Well that helps.'

'It will help if your killer's source was the hospital, because even in such a huge hospital complex as this only one or two theatres will habitually use both number 22 blades and 5/0 silk. When you think of it it's a funny combination – very fine silk, but a clumsy blade. The blade is robust enough to be used for adult, abdominal surgery. But the silk's far too fine for that. It would break. It's far more suitable for plastic surgery. If you found a theatre which used this particular combination – say it did plastics a couple of days a week and abdominals for the rest of the time, it might help you to home in on someone a bit quicker. The only trouble is that the other theatres may well keep this combination in stock.' She hesitated. 'I don't know what Barney will make of the combination, but to me it suggests even more that your killer was unlikely to be a medic.'

'Maybe,' Forrest said thoughtfully, 'Wilson's murder was something else. Not sadistic mutilation or anything like that. Maybe it was a sort of yah boo at the medical profession rather than an act committed by a medic or a mock-medic.'

Suddenly, without warning, Karys went cold. It was the childish phrase Forrest had used that had triggered it off. Yah boo. She could visualize the sort of person with awful clarity, tongue lolling and eyes rolling ceilingwards. Poking fun at the self-conscious status of a surgeon. It forced old memories back into her mind so she knew she would return to sleepless nights. The more she tried *not* to think, the clearer the picture became. She knew the type of warped mind that would have found the murder of Colin Wilson funny, the mock-hernia operation on a dead man something to laugh about. She understood the person only too well. In fact she was so familiar with his mind that she could picture him suturing the wound of a dead man, snipping the stitches with sharp, pointed scissors.

Forrest was staring at her.

The sandwich suddenly seemed immensely unappealing. She put the half-finished one back on her plate, nauseated. She must say something. 'How specific could they be about the plastic bag?'

'It came from the hospital trust. There was a code. Along the top. According to the hospital manager it almost certainly came from one of the operating theatres within the last few months.'

'I see. Any particular theatre?'

Forrest shook his head. 'They couldn't go that far.'

Karys smiled at him, showing a neat row of small, white teeth. Forrest noted them and thought them her most attractive attribute. His wife, with her voluptuous, hour-glass figure and attention to make-up would have called Karys plain. Plump and plain. And David Forrest, with Maggie on his arm, might once have agreed with her but now he realized there were lots of things he liked about the pathologist. He liked her plumpness; it relaxed him. He liked her shining brown bob, even the heavy glasses that seemed to blot out the intelligent, serious eyes which could, on occasions, look merry and full of fun. In fact, he liked almost everything about her, except that fierce, defensive, repel-all-boarders look, but particularly he liked her teeth. He grinned at her encouragingly.

'I don't suppose Paget got us some dessert?'

She opened the top drawer of her desk. 'Chocolate?'

He took the couple of squares from her. 'Thanks.'

'It's a weakness of mine,' she confessed.

'Mine too.'

They sat in companionable silence for a while. When Forrest's mouth was empty he ventured yet another question. 'Can I ask you something else?'

'Of course.'

'The mutilation,' Forrest began. 'What was the point of it?'

'Talk to Barney,' she urged. 'If anyone should be able to penetrate the murky depths of a warped mind he should.'

'And if he's wrong?'

'That's a chance you'll have to take. But Barney isn't usually wrong.' She looked up. 'He is clever, you know.'

'I just wish he wasn't so aware of it.'

'He's always been like that.'

Forrest wanted to probe. How well had she known Lewisham? Had they been friends? Lovers? Glancing at the set expression on Karys's face he did not dare ask anything.

He drained his mug and put it down deliberately hard on the desk but Karys did not offer him a refill. He knew she was anxious for him to leave. She even glanced surreptitiously at her watch, twice, clumsily pretending to adjust the sleeve of her gown. Forrest stood up. So did she.

'I'll see you to the front door.'

Just as they reached it the telephone rang. 'Don't worry,' he said. 'I'll see myself out.'

Even so he heard her first words. 'Darling. Yes, I'm fine. Only having lunch. No, on my own now.'

Typical, he thought. Just as he was getting to like her. Up pops a boyfriend. And he felt a little cheated. There should have been a photograph of him, even if only to warn him to keep his distance and his still raw emotions tightly reined in. But their lunch together had been purely work. So why hadn't she told her friend that she'd shared it with him?

Feeling a touch of poetic justice he closed the door very gently behind him.

Brenda got him the blades. She'd been getting them for him for years. She picked them off the trolleys when the operations were finished. No one minded, she'd told him. They'd no use for them. They were disposable anyway, meant to be thrown away after each operation. Useless.

Not to him.

She'd told him she cleaned them very carefully, rinsing away the blood and flesh under the tap before scrubbing them with a nylon nailbrush and finally putting them through a cycle of the autoclave which sterilized them. Then she collected them into a small plastic box with a sliding plastic lid that had once contained sutures. As she had handed them over Brenda had given him one of her plump, comfortable smiles. 'I have to do it properly, Malcolm,' she'd said with a wink. He'd nodded his head, impressed by her thoroughness.

'The steam sterilizer kills all the bugs, you see. So you're safe, absolutely sterile.'

He'd stared at the shining blades with new respect.

It had been Brenda who had introduced him to the fact that there were different sorts of blades. Up until then he hadn't taken much notice. He'd realized there were various shapes and sizes but he'd never really thought about it. And then one day Brenda had been waiting for her son-in-law, Terry, to pick her up. He'd been a bit late so she'd had a bit of time to spare and she had shown him the tiny number etched on the blunt end of the blade, the bit that clipped onto the handle. She'd got him that too. Two – a big one and a small one.

'This tiny little blade has a number six on it. Do you see?'

He'd leaned over her to peer short-sightedly at the blade, held between her wash-reddened fingers, and he had seen what she was talking about. He'd looked questioningly at her, then uttered just one word, 'Why?'

'So we use the right blade for the right job. They all have separate little jobs to do. This clever little blade might be used to remove a child's appendix or something similar.' She'd held it up in front of his eyes to show him. 'It's such a delicate blade, Malcolm, in the right hands. And small enough to perform a very tiny operation. It's so smart it could repair a hole in a newborn baby's heart. Now this one.' She'd picked up the largest blade he had. Too big for him to use very often, although it cut as finely and precisely as the others. 'This one might be used to do a big operation on a fat man's stomach. What do you think of that, Malcolm?'

He'd grinned at her. He would enjoy playing with the blades even more now that he knew a little bit about them. He selected another one. 'And what about this one, Brenda?'

The one he'd picked was long and thin and sharp. Cruel, he thought. If one was strong enough for a fat man's stomach and the other delicate enough to operate on a baby's heart then this one was cruel. So what would they use such a cruel blade for?

Even Brenda's fleshy face had changed while she handled it. 'Oh, that one might be used to make a little nick in something. To pop a catheter in.'

Malcolm had watched her speaking. He didn't like the casual way she had said that 'pop a catheter in.' Surgery was serious work. Surgeons were skilled and brilliant people, worthy of respect. They didn't just pop things in. She shouldn't have said that word. She shouldn't be so flippant about it. He didn't like people not taking things seriously enough. It upset him.

Maybe Brenda had picked up some of Malcolm's disapproval. Maybe she had heard a car outside. Or maybe she just felt suddenly uncomfortable at the way he was staring at her. She made a great show of peering through the window as though she couldn't wait for Terry to turn up. And when, a fraction of a second later, he did, she tossed the spiky blade carelessly into the box and jumped up.

Malcolm could tell from the way she sidled towards

the door and said very deliberately, 'Terry's here now,' that she was glad to go. And for the first time ever he was glad to see her go. Not only because she had upset him and because she had been careless with one of his blades, but because he badly wanted to play with them, line them up and study the numbers, look at the shapes and see how many sorts he already had. Then he would try to guess what they would all be used for. He would group them like soldiers, the same shapes together.

Next time Brenda came he would ask her how many different sorts of blades there were so he could check whether he had them all, a full set. But he was suddenly seized with the worry that if he wasn't nice enough to her there would not be a next time. She would not come again. And he did not know where else he would be able to get the blades from. He just managed to get the words out as she turned the door handle. 'Please, Brenda, please, come back. Bring me some more. Please. Promise.'

She was a nurse, schooled to react to the pity inside her. And she did pity Malcolm. He was a sad, lonely creature. Different since his mother had died – more inadequate, more pathetic. Instantly she beamed at him, forgetting the earlier moment of discord.

'Of course I'll come back,' she said kindly. 'I'll come back one afternoon next week. But don't wait in for me, Malcolm. I don't know which afternoon I'll be able to come. I'm not sure what hours I'll be working. It depends on the operating lists. But don't worry. I will bring you some more blades. I can leave them in their box on the hall table if you're out.'

She couldn't know that Malcolm wouldn't dare go

out any afternoon next week until she'd come. Terrified he might miss her he would sit in his room with his door ajar, watching down the stairs towards the front door so he would hear her knock. He couldn't go out because if he did miss her someone else might steal his box of blades. Already he'd decided – he'd better stay in, all week.

He listened while she clattered down the stairs before selecting two of the blades, the small, clever one with the number 6 etched near the handle part and the long thin one with an angled end and an 11 on it. He liked the way they clipped onto the handles Brenda had given him. He clipped the thin one onto the small handle and sat back. Now he was ready to work.

Chapter Five

Caroline Fielding elbowed her way through couples carrying pink and blue wrapped bundles towards the reception desk. She flipped her ID card at the receptionist, a pretty Asian girl with scarlet lipstick and nails to match who asked, very nicely, how she could help.

'I want to find out which doctors and midwives were on duty on a particular night.'

'You'll have to speak to the nursing officer,' the girl said. 'I'll ring her for you, shall I?'

'Thanks.' Fielding managed a tight smile. The conveyor belt of babies being taxied home was making her uncomfortable.

The receptionist pressed a few buttons, spoke into the telephone, sat back and watched DS Fielding with large, dark eyes. 'I know,' she said, picking up on Fielding's discomfort. 'Makes you sick, don't it?' Her eyes scanned the crowds of cooing new parents. 'I wonder how many there'd be if men was the ones having the babies?'

Fielding gave a non-committal grunt and the receptionist continued in her broad, Brummy accent. 'Got any kids yourself?'

Fielding shook her head. 'No time.'

'Me neither.' She ventured a wide bonding smile.

Fielding was relieved when a stout woman in a dark red suit strode towards her. No mistaking her authority. Even the doting parents parted in front of her like the Red Sea before Moses. She came straight up to Fielding and introduced herself without preamble. 'I'm Mrs Kray, the Nursing Officer.' Her eyes scanned Fielding's ID card and her face altered. 'Why don't we go into my office,' she suggested.

She made no conversation as they proceeded along the corridor and preceded her through a door clearly marked with her name and flicked the board on it to 'Do Not Disturb'. She motioned Fielding to sit in the armchair opposite her desk.

'Now what's all this about?'

'You've heard about the body, found just over a week ago on the hospital site?'

'Yes. But I don't see what – '

'Look, these are purely routine enquiries. The murdered man's wife had a baby at this hospital earlier on this year.'

'Ye-es? I still don't see – '

'As I said,' DS Fielding could, on occasion, be very patient, 'it's purely routine. I just wondered whether the birth of his daughter might have brought him into contact with anyone who might have a connection with his murder.'

Mrs Kray gave her a sharp look. 'I haven't a clue what you're saying,' she began.

Fielding pressed the point. 'Did everything go all right during the delivery and afterwards?'

'I'd have to look through the records.'

'Would you?'

Mrs Kray heaved a sigh and spoke into the telephone. 'What was the date of his wife's delivery?'

'The twenty-first of January.'

'It'll take a while to locate the records.' Irritation made her face tighten. They were left, facing each other, awkwardly waiting for the secretary to bring the notes. 'Any children yourself?' Mrs Kray asked DS Fielding conversationally.

It seemed all anyone could talk about in this place was babies.

Forrest, in the meantime, was tackling a joint press conference with Barney Lewisham. Press conferences were a policeman's nightmare, when an unguarded answer could set fifty pens streaking across the page. But to manage one with a forensic psychiatrist by his side who was determined to be the star of the show, magnified the nightmare at least twenty-five times. The girl with the flame-coloured hair sitting in the centre of the front row was not helping matters. In fact, she seemed to be playing a different game altogether, appearing less interested in Colin Wilson's murder than in the psychiatrist himself.

The situation annoyed Forrest and he blamed the woman with the red hair. Titian, Maggie would have called it. Red, he called it. He had noticed her as soon as he had sat down behind the large table set on the stage of the local infant's school hall. A makeshift newsroom. The media ghouls needed somewhere large – there were so many of them. Typical, he thought sourly. Give them a gruesome murder and they'll come flocking. He scanned the faces wishing, not for the first time, he could bypass these press conferences completely and simply issue a statement. He wouldn't deny they were necessary and the public needed to be informed – even if the only real outcome was to encourage heightened vigilance. Sometimes they bore unexpected fruit. People did read newspapers.

He sensed hostility behind the girl's narrow green eyes and knew that his dislike of the casual way she sprawled in the chair, legs splayed, one thumb hooked into the pocket of her brown jeans, had communicated itself to her. It wasn't a good idea to antagonize the press.

As he had expected she was the first to speak. 'Exactly what progress are you making in finding the killer of Colin Wilson?' Her voice was loud, clear and very haughty.

Without much hope, he tried to distract her with the euphemism that the police were proceeding with their enquiries. But she was tenacious – and intelligent.

'We understand you are centering your investigation in and around Queen's Hospital.'

Forrest felt forced into conceding the point. 'That's right.'

Her green cat's eyes stared into his. 'Why?'

'It's where the body was found.'

Maybe the girl really was a cat. She sat, pencil poised, almost purring.

Lewisham cut in. 'Because, apart from the connections already discussed in previous press conferences we now believe a scalpel was used on Colin Wilson's body.'

They had already decided the time was ripe for them to disclose this snippet of information and there was no reason why it should have been Forrest rather than Lewisham who dished it out. All the same, Forrest was annoyed. Lewisham had his part to play in this little charade, but this hadn't been it.

'A scalpel?' The red-headed girl was leafing through her reporter's pad. 'But you told us on the . . .' the green cat's eyes dropped 'twenty-fifth of November that Colin Wilson had been strangled following a blow to the back of the head.'

'That is correct,' Forrest chipped in testily. 'What we did not know – for certain – was that another wound had been inflicted with a surgeon's scalpel.'

'What part of the body was – ' she was directing her question to Lewisham – 'mutilated?'

Without even a swift, checking glance at Forrest, Lewisham said baldly, 'The groin.'

Gasps and plenty more scribbling followed. But the girl did nothing except bite her lip. Maybe she had a tape recorder as well as a pad.

'Do you mean the injuries were of a sexual nature?'

Lewisham gave a condescending smile. 'No. I do not.'

'So what can you tell us about the killer?'

Was she ever going to let anyone else in with their questions?

Concisely Lewisham repeated what he had told the police force, adding nothing but leaving nothing out. Forrest felt his face grow tight. What right did these bloody journalists have to question him like this? Why did they feel it was their God-given duty to lay everything open on a slab? The word evoked a vision of Wilson's pale body, stretched out, awaiting post-mortem. He blinked quickly to blot it out.

The red-headed girl shot Forrest an appraising look and he felt his face grow hot. But her next question was again directed at Lewisham. 'Do you think this is the work of an employee of the hospital?'

Lewisham leant forward. 'I believe,' he said, peering over the rim of the half-moon glasses, 'that it is a distinct possibility. Almost certainly our killer is someone familiar with the hospital site. And perhaps someone who worked there in the past or indeed the present.'

More furious scribbling.

Forrest felt he had to say something. 'And that is why we are concentrating our enquiries around Queen's Medical Centre,' he reiterated firmly.

The girl smiled at him then, and again Forrest had the uncomfortable feeling that she read the resentment flashing through his mind. So much so that he felt grateful to a second journalist, a thin young man dressed entirely in black – jeans, jacket, shirt – who asked how the dead man's family were taking it, had there been any comment from the hospital board committee, had the police any idea of motive or had it been a random killing? Forrest answered fluently and predictably, with recovered equanimity. The widow was – upset. His mind flicked back to the brief, painful interview he had had with Laura Wilson; young, bemused, vulnerable, holding her plump daughter tightly on her hip. The hospital committee had expressed – regret. They were not in a position to comment on the motive for the killing. Lewisham added his comments: a warning that the killer might strike again. By the end Forrest felt he had, at least, sounded like the Senior Investigating Officer.

*

Karys was still struggling to shake off the feeling that had haunted her ever since she had performed the post-mortem on Colin Wilson. It had begun in the usual way: her old nightmares returned, when she was awake, not asleep; with a cold feeling trickling down her back, as though, if she turned quickly, he would be there, behind her, with that strange, mocking look on his face. As though he could penetrate her most secret thoughts. For years now she had wished she could forget him – shake off his influence, return to the person she had been when she had first stepped inside Queen's Medical School. But even drawing on all her reserves of optimism she knew she was playing a losing game. And Tonya knew too.

Two days after Wilson's death Tonya had slammed her mug of coffee down on the kitchen table. 'Are you going to tell me what's up? Or do I have to prise it out of you?'

Karys had given her flatmate a weak smile. Tonya was one of the few people who knew the whole story, from chance beginning, to sorry end. Only it wasn't the end. People's characters don't change. Flaws stay. We only learn, with age, to disguise them. Karys would have given anything for no one to know her flaws. But someone had to know. And like the true friend that Tonya was she had attempted to dissolve Karys's guilt.

Tonya had sat and watched Karys over the rim of her coffee mug. 'You like this – Forrest – don't you?' she said perceptively.

'He's OK. Yes. I like him, but not like that. He's nice. That's all.'

Tonya gave a knowing look. 'What does he look like?'

'Nondescript. Tallish, thinnish. A nice smile.'

Tonya pounced on this. 'What do you mean – a nice smile?'

'Sort of personal. Warm.'

'Hmm. Hair colour?'

Karys thought for a minute. 'Nondescript,' she said again. 'Sort of not quite blond, not quite brown. Mousey, I suppose. Getting a bit thin on top.'

'Eyes?' her friend demanded.

'Blue,' Karys said, then added, 'Nice.'

Tonya made a face. 'When are you going to learn? They're not all like *him*.'

Karys gave her a faint smile. 'I know that, Tonya. The trouble is I don't know how to tell the difference. Someone as poor at human judgement as I am really shouldn't tangle too much with the opposite sex, don't you think?'

Tonya snorted. 'No. I bloody well don't. For goodness' sake, you were young then. You just got in with the wrong bloke. He was a piece of shit, using that against you. And to be honest, Karys, I think he was clever. Bloody clever.' She gave her friend a sly glance. 'They're not all like that.' She paused. 'But this Forrest – he's not going to split us up, is he?'

Karys took a long look round their kitchen, at the expensive wooden Danish units, stained bottle green with the grain showing, at the rows of herbs, spices and, at the good-quality French saucepans haphazardly arrayed along the shelf. Didn't Tonya realize? This was home. This was comfort. Not for anything would she risk losing this.

Tonya put her hand on her arm. 'Don't start imagining things, Karrie. Forrest isn't *him*.' She got up to refill her coffee cup. 'Your problem is you see him behind every bush. He's your big bogey man.' She came back to the table. 'It's guilt, you know. You're going to have to see someone about it. And from what you've told me I would guess you aren't half as guilty as you think.'

'In both cases?'

'In both cases,' Tonya answered firmly. 'So if I were you I should get on and enjoy life.'

'If only.'

Volatile as ever Tonya got angry again. 'It's been eight years, Karrie. Eight bloody long, self-flagellating years. And you're still punishing yourself. For nothing. *You* didn't do anything. *He* did.'

'At my suggestion.'

'You don't even know that. Not for sure.'

'I know. Just like with Sam. I make a joke, someone dies. People take me seriously, Tonya.'

Forrest was having nightmares too, spliced into dreams. Half awake. Half asleep. The case was not progressing as he knew it ought. It was making him jumpy, irritable and sleepless. Instead of counting sheep, he ran through his meeting that evening with DS Shaw and DS Fielding.

'The trouble is, sir,' Shaw had said, 'none of us knows what we're looking for.'

His answer – lacked substance, full of cliché, OK in detective novels, hopeless in a real life case; 'Anything out of the ordinary.'

Shaw had spread his hands. 'Everything seems to be out of the ordinary. I mean there's deaths everywhere you look. People shacked up on casualty trolleys, kids still waiting to see a doctor three hours after they arrive. There's loads of apologetic letters to parents and other relatives. The place is a disaster area.'

'Well, it wasn't like that at the maternity hospital. It was all sweetness and light, and pink and blue blankets.'

Forrest had been glad to turn to Fielding. 'Nothing there then?'

'No, sir. The Wilsons' baby was born without problems. A normal delivery. Father present.'

'Right.' Forrest tried to convince himself he had sounded decisive. 'Then I want both of you to comb through everything at Queen's. I don't know what we're looking for, Shaw. Maybe nothing. But you've got as many men as you need. Take the bloody place apart. Layer on layer. I want Wilson's killer caught.'

He repeated the phrase in his mind: I want him caught . . . before he does it again.

It was this barely formed thought which had brought in its wake a return of the depression that had felled him when Maggie had confessed to loving another man. A few days later she had left him. But that was personal. This was not. Then he had been able to escape to work, now he could not. It was work that was the problem. A long tunnel with no light at the end. He had prided himself on being immune from involvement with his cases, it was just a job. But he knew he was not, it was all he had – now. Maybe he was getting too old and vulnerable. But he was not old – he was only thirty-five. Physically and mentally fit. He had thirty more years of hard work left in him. Maybe it was just the divorce that had made him lose confidence. Temporarily.

If only they could have just one, firm lead which took them somewhere. Anywhere would do as long as it was somewhere.

Forrest tried to console himself by blaming the hospital site. So big, so many people, so many comings and goings. And, of course, no one had seen or heard anything.

Even quite promising leads had turned up nothing. The address to which Colin Wilson had been sent to repair the leak had again turned up nothing. Wilson might have been lured and killed there. The surgeon's slash might have been made and sutured there. But there was no evidence.

Wilson's van had been another potentially promising lead. A ten-year-old Vauxhall Nova. Lewisham had been right: Wilson's mobile-phone number had advertised his plumbing services on the vehicle's back door. It would have been easy for anyone to copy it down. The van, like Wilson's body, had soon been found four bus stops away from the house he had been lured to, on the same number one bus route, just through Moseley village, the Greenwich village of Birmingham where all the chic types and artists hung out. None of them had seen anything either. 'Too bloody stoned if you ask me,' DC Murray Lowen had reported. The van had been picked up and stripped by forensics to find – again – nothing. No blood, no hairs belonging to anyone but Wilson, his wife and his baby daughter. Yet the killer must have driven the van to have dumped it. He had probably sat on the number one bus for his ride home. But no one had seen him.

The street of flats which had housed the van overnight should have borne some fruit. Surely someone should have spotted the van being dumped. They had made extensive house-to-house enquiries. Of course the good citizens offered various helpful explanations as to why they had seen nothing: if it had been after dark, their curtains would have been drawn; they might have been in bed; they didn't go out much in the day when the weather was cold or miserable; they had been watching television, or asleep. The only fact that had surfaced was that the van had not been there in the afternoon when darkness fell and had been there when they had drawn their curtains back in the morning.

Forrest went over and over the statements searching for answers to even the most basic questions. Where had the 'surgeon' performed his operation? Where did he get his materials? Even at home, through the hours he was supposed to be sleeping, Forrest forced himself to work on, trying to understand. Oh, for Poirot's 'little grey cells', Holmes's sudden inspiration. Even his cocaine.

Waterman believed the solution would come from analysing the psyche. So Forrest sat alone, in darkness and in silence and forced himself to consider the murderer's mind. What could conceivably have made a human being act in this way? In his small, bare sitting room stripped of furniture for his wife's new love-nest he almost smiled because the answer to that question was *nothing*. Murder – yes, in a fit of temper, red hot hatred, to protect a loved one. He had thought of killing when his wife had glowingly described her love for another man. He had wanted to punch, kick, hammer the hell out of the man and strangle her. But they had just been thoughts, a lava flow of hatred which had cooled down before any action – except legal action – had taken place. The civilized man's resort.

So, Forrest reasoned, if there was no experience in this world that would make him commit cold-blooded murder before maiming his corpse, what did it tell him about the killer? That he was unbalanced? So, we search for a madman.

He stared for a long time at the blank wall, recalling the picture that had sat there, before his wife had removed it, leaving nothing to look at but a picture hook. It had been a strange choice of picture for a sitting room, even for his wife. A print by someone called Magritte. He had always called it 'Raining Men'. That's what it looked like to him, men in bowler hats raining on a terrace of uniform mustard-coloured houses. His wife had told him the title on many occasions, but now, for the life of him, he could not remember what it was. He recognized it sometimes when he passed shops that sold avant-garde posters, shops that reminded him very much of his wife, always trying to appear 'arty', a woman of taste. Forrest smiled ruefully. Maybe she had been a woman of taste. Maybe that was why she had finally left him for someone else, someone who had recognized qualities in his wife that he had failed to appreciate. Although how the chinless French teacher she had taken up with could possibly be described as . . .

He stood up, suddenly angry. This was no good. No bloody good at all. He glared at the nail. He must get a new picture or pull the nail out of the wall. He just stopped himself from banging his head against it and deliberately turned his mind to Karys, using her to blot out the painful anger that shot right through him.

He immediately felt calmed by the memory of her thoughtful grey eyes, her soothing voice. Dammit. She was as good as a tranquilliser.

But almost as quickly as he had conjured up the image he dismissed it. He was being unfair to her. He really knew nothing about her. Most of his impressions had been dreamt, imagined, filled in by a wishful, lonely, embittered mind. Forrest picked up a bottle of whisky from the mantelpiece and poured a stiff tot into the stained glass at its side. He lit a small cigar and felt terribly alone. More lonely than at any time since Maggie had gone. He needed to talk. He had been wrong; he had thought the loneliness would lessen and finally abandon him, but it hadn't. It had become more and more intense until now it was unbearable. The quiet semi gave him too much time alone to ponder – even at such a busy time as this when he spent most of his waking moments on the investigation. The truth was he was glad of the overtime. Not for the money. He had no real need for much now. A clean break of a divorce had left him financially solvent. But being alone gave him too much time to think. And thinking, right now, was unpleasant.

Even with the help of the whisky he tossed and turned through the night. Maybe there had been no point in him going to bed at all. In the early hours Forrest finally gave up any attempt at sleep. He did not dare take the sleeping pills the doctor had prescribed because he had to be alert the next day. So instead he brewed some tea and peered through the window as though by divine revelation he would see who was to be the surgeon's next victim.

*

The 'surgeon' knew very well who his next victim would be. She had been selected with all the care and precision that marked his entire campaign. Like a theatre list things had their proper order. There must be nothing haphazard about his operations and he chuckled as his mouth formed the word, operations.

But he had had a problem! Rosemary had married and cunningly changed her name. So Student Nurse Rosemary Shearer was now Staff Nurse Rosemary Baring. She had moved hospitals. Subtle questioning in the right quarter revealed that she had not done well. She had managed to qualify before marrying but, with a subsequent divorce, her career had taken a nose dive and she was now to be found working on the other side of Edgbaston in a private nursing home that specialized in cosmetic surgery. The 'surgeon' took a recce one afternoon and was initially impressed. It was a swish place, neat red brick, with clean white window frames and a hand-painted sign advertising proudly, The Cater Clinic. The 'surgeon' clapped a hand to his mouth and giggled. He could picture the work that went on in their theatre: varicose veins, face lifts, breast, ear and nose jobs. He giggled again. He had an idea. He flexed his fingers, excitement making them tingle. Maybe he would have a go at some cosmetic surgery too, perhaps a breast reduction. He was tempted to laugh out loud. Did she need a breast reduction? He must take a look at her. He pulled up in the far corner of the car park, wedging himself between a Mercedes and a BMW, noting other cars that were in reserved spaces, the manager's Jaguar, the doctors' Audis, a Rolls-Royce pulled up right outside the door in the space grandly marked, Consultant Surgeon. That was what they liked about private practice. Treated surgeons the way they should be treated. He looked round him. Maybe they should have a parking space for him too. Like war memorials honouring 'The Unknown Soldier', they should paint a sign, 'The Unknown Surgeon'. Looking along the row he wondered whether Rosemary had a car. At the bottom end of the car park were a couple of clapped out vehicles. Maybe one of them would be hers. He wondered why she had left the National Health Service. Money? Or some other reason?

He turned round and drove home.

It was a week later that he first sighted her, late on a bright afternoon in December. He had needed to get a description, a precise description. Plenty of nurses worked here, and he needed to be sure. It was not so difficult. People, in general, were not so suspicious they would not confirm an identity. He had half formed a picture of her in his mind, with the result that he felt a flood of recognition as she came out of the staff entrance of the clinic looking tired after, presumably, a long and busy shift. She stood in the fluorescent light of the ambulance entrance and seemed to draw in a deep breath before lighting a cigarette and dragging the smoke down into her lungs. She had not, he noted with further malice, worn well. For a woman of twenty-seven she should have looked younger, less haggard. Perhaps there was some justice in the world after all – other than his. Already her face looked old, her hair lank, thin and dull. She even stooped a little, the posture emphasized by a long black mac which reached almost to her ankles. The buttons were open, the belt trailing to the floor. She looked already defeated as, of course, she was.

He watched her cross the road to the bus stop, ticking off the first of his questions. No car. At the edge of the road she waited and stared at the pavement with an air of pessimism, as though she believed no bus would ever come. When one did arrive she didn't look around but vanished inside, so she failed to see him and missed her only chance of salvation. As the bus moved off the 'surgeon' saw her face quite clearly. White skin, heavy lidded large brown eyes, straggling shoulder-length dark brown hair. Her eyes drifted across him without recognition, not even registering his presence. The bus moved off and he was left still sitting in his car, staring at an empty pavement.

Chapter Six

23 December 1999

Lewisham turned up unannounced in Forrest's office, on Thursday, a couple of days before Christmas. Forrest had gone for a cup of coffee. When he came back to his room the psychiatrist was sitting in his chair. It gave Forrest a shock and put him at a disadvantage.

'I've had a good chance to study the reports,' Lewisham said, without preamble. 'I know more about Wilson's killer.'

Forrest felt his hackles rise. Mumbo-jumbo, he thought. He will tell me nothing more than I already know. Politely he inclined his head. 'Go on,' he said. 'I'm all ears.'

'For a start, he's left-handed.'

'What? The pathologist said nothing about that.'

Lewisham permitted himself a smug smile. 'I know Doctor Harper says nothing in her report about our killer being left-handed, but he is. I've studied the direction of the cuts, looked at the knots, the tie, the area of bruising around the neck. And finally I've worked it out for myself.'

'Are you sure?' Forrest hadn't meant his voice to sound so hostile.

'Positive. I'm a bit surprised she didn't mention it.'

Forrest frowned at the implied criticism of Karys.

'He is of average stature – somewhere between five eight and five ten, physically strong and clever, but not an intellectual.'

'How can you say all this?' Forrest burst out.

I believe you would have no trouble following my reasoning.'

'Try me.'

'Right. The stature can be worked out by contemplating the problem of getting a body up to a certain height. Assuming, that is, that he does not have an adjustable operating table.'

Forrest blinked.

'I have decided that a body could be lifted fairly easily up to a height of three feet. Maybe three feet six. Again, the direction and depth of the cuts indicate little pressure on the scalpel.'

Forrest could see flaws in the arguments. 'The murderer could have kneeled,' he objected.

Lewisham infuriated him by giving him another supercilious glance. 'Our "surgeon" would not kneel to conduct his operation,' he said. 'Authenticity, Inspector Forrest. It means a great deal to him. He must stand.' He lifted an index finger to point straight at Forrest. It had the effect of casting a hex. 'I tell you, Forrest. I *know* this man.'

Forrest began to see the way Lewisham worked. He entered the 'surgeon's' evil mind, and from that viewpoint he scanned the possibilities and probabilities. Forrest looked into Lewisham's strange, marmalade-coloured eyes and was fascinated. 'Anything else?'

Lewisham leant forward. 'Did you find any hair on Wilson's body that was not his?'

Forrest shook his head. 'Regretfully, no.'

'Good. That means he did wear a hat.'

Forrest had visions of a fashion item. 'A hat?'

'A theatre hat.' Lewisham rubbed his hands together. 'One of those disposable paper things. They use them in theatre. Covers the hair. Excellent. You see it means my instinct that our friend has to have these touches of authenticity is correct.'

The man's enthusiasm was infectious. Forrest smiled. 'Is that good?'

'Oh yes,' Lewisham said. 'It's how we will eventually trap him, through his desire to be recognized as a fellow professional.'

'You're taking this too far.'

'You think so?' Lewisham stood up. 'Have you never understood that when a mind is psychotic it is also logical? It may not be my logic. It may not be your logic. But once you understand the extent and reality of delusion everything is clearly spread out.'

'You've lost me.'

Lewisham stepped closer. 'That's the problem,' he said softly. 'One has to be prepared to deviate, to follow the strange mind along the maze. Only then can you understand. I have found this already. Policemen are far too bound up with the pedantic, the literal and the logical. Don't even try, Inspector Forrest. Let me wrestle with our killer. When I have him by the throat, then I shall consult you. Well,' he said in a sudden turnabout. 'If I don't see you again, have a nice Christmas.'

Forrest returned the greeting with a sinking feeling at the bottom of his stomach.

Christmas.

*

By sheer coincidence it was that same night that the 'surgeon' felt fully prepared for his next case. He had watched Rosemary for a couple of weeks now and he knew her routine as well as his own. Earlies at the Cater Clinic meant she caught the bus for a couple of stops to the flat she shared with another girl. Once, he had caught a glimpse of her flatmate, a short, neat woman with dark hair.

But if Rosemary worked the late shift, she finished at ten p.m. and usually went for a drink. Tonight she would finish at ten.

He sat in his car and waited.

At five minutes past ten she swung through the doors, her head down against the world, the weather and the flying snowflakes, her coat wrapped tightly around her. Just outside she fumbled in her pocket for a cigarette, lit it, and took a couple of deep drags before hurrying along Pritchard's Drive to the pub at the top.

Regular habits have their advantage. He knew what she would do next.

He kerb-crawled behind her. She never even looked back but hurried inside the pub.

He did too.

She ordered a drink, a half of lager.

He did too. From the other side of the bar.

It was early, but because Christmas was approaching and exams had finished the bar was closely packed with celebrating students. She was not part of them. She drank up quickly, hardly looking around. Certainly not at him. He wondered whether she would have a second drink. Sometimes she did. Tonight she did not and left the pub.

So did he.

She walked through the door. He smiled. She thought she was going home, to the dark, rough area to the north of Edgbaston. She approached a square, derelict block of 1960s flats awaiting demolition before redevelopment. Ideal for him. Already encased in corrugated sheeting and adorned with 'Keep Out' signs.

Rosemary glanced round uneasily, aware of the desertion of the streets, of the darkness, the lateness, the isolation of her route. Less than three hundred yards to the busy, Hagley Road. She hurried.

He could read her mind.

He pulled the car up – just in front of her, got out and approached her. Spoke. 'Excuse me, aren't you Rosemary Shearer, that was?' When she nodded and explained that Shearer had been her maiden name, he went on, 'Didn't you once work in the operating theatre?' Her expression was at first, startled.

'Yes.' She laughed. 'I did.'

He was friendly. 'I thought so. I used to work with you.'

'Oh.' She didn't remember.

She wouldn't remember.

'Well, goodbye.'

He moved past her. Then struck. From behind. So practised she dropped like a stone, her body thumping onto the pavement, then lying still. He dragged her behind the corrugated tin screen. He pulled a stocking from his pocket. So quick. So easy. And so, so effective. When he was sure she was dead he moved his car in close.

To work.

*

It was perfect textbook stuff. Mask on. Hat on. Gloves on. Gown on. He ran through the checklist, speaking as he worked, both to himself and to his patient. She lay obediently still. He removed her mac then her sweater, dropped both to the floor and kicked them out of the way. It would not do to contaminate his gloves. The bra, though, he had no option but to unhook. Then his patient was ready.

He stood for a moment, staring down at her, his mind working out the correct incision. Approach, they called it. Correct approach. Then he draped her entirely with green theatre towels.

'Scalpel.'

He liked to speak out loud. It gave him the illusion that he had a full team of staff watching him, admiring his skill with the blade, giving him the accolade he deserved. Then the first cut. Always the most exciting part, watching the skin part for him, revealing its secret underlying tissues. Though she hardly bled, only the tiniest of oozes. Shame that.

Different from last time, he used his hands to separate Rosemary from her breast, peeling back the tissues, exposing bone, mopping rapidly congealing blood from now obsolete blood vessels.

She had not needed a breast reduction at all. She was not a big girl.

The stitches gave him a bit of a problem. Not a nice, neat cut this time but a great big, untidy, jagged wound, inches wide. Difficult to suture. He wondered how other surgeons coped, but then their patients would heal, his would not. Shame that.

The entire procedure took well over an hour and he was tired by the end. Tired, yet exhilarated. This had been *major* surgery. Not some poxy little cut. Major surgery. It felt good.

Over his mask his eyes searched out the bright colour of yellow bags in the corner, and he smiled. Life had never felt so fine. Slowly he was feeling calmed by his work. He would return his patient to the hospital tonight. While it was still dark. He knew another place. Maybe it would take them a little longer to find this one.

It was so easy to drive her to the hospital site, pull up by the planned development, lift her body and dump it among the rubble.

Chapter Seven

24 December 1999

A blanket of cloud had descended over the city bringing with it a dull sheet of wet snow, unusual for Christmas Eve. Malcolm had pinned back the net curtain and was watching for Brenda, trying to ignore the sleet which tumbled from the sky lying for a moment on the pavement before melting into patchy blobs. He was worried that the weather would put her off and that she wouldn't come. Besides, people with families were often busy on Christmas Eve. There was a lot to do: turkey to stuff, presents to wrap. Too much work to spare the time to call on . . . Malcolm sat and fretted all morning.

In the afternoon he laid out his blades. He must have some pleasures. Carefully he lined them up. So many of them now. He must have at least forty. He counted them. Forty-one. He wondered if he had a full set. If Brenda did come he would ask her. Desperately he glanced across the room at the window. She would not come. He would be forced to wait until well after Christmas to add even one blade to his collection.

He was seized with a sudden fear. Were there any missing? Long ones, pointed ones, baby ones or big blunt ones?

Malcolm had a love of order and he loved to count.

Altogether there were twenty-three different shapes. Some curved, some straight. He put all the curved ones together, in order of size. Then all the straight ones, in order of size. His hand hovered over the lines. Which one would he concentrate on this afternoon? As it was almost Christmas he chose the largest and laid it out carefully, away from the others, on a piece of dark cloth that showed up the silvery stainless steel to perfection. He clipped the blade to one of his handles and held it, as Brenda had showed him, almost like a pencil, between the forefinger and thumb. Then with a delicate, practised manoeuvre he stroked the air, hardly hesitating, before closing his eyes. Whatever this one had been used for could be done again. To cut out a cancer? An appendix? A diseased length of bowel? And had the patient lived or died? That must make a difference to the vibes given off. Malcolm's pale eyes flipped open. Had this very object, in his hand, been responsible for someone's death?

He couldn't remember when he had first thought of the idea, to use the blades as a medium uses a crystal ball. But instead of peering into the future he looked into the past. And saw what they had done, the wonderful, wonderful work. Saving lives. Or not. It didn't always work. Today there was nothing. Maybe this blade hadn't been used before being discarded. He knew that the theatre sisters laid out many instruments on the operating trolley that were not needed. He closed his eyes again.

A little thought pushed into his mind, stopping him concentrating properly. Last week he'd said something to Brenda about cleaning them properly. Half as a joke he'd asked her if he could catch AIDS from them. She'd been really angry with him and her voice had been sharp and very unfriendly.

'What do you take me for, Malcolm?' She'd looked disgusted with him. 'You are such a fool,' she'd said unkindly. 'I'm sure you weren't this peculiar when you worked at the hospital.' She'd glared at him. 'It must be living on your own. Why don't you get a job? Do some work for a living. I can't understand you just sitting here day after day, doing nothing. The AIDS virus can't live outside the body, any old muggins knows that. And anyway, common or garden soap and water or bleach would kill it, let alone the stuff I've had it soaking in. And I've sterilized them in the bloody autoclave.' Her face had looked hard and nasty. A bit podgy. A bit piggy. 'I don't *have* to bring you the blades, Malcolm, you know. It's quite a nuisance collecting them up and cleaning them and then trailing all the way out here with them. Besides . . .' Her expression was hostile. 'What do you want them all for?' She'd glanced suspiciously round the little flat.

'I told you,' he'd answered grumpily. 'I do marquetry. You need sharp blades for that, so as not to split the veneers. You can never have enough of them. They go blunt.'

'I've never seen you doing any marquetry, I've never seen so much as a sliver of wood round this place.' Brenda's eyes had narrowed suspiciously. 'You're not having me on, are you?'

Malcolm squirmed. He didn't want Brenda to know. 'I, umm, tidy it all away before you come. It makes a mess.'

Remembering all this and watching the miserable weather, Malcolm was sure she would not come.

But she did.

She came at three, the cold, seeping from her clothes making the small flat cold too. 'You're lucky,' she said, flinging her arms around herself, stamping her feet and shivering. 'I finished early and thought I'd bring you your Christmas present.'

Malcolm was in a fret. What had she brought him? A present? A blade he didn't have?

Like a child he fidgetted while she rooted through her huge handbag. Then he remembered, he hadn't bought her anything.

Brenda fished something out of her bag. 'There,' she said proudly.

Malcolm stared in disappointment. Even wrapped he knew it wasn't the right shape for a box of blades, and he wanted nothing else. He tried to stammer out some thanks but Brenda wasn't even listening.

'Now don't go opening it before the great day.' He could have sworn her button-black eyes were scanning the room for her present. He felt a swift flush of anger. It wasn't right for her to expect things from him. He didn't have much money.

She stopped looking around the room and gazed at him. 'Promise me you won't,' she said.

'What?'

'Open it before Christmas.'

'No.'

She brushed his arm with her hand. 'No what?' she said, giggling.

Giggling! Malcolm stepped back. She'd been drinking. He could smell it on her. See it on her, cheeks flushed, eyes slightly bloodshot.

'No you won't promise, or no you won't open it?' she teased.

'No I won't open it,' he said sullenly. And now he had a dilemma. He did not want to appear ungrateful but he must ask. Did she have any blades for him? Maybe she had some in her bag and with the distraction of the Christmas present she would forget to give them to him. He almost wet himself in anticipation. She was getting ready to go, already pulling aside the net curtain he'd nailed across the window to stop people peering in. It tore a little. She waved to a man in a van. Peering over her shoulder Malcolm saw him wave back. A black-haired man with big shoulders.

'Well,' Brenda said, turning round to face him. 'I really ought to be going. I've got loads to do with it being Christmas. Terry, that's my son-in-law, and Shani, my daughter, are coming for the day.' She mock-sighed. 'She's a lazy girl, Malcolm. Lazy and very fat. Unlike her mother.' She chuckled and put her hand over her mouth but Malcolm knew she did not really regret having insulted her daughter. Just pretended to. 'I'm doing the cooking.' She winked at him. 'But they'll have to do the washing up.' She winked again. 'I just might have had a drop or two of the sherry and break the glasses.' Malcolm watched her curiously. It was funny. She, a grown woman, was excited over Christmas. He puzzled over it for no more than a second before he continued in his agony of indecision. She'd given him a present. He couldn't ask for something else.

But she might forget them.

He gave her a desperate look but she had moved back to the window, and was smiling down again at the

118

bloke in the small, white van. Malcolm added curly hair to the description.

Brenda giggled. 'Good-looking guy isn't he, Malcolm?'

Should he ask her?

Indecision was giving way to crossness as Brenda gave the man in the van another wave and the one-minute sign with her forefinger before she dropped the curtain. Malcolm stiffened. Not only had she torn it, she hadn't even bothered to rearrange it. There was a corner still tucked up, quite a big corner, leaving a triangular gap where anyone could stare in, and see quite a lot. Anything. It bothered him so much he was finding it hard to concentrate on what she was saying with that silly wet smile all over her face. His fingers wove in and out of each other as though they had a life of their own.

Perhaps Brenda sensed his antagonism towards her hero. Maybe that was why she continued her teasing. 'My son-in-law, Terry, who drives me,' she said, 'thinks you're a strange sort of bloke, Malcolm. And you should remember you're relying on his good nature to bring me here.' Instinct made her tack the phrase on the end of the sentence. 'And the blades.' It was a sudden revelation. It was not *her* visit that Malcolm appreciated, but the second-hand surgical blades she brought in her bag.

Resentment as sharp as a current of electricity shot through Malcolm towards this man who thought he was strange. There was nothing strange about him. He just liked privacy. And certain things. His eyes want to the turned up corner of the net curtains. He didn't want people looking into his flat. He might be on the first floor, but people might still look, mightn't they? He eyed Brenda suspiciously. Maybe she had left the peep-hole on purpose. Deliberately and very slowly he moved past her and pulled the curtain down – hard. Then he replied to Terry's jibe about him, but he watched her very carefully as he answered quite casually because she could, of course, be making the whole thing up – just to tease him. Brenda liked a joke. 'Thinks I'm strange, does he?' He failed to sound nonchalant, he knew he sounded anxious and pathetic.

'And I'm not sure I don't agree with him,' Brenda continued, with that mocking, laughing expression still on her face. She picked up the net curtain again and suddenly Malcolm knew she had left herself visible on purpose. Almost as though she didn't quite trust him. The thought still occupied him as Brenda picked up her white plastic handbag without even promising she would ever be coming again.

She was halfway to the door when he managed to stutter. 'The b-b-b-blades?'

Brenda gave him a searching look. 'They mean a lot to you, don't they?'

He nodded, feeling as trapped as a bird caught in a net.

She gave him a cruel, teasing glance. 'But it's Christmas, Malcolm. I've already brought you a present.' Her eyes fell on the small, wrapped gift. 'You can't want another one, surely? And you didn't get me anything.' Her mouth drooped slackly in a red, lip-sticked pout.

He closed his eyes. She hadn't brought him any blades today.

'Besides, over Christmas, we don't do any operations.'

That seemed to confirm it.

'What are you doing for Christmas, Malcolm?'

Without knowing why he made up a sister.

'Going to my sister's.' He was pleased with that. It
sounded so normal.

But Brenda gave him a suspicious look. 'I didn't
know you had a sister.'

'She lives in . . .' he cast right through his mind –
'Erdington.'

'That's where that man came from – the one who
was killed.'

The lie was tripping him up. 'He was from a different part.'

She didn't believe him, he could tell that.

'But when your mother was ill – and died – you said
you were the only one who could look after her.'

The trouble with lies was they got longer and
longer, like the nose on Pinnochio's face.

'They didn't get on,' he said sullenly, convinced
now that Brenda was trying to trap him.

From outside came a blast from a car horn.

Brenda tired of the game. She fumbled through her
bag. 'Here you are.' She dumped the box on the table.
'Merry Christmas. In fact a Happy New Year too. I'll see
you around, Malcolm.'

As she clattered down the stairs Malcolm heard a
second blast from the horn. He could kill that Terry.

The 'surgeon' was right. It did take them a little longer
to find this body. All through the day he had listened to

the news, waiting for the story to break, imagining the headlines. He wanted them to *know* it was him again. For Christmas. He would enjoy this little game of hide and seek much better when the police knew what they were participating in.

In fact it took them more than twenty-four hours to find Rosemary Baring. Her body had been a little too well concealed on a building site, behind a high fence, beneath a huge, bright sign that announced a building firm would soon be commencing work on a brand new multi-million-pound maternity block. Being Christmas Eve the site was deserted.

David Forrest spent an uncomfortable Christmas Eve, working late at the Incident Room, watching the junior officers eye the clock muttering about children and Santa Claus. He spared a couple. The rest, including DS Fielding and DS Shaw he ruthlessly forced to work until nine o'clock. After all, neither of them had kids. He tried to convince himself that it was an ordinary working day but people kept shouting out greetings, making jokes about the turkey, forgotten presents for the wife. He sat, quietly reflective, in his office, remembering Christmases past. He had always loved the festive season: until his father's accident; until Maggie had left him. Now for the first time ever Forrest had no one special to buy for. His father had had the obligatory bottle of Scotch, hastily wrapped, his mother a cardigan he couldn't even remember choosing from M&S. He'd made a vague commitment to visit them sometime during Christmas Day and knew, with irritation, that they would hold back the festive meal, watching out for him as though he were the Blessed Child. With a wry smile he acknowledged the fact that, to them, he still was. At five minutes to eleven he switched the computer off. Less than an hour to go. Then twenty-four, no, forty-eight more hours and it would all be over for another year. As he left his office he wondered what Karys was doing tonight.

Karys was toasting her feet in front of a fake-log gas fire and sipping mulled wine. 'You know,' she said to Tonya, 'I feel one hundred per cent happy. Utterly contented.'

Tonya leant back in her chair. 'Maybe,' she said, 'Christmas is the time to forget family, and to close the doors against work.' She gave a deep sigh. 'So what shall we do tomorrow?'

'I'm on call,' Karys reminded her.

'Surely you won't get bothered?'

'No.' Karys fell in with her. 'No one would commit murder over Christmas.'

But statistically she knew this was not true.

Christmas Day 1999

Forrest tried to inject himself with Christmas cheer as he turned into the drive of the neat semi. He even practised his smile, tilting the car mirror down to reflect his mouth. It worked. Smiling actually made him feel happier. He parked the car and rang the doorbell, watching the blinking fairy lights draped across the front window. His mother opened the door with a small shriek of pleasure and threw her arms around him.

'A Merry Christmas, love.'

He kissed her cheek and breathed in the scent of the house – floral disinfectant that his mother used to douse the commode. The atmosphere was so different from the place it had been before his father's accident. His father had once been an outdoors man, a man who had preferred to be at the top of a mountain than at the foot, someone who would rather run than walk, a man who had once burst with energy and vitality. Now he felt the cold, hated the breeze on his face, frequently kept the curtains closed all day to 'keep out that blinding sun'. The accident, and its aftermath, had been a cruel blow to such a man. It had destroyed and changed him beyond recognition, both physically and mentally. Forrest had to fight to remember the father he had once had.

He caught sight of him, red paper cracker hat askew and felt a lump of affection well up.

'Hi, Dad. Happy Christmas.' His father gave a tight smile. That at least had not changed. He still fought shy of open displays of affection. But it was Christmas. So the son patted his father on the shoulder and sat opposite him, across the dining table. They would have Christmas dinner now he had arrived.

His mother bustled between kitchen and dining table. 'A beer, David?'

'Better not,' he said. 'On duty.'

'You're always on duty.'

'Well, there's a major investigation going on. Might get called away at any time.' He smiled at the pair of them.

He had just carved the turkey when the phone call came.

Rosemary's body had been found by a group of boys anxious to test out their brand-new mountain bikes. The building site was perfect for them. It only took a push against the corrugated wall and they were through to a tailor-made course. A rough, untidy place which served the gang of youths well. It was lumpy, with steep drops and sharp curves; a loose, dangerous shale on which to practise their skids.

And one did. Skidded round a berm to tumble against the yellow plastic bags taped together. Like the medical students before him he quickly identified the shape of a body and probed with curious fingers. Triumphant at being the one to make the discovery he called his mates over to take a look. Initially they were inclined to scoff and disbelieve.

'You're a damned liar, Jarrod.' It was Cliff, his spotty best friend who spoke first.

But it only took a fraction of a second for them all to realize he had been telling the truth. Then they were excited. This was drama. Real life drama.

They quickly understood the implications. This body heralded fame. Their chance to be on the telly; to give their story. For the corpse they felt neither sympathy nor revulsion, only curiosity and pride at having been the ones to discover it.

Luckily for Inspector David Forrest they knew just enough about police procedure from television soaps not to touch anything. So they didn't. Jarrod and Cliff earned the dubious reward of mounting vigil while the other two sped off on their bikes, skidding round corners until they reached a telephone box, fulfilling a life-long ambition to dial 999.

They were rewarded quickly by screaming police sirens.

It was better than the telly.

Whatever day of the year it was, Karys always visited the scene of a crime as soon as possible. So she was there within half an hour, pulling the Merc up behind the police incident van full of officers cursing the job that tore them away from their families today. Karys ignored them and slipped on overshoes and a paper suit before elbowing her way through the throng of voyeurs attracted by the police sirens and flashing lights, even on Christmas Day. Luckily the high fence ringing the building site made a good cover. She ducked beneath the fluttering blue and white 'Do Not Cross. Police' tape with a strong feeling of déjà vu.

Forrest gave her a wry smile. 'Sorry to drag you out on Christmas Day, Karys.'

'It's all right David.' Normally she would have returned the commiseration but she knew more about him now, knew he did not have a family with which to share the festivities. She also knew he had been dreading this moment: the finding of another body.

So had she.

Forrest was looking drawn, as though he hadn't slept much in the past few days. He made an attempt to be professional but friendly. 'I thought I'd better hang on for you, Karys. It's obviously the same guy.'

Her eyes slipped past him to the yellow plastic bag.

'I'm glad you did.' She suddenly felt terribly sorry for him. Had they caught the killer of Colin Wilson they would not be standing here, about to unwrap a second victim. He would see this as a personal failure. She resisted the temptation to put a friendly hand on his arm, but she longed to even though the two Detective Sergeants were both watching her. Instead she gave him a warm smile. 'Come on, David,' she said. 'It's damned cold out here. Let's have a quick look and then move this to the morgue.'

She had brought with her the hunting knife. She slit open the bags like the belly of a fish and watched an arm, a head and a leg, appear. Rigor mortis was beginning to wear off. There was some movement in the corpse. Karys watched, mesmerized. It was the body of a young woman, her upper half horribly naked, the mutilation this time the total removal of the left breast. The 'surgeon' had found it impossible to suture that wide, grotesque wound neatly. But he had tried, with huge, clumsy black silk sutures. Thick ones this time. Karys didn't move for a few seconds. The chill threatened to fix her in the stiff pose. Only by drawing in a deep breath of pure cold air could she force her brain to function again and move her eyes away from the ugly wound to the rest of the body. The woman's lower half was clothed in a short, grey skirt spattered with blood, below that she wore knee-length black leather boots. There was no coat: Closer scrutiny revealed partly congealed blood had pooled at the bottom of the sack.

Even a pathologist can feel sick and faint sometimes.

Her eyes finally found Forrest's and all her

127

emotions were mirrored there, horror, sympathy, revulsion. Fear.

It was his fear that surprised her most. It was the fear of failure. Failure to catch the 'surgeon' before he worked yet again.

Hers was a different fear altogether. It was fear of the killer himself.

Forrest had waited in dread for this moment. And now the dread was compounding. There would be a third, and a fourth. He felt his resolve strengthen. There would be no more. He gave Karys a strained smile.

'Do you know who she is?' she asked.

'Not yet, at least, not for sure, but we've had a call from a frantic flatmate saying her friend hasn't come home for two nights.' He looked depressed. 'She's a nurse.'

'From the hospital?'

'No. From the Cater Clinic.'

The name meant little to her apart from being a private institution rather than NHS. 'The nurse's name?'

'Rosemary. Rosemary Baring.'

She touched his arm then. 'David,' she said urgently. 'You must go back. These aren't random killings. They're planned. I'm sure. There's some reason behind them. I don't know what it is but it has a connection with the Health Service, doctors, nurses, something.' Her eyes were drawn back through the entrance of the building site, towards the police tape, fluttering in an unkind breeze. Through the gap she could see the angular grey shapes of the hospital, beyond that the tall clock that marked the university buildings and, the entrance to the Medical School, deserted for the Christmas vac. For the first time ever the sight made her apprehensive.

She licked dry lips and listened to David Forrest's reply. 'We've already worked on that theory,' he protested. 'We've spent hours, days, weeks shadowing the place. Officers have been round most of the theatre suites, interviewed I don't know how many doctors, nurses, technicians. You name them.' His eyes too trawled the skyline. 'There's nothing there.'

'There has to be.'

She did the necessaries quickly. It was too cold out here to work efficiently. Besides, Karys liked the privacy and the frosted windows of the mortuary, she felt safe behind them. Despite the festive season it wouldn't take long for the vultures to circle. She had a horror of a photographer getting a picture of this . . . her eyes focused on the raw, ugly wound.

Forrest followed her to the car. 'The post-mortem?' he asked awkwardly.

'How about tomorrow morning? Nine o'clock?'

'Thanks. The sooner we – '

She unlocked her car. 'That's all right, David,' she said. 'It does happen to be my job, Christmas or not. See if you can get the next of kin in for eight thirty, will you? I prefer to get the identification over with before I start work.'

Malcolm was enjoying his Christmas dinner. He'd treated himself to a chicken Kiev from the supermarket. They'd had a special offer on and it had only cost 99p. For a treat he had even allowed himself to slice through the chicken using one of his precious blades. After all. It was Christmas.

He revelled in the way it cut so cleanly, even coping with a nasty tough bit. There shouldn't be a tough bit in a chicken Kiev. Perhaps that was why the shop had sold them off cheaply, not as a Christmas present at all. The thought threatened to cloud his day. He shut it out.

It was tricky, but he managed to pull the cracker on his own, congratulating himself on winning the prize, the hat and the joke. The Women's Institute had put the cracker in with the Christmas hamper. Well, he called it a hamper. But really it was just a carrier bag with a robin cut from an old Christmas card stuck on the side. In the bag they had put a tiny Christmas pudding which was bubbling away on the stove, a packet of tea, some Rich Tea biscuits and the cracker. The woman who had dropped it off had had two rosy cheeked toddlers with her and had thrust the bag into his hand, refusing his invitation to come in. 'Can't,' she said; sharply he'd thought. 'Happy Christmas,' she'd added as an after-thought. And then the excuse. 'Have to get the other kids from school.'

They always made excuses not to come in. Malcolm didn't think the woman was frightened, she was just in a rush. Everyone was in a rush.

Except him.

Brenda had drunk four schooners of Sherry before she even attempted to slop the dinner onto the plates. It was always like this, Christmas dinner. A haphazard affair. But Shani didn't mind, as long as she didn't have to do the cooking, and there was plenty of it. She sat, like Mrs Blobby, knees a foot apart, smiling and watching the telly. Shani was always smiling. Even as a big, fat baby she had always smiled.

'Not one of those skinny miserable things,' Brenda had boasted, then.

She was going to ask Terry to carve the turkey. That would fetch him into the kitchen. She would tease him as he sharpened the knife. Brenda loved to see a man carve the turkey. Looked so macho.

She stood in the doorway, glad of the saucy French maid's apron Shani had presented her with that morning. Tassels on tits, a belly button and French knickers stamped on PVC.

'Be a darlin',' she said to Terry, giggling and hanging onto the door frame. Lucky it was strong else she'd have toppled.

Terry made a fine, showy job of sharpening the knife, rubbing it along the stone with a muscular vigour. Brenda sidled up behind him and wrapped her arms round him low down below his waist.

He brandished the knife. 'You want this bird carved, Ma?'

She giggled again, pretended to fall against him.

He took the knife along the sharpener.

She pretended to be nervous now. 'That knife's sharp enough,' she said. 'For a turkey.'

Terry turned suddenly, almost throwing her off balance. 'Sharp as the surgeon's blades?'

She gave him a coquettish look. 'Don't know about that, our Terry.'

He pretended to draw it along her throat. 'Sharp enough for that?'

'Don't know about that either, our Terry.'

She didn't flinch but glanced upwards, towards the ceiling light. Yesterday she had positioned some mistletoe right up there. She put her arms around his neck. 'How about a nice Christmas kiss for Ma?'

For a treat on Christmas afternoon Malcolm had taken all his blades out of the box and was sitting down, polishing them. Carols were playing on the radio. Some of his old favourites. 'Oh, Come All Ye Faithful', 'Once in Royal David's City', 'Away in a Manger'. The traditional ones. He hummed along, contented.

There was a knock on the door. He shrank against the table. He didn't want anyone around. Brenda wouldn't be visiting today, she would be with her family: that horrible Terry and her daughter. Malcolm screwed up his face trying to remember her name.

'Malcolm.' It was the old bag from downstairs. Mrs Stanton, the landlady. He didn't answer. 'I know you're in there. Malcolm. I can hear your radio.' She sounded cross. 'Why don't you come down? Join me and a couple of others for a few drinks and a game of cards.'

Malcolm swallowed. She was waiting on the other side of the door.

'Come on, Malcolm. It's Christmas. You don't want to be on your own for Christmas.'

But he did. He did.

'I've a nice drop of sherry. Or a beer if you'd prefer.'

Malcolm eyed the door, terrified he hadn't locked it. He tried to see whether the key had been turned but he couldn't tell. Not from here.

Another knock. 'Come on, Malcolm. We're all downstairs, in the sitting room.'

He must say something. And as usual he chose the wrong lie. 'It's all right, Mrs Stanton. I've got some company myself.'

'I know you haven't.' She was a sharp-nosed bitch. 'No one's come up or down these stairs all day. I know you're on your own.'

Malcolm whimpered. He didn't want to go downstairs, sit with the others, try to make conversation. He didn't have any conversation and they didn't like him anyway. He looked longingly at his neat row of surgical blades. Why couldn't they leave him alone?

Another knock. Angry now. 'Malcolm.'

'It's all right, Mrs Stanton.' He chose another lie. 'I've got a headache.'

'And I've got an aspirin.'

A further long pause. She was still waiting, outside the door. Then an angry, 'Oh, suit yourself,' followed by high-heeled shoes tapping down the stairs.

Malcolm heaved a sigh of relief.

Chapter Eight

26 December 1999

The mortuary was eerily empty as Karys unlocked the door. Paget had yet to arrive so her only company was a few refrigerated corpses awaiting burial and the body of Rosemary Baring. Karys changed into her post-mortem gown then wandered along the corridor and pushed open the door to the viewing room. Paget had come in yesterday specially to lay the body out. He had covered her with a purple velvet and gold shroud that evoked the church, hope, immortality. But to Karys it was a vain hope. Death, to her, seemed all too final. She put two hands on the cover preparing to look at the girl's face but it was a mistake. Like a witch's magic sand on the fire, it evoked cabbalistic memories of the sheet shrouding her first body, the one designated to teach her anatomy. She and Barney had been assigned to the same corpse. That was how they had met. From that it had been a short step to him becoming her boyfriend, her second ever boyfriend. A sheltered and protected only child, the product of a convent, single-sex education, quiet and introverted by nature, university had been her chance at life.

She could still remember meeting Barney's eyes, coolly friendly, half formal, appraising. That first morning, suddenly hit with all that studying medicine would mean, she had been reluctant to remove the winding sheet. She had glanced up to see him watching her, challenging her to do it. She had gripped the cloth with both hands as she was gripping this cloth now, and had calmly pulled it back. When she had looked at him again his expression had not changed. He was still mocking her squeamishness.

He knew she was apprehensive. She knew he was not. He was eager.

It might have been easier if she had lived in the rough and tumble of the halls of residence and got to know some of the other students, but her parents had been reluctant to let her go. They only lived four bus stops away from the medical school and so she had kept her pink and white bedroom at home. Not for her the posters and late-night drinking sessions at the medical society bar. Barney had been the only fellow student she knew well during her entire first year. She knew she had quickly been labelled a 'weirdo', someone who kept herself to herself. Distant.

On the second day he had asked her if he could take her out for dinner. She should have suspected something. The other students were rowdy, full of plans for an evening's entertainment at the Freshers' Ball, which she couldn't face. Why would Barney want to take her out instead of going to the ball himself? Little, plump, plain Karys, with the shell she had crawled into. Puzzled, she had nodded. 'At eight,' he had repeated. 'At eight. Dead – on – eight. I'll pick you up.' And he had taken detailed instructions as to how to find her parents' house.

That night she had moved through the perceived motions of a date. She had had a bath and washed her hair, blow drying it carefully so it bobbed neatly to her shoulders. She had refused her mother's carefully prepared supper and munched an apple instead. She had drunk camomile tea to calm her down. She had smeared pale foundation over her paler complexion, fiddled with a brown mascara wand and touched up her eyelids with beige eyeshadow speckled with gold flecks. She had thought she looked nice.

Then she had sat down in the lounge and waited, listening to the clock with its Westminster chime hammer out the hour of eight.

And waited. Until a quarter past.

Her father, embarrassed, had hidden behind his paper. Her mother had grown angry and said something about 'being used', 'cheapening' herself and being 'worth far more than this'. Karys had sat, silently, through more than an hour of television soaps, feeling more and more emotionally frozen until she had finally returned to her room to hang up her dress and sit on the bed, stare at her reflection and wonder. What was wrong with her? Why was she so different? Abnormal? It had been then that she had first acquired the chocolate habit. Two bars, stolen from the fridge. Fruit and nut that night, later any chocolate would do for compensation.

The next morning she had once again faced Barney across the corpse and expected an apology. But Barney had said nothing. Neither did she but he had watched her with that same, mocking smile.

At the end of the day he had again asked her out to dinner without mentioning the previous night. When she had remonstrated Barney had looked puzzled. 'But I asked you for tonight,' he said, sounding genuinely hurt. 'Surely you didn't think . . . I was at the Freshers' Ball last night. I couldn't have gone anywhere with anyone last night.' And then he had laughed that half crazy, loud laugh with his mouth forced open as wide as it could possibly go. 'Well, you are a silly thing. You got it wrong. You were confused. I meant tonight.'

She had stared at him and wondered, made the assumption that *she* had been wrong. She must have got the night wrong. Barney couldn't have done. Not with all the talk having centred around the Freshers' Ball. Why would he have deliberately misled her? There could be no purpose. No logical purpose.

And so that night she went through the rigmarole again: the bath, the hair, the clothes, the make-up. Again Karys had heard the Westminster chime of the clock in the dining room strike eight and had felt sick and humiliated. At ten past she had been about to go upstairs when she heard a car screech to a halt outside. She'd run to the door and flung it open. And there he was, still wearing that same sardonic smile.

'Hello, Karys,' he'd said casually.

That night she'd confessed to him what had happened. He had seemed so nice, so friendly, so sympathetic. But it had been a mistake. A terrible mistake. Of all the people she might have told he had been the worst, prepared to use it against her.

Three nights later there had again been a mix-up over the night. But this time, having found some confidence, she had stuck to her guns.

'I'm sorry, Barney,' she'd said. 'It was you who made a mistake. Let's call it a day. I really don't want to get in a tangle again. I'd rather not see you again – except in the Med School.'

His answer had seemed odd. 'Don't say that.'

'I mean it. I *know* you said Saturday, not Sunday.'

'OK. OK. So sometimes I'm wrong.' He'd fixed his eyes on hers. 'I'm sorry, but please. Please. Don't say you don't want to see me again.'

Reluctantly she had agreed to extend the relationship, and for a few weeks he had been a different Barney. Reliable, pleasant, reasonable. He did not stay that way.

The evenings gradually became strange again. Cinema tickets were produced to prove that she had got the night muddled up. Again she had remonstrated, made up her mind to stop seeing him. Again he had pleaded with her. Differently this time. With a threat. 'If you don't . . .'

She had challenged him. 'If I do – then what?'

They had been standing in the huge hallway of the Medical School, arguing, students milling round them. It had been noisy, so noisy that she had wondered whether she had imagined his reply.

'I'll shoot myself.'

She had felt the ice-cold wind of fear. He was going to use the knowledge she had confided to him. Use it to gain ascendance over her, to tie her hands.

'You wouldn't really do it.'

'Oh but, Karys,' he had said, his strange, marmalade-coloured eyes gleaming, 'you don't know that I wouldn't.'

And she didn't.

That was when she had begun to lose concentration and fail exams. Her tutors had commented on her lack of commitment. She was confused, terribly, blindingly confused. Even her mother and father began to tell her she should not be trusted with human lives. She would be a danger to patients. Maybe that was why she had finally elected to abandon the living and work instead with the dead, choosing pathology for her career. Maybe that was why she had never had any sort of relationship with a man, after Barney.

After the terrible climax of their relationship Karys had snapped and taken an overdose of aspirin. Hospital discharge had swiftly been followed by an attempt to resign from the medical school, a visit from the Dean which had led, in turn, to an astute psychiatrist who had finally told her what no one else had perceived – least of all she – that it was not her but Barney who was most disturbed.

It had taken her a further year to blot out enough of his influence to return to her medical studies. By then she could see it all, the evil, the spite, the danger of a pathologically dominant personality, the deliberate manipulation of her mind. When she had returned to Medical School she had slipped a year behind Barney and had seen little of him – the psychiatrist had warned her to give him a wide berth. When Barney had qualified and had moved away she had made no attempt to make contact.

She came to with a shock and found herself staring down at Rosemary Baring's pale face. Keys were being inserted in the mortuary door, but her own were still in the lock. Paget wouldn't be able to get in. She hurried to open the door. Even as he entered she could see a white car pull to a halt outside. Forrest was here, probably with the girl's next of kin and a WPC. She waited in the doorway.

Rosemary Baring's father was a man in his forties, tight-lipped, dark-haired. He looked irritated, not shocked, not in a state of inconsolable grief. Just irritated. In silence she led the three of them along the corridor.

She was a little surprised that Forrest didn't waste much time on preambles. No 'regrets at this terrible tragedy', no empathizing with the father's grief. Perhaps he thought the man would want to get this trauma over with as quickly as possible.

Rosemary's father said little as they walked towards the tiny 'recognition' room. Just before she pulled the cloth away she risked a swift glance at the man's face. It was wooden. Completely devoid of any emotion. Karys was suddenly curious. This man didn't feel any grief. He gave a curt nod. 'That's her all right.'

It wasn't until the WPC had driven him away that Forrest offered an explanation. 'Mum and Dad divorced years ago, with some acrimony. Father hadn't seen his daughter for a few years. Bit of an argument about who was actually coming down here.' He looked distressed. 'Neither wanted to.'

It wasn't much of an epitaph for a murdered young woman, she was thinking.

The post-mortem on Rosemary Baring was horribly familiar. Again Karys found herself pondering from the foot of the slab, pushing her glasses on so hard she felt an ache in the bridge of her nose. Again there was the same, embarrassed silence as the others, police, attendants and Scene of Crime Officers, waited for her to begin. Even a cursory examination showed Karys similarities with the murder of Colin Wilson: the same blow to the back of the head; the same ligature tied around the neck. Not a tie this time, but a ladies' stocking, a fine, pale filmy affair but tied just as tightly. As she bagged it, Karys reflected it was almost certainly not Rosemary Baring's.

The real difference this time was in the 'surgeon's' handiwork. And it was a terrible difference. Not a neat, straight superficial cut, not a pretend hernia but something else – a full mastectomy, a ragged wound with ugly black sutures. The 'surgeon' was getting more adventurous.

Something occurred to Karys as she worked. 'What sort of a place is the Cater Clinic?'

'Private nursing home. Cosmetic stuff.'

Forrest was struggling with his emotions, his eyes focused on Karys's face rather than her butchering hands.

'Expensive?'

'I expect so.'

'I see.' She heaved a deep sigh and continued in silence.

She completed the examination before turning back to him and relating her findings in a calm, factual tone.

While Paget was slotting the body back into the mortuary fridge and the SOCOs were busying themselves with their samples and they were finally alone, Forrest allowed some emotion to leak out. He rubbed his palm across the thinning patch on his head. 'Karys,' he said, 'how the hell do we stop him?'

'By finding him.'

'So where do I start looking?'

She caught the despair in his tone. 'Haven't you turned *anything* up?'

'Not a thing.' He gave a rueful grin. 'In fact I've even sunk low enough to trust the forensic psychiatrist. I mean, what else do I have?'

'I think you have little option, David, but to trust Lewisham.' She was glad to stop staring at the mortuary table with its recent staining. 'Whoever is doing this is a complete nutcase. As I said before, Barney may be a conceited prick but he is clever, if anyone can help point the finger it'll be him.' She started rinsing her hands under the tap. 'Has he ever come across anything like this before?'

Forrest shook his head. 'No he hasn't. But then I haven't told him about . . .' he jerked his head towards the operating table. 'The man's a ghoul with a perverted sense of pleasure. He's getting quite excited about the case.' He hesitated. 'I suppose I'd better ring him.'

'Not today, surely?'

They both realized at the same time that it was Boxing Day.

Forrest voiced his thoughts first. 'Look,' he said awkwardly. 'I expect this is the worst time for you – you've just done a PM – and I've got loads to do, but it *is* Boxing Day. The pubs are all open,' he gave a swift, embarrassed glance at his watch, 'and it's almost lunchtime. I don't suppose you'd have something to eat with me?'

'I'd love to,' she said firmly.

She might be risking dry turkey, frozen roast potatoes, shop-bought Christmas pudding. But perhaps it was time for her to start living again.

Chapter Nine

She had been right about the dry turkey, the frozen roast potatoes and the shop-bought Christmas pudding tasting of synthetic brandy essence. But worse, away from the mortuary and their work she and DI Forrest had nothing to talk about. Her diffidence came to the fore and he didn't help. She couldn't know he had steeled himself not to ask her personal questions, the things he longed to ask: was she married, engaged, in a long-term relationship, did she live alone, have children? Avoiding these normal everyday topics gave them little to discuss and the case hardly seemed an appropriate subject for the noisy, jolly pub festooned with reminders of the festive season – tinsel, balloons, a Christmas tree in the corner. After four false starts Forrest began to tell Karys about his father. It seemed a safe subject.

'He had an accident,' he said.

'Oh?' Karys wished she could think of something more intelligent to say.

'He's in a wheelchair.'

'How awful.' She listened to her own voice. Banal, silly. She bent her head over her glass.

'I don't know how he copes.' Forrest blinked quickly, as though something had lodged in his eye.

'What kind of accident?'

'Driving. He was a lorry driver. He ran head on into a BMW and got stuck in the cab. Someone pulled him out. The accident wasn't his fault though, a car had broken down.'

Karys looked up. 'And?'

Forrest felt defensive. 'And what?'

The trouble was she didn't know except that there was anger in both his voice and face where there had been none before. Maybe it had been the rescue, not the accident, that had made him angry. Curiosity overcame her reticence. 'What happened then?'

Forrest touched his mouth with the serviette as though he was editing his words. 'They told us afterwards if he hadn't been pulled out of the cab so roughly he might not have been paralysed.'

Karys winced. 'He might have been in more danger, if he'd been left.'

Forrest raised his eyebrows at her. 'How?'

'If the cab had burst into flames. If he'd been bleeding.'

Forrest shook his head.

'Well the cab might have been hit by other traffic.'

'He should have been left there.'

'The rescuer might not have *known* that.'

'That's what was said at the inquiry. But, he *should* have known, he was a doctor.'

She felt bound to defend this unknown colleague. 'He still might not have known. I'm sure he chose what he believed to be the best option.'

Bitterness flashed through Forrest's eyes. 'That's the trouble with you lot, you all stick together. Outsiders never really find out the truth.'

The truth of this made Karys avoid his eyes. He was right. More right than he could possibly know. Feeling forced to say something, she asked lightly, 'So did you sue?'

'We took advice,' Forrest said gruffly. 'A solicitor advised us.'

'And?' Her embarrassment was fading, replaced by the aggression most of the medical profession feel for plaintiffs who dog their every wrong step.

Forrest squirmed. 'He said if the guy hadn't pulled Dad away there was a chance the vehicle could have exploded. He was carrying corrosives. The tank had burst.'

'So you understood he had no choice?'

Forrest countered angrily, 'He could have done it more gently. My dad needn't have been paralysed.'

'I expect he was in a panic in the heat of the situation, David.'

He watched her with suspicion.

'You can't blame him.'

There was another long silence before Forrest finally lowered his eyes. 'But I do.'

Karys shrugged. 'It's the anger we carry with us that weighs us down, that becomes the impossible burden.'

'Says who?'

She gave a ghost of a smile. 'Says me.'

'Oh.' Forrest looked surprised. 'I thought it was a quote. Some poet.'

Again she shrugged. 'I'm always making up "profound" statements, David.' She smiled across at him, warmth pervading the space between them. 'I'm sorry about your dad. It must be a burden on your mother.'

He gave her a puzzled look. 'It's really strange,' he

said, 'but she doesn't seem to mind. Sometimes I almost think she – '

'Likes it?'

He felt relieved she'd said it. 'Yes.'

'Maybe it's like having a replacement child.' A fleeting glimpse of her mother's swamping concern when she had been sick reminded Karys she, too, had been pleased at the return of her dependent child.

'But that's . . .'

'Natural.' Karys gazed far into the distance. 'Women naturally feel they have a role as a mother.'

Something lost and sad about her face made him long to ask her whether she had children and if not whether she would like some. But it seemed an intrusion. Instead he turned the conversation back to himself. 'My wife never wanted children.'

She turned those huge, owl glasses full on him. 'Didn't she?'

'No. Always too busy doing some great project.' He raised his beer to her. 'Artistic woman, my wife.'

She noticed he had not said 'my ex-wife' as men did who were glad – or relieved – to have shed the burden of a spouse. 'You must miss her.'

Surprisingly Forrest grinned, looking less the thin-haired, middle-aged Detective Inspector. Something of the boy peeped out. 'Not any more,' he said. Then he said, 'But I don't like living alone.'

Afterwards he reflected that that had been the perfect moment for her to have replied. 'Neither do I.' He had hesitated, hoping she would echo it. Instead she had regarded him solemnly, and said nothing.

'Karys,' Forrest said suddenly. 'Something came to you. While you were doing the PM.'

She gestured with her hand. 'It's nothing. It won't help you.'

'Just tell me,' he said.

'It was what you said about the Cater Clinic,' she said. 'No more than a stupid thought. Cosmetic surgery? Breast surgery. I just wondered whether the fact that she worked at a clinic specializing in cosmetic surgery was the reason he chose to – well – mutilate her breast.'

Forrest was silent.

They drank their coffee quickly. Forrest stood up first. 'I have to go,' he said. 'There's a press conference,' he glanced at his watch, 'in half an hour.'

Karys gave an abstracted smile. There was yet another awkward pause. It would have been another perfect opportunity for him to have said, 'It's been nice. Let's do it again.' Careful, polite words that would have been unobtrusive, unthreatening but he was too aware that his knowledge of her had not advanced one milli-metre. She was still an enigma, still a stranger. So he said nothing but picked up his coat from the back of the chair and headed for the bar to pay the bill. Karys let him walk out, giving him five minutes to drive away from the car park before she wrapped a black wool coat around herself and followed him through the double doors.

Forrest knew he was in for a rough time even as he took his seat behind the desk and scanned the rows of waiting journalists, a surprising number for late on a Boxing Day afternoon. The full attendance underlined the newsworthiness of the case. Once a killer had struck twice he had earned the title of serial killer, add to that dark hints of mutilation and it would fill the front pages of next morning's newspapers, both local and national. As he sorted through his notes his eyes landed on the flame-coloured hair of the girl in the central front seat, right in front of his nose, sitting bolt upright and staring directly at him. He held her eyes for a brief moment and wondered if he was mistaking the dislike he read behind her green cat's eyes, and why he felt the emotion mirrored in his own. He didn't even know the girl. But there was tangible antagonism between them. He had to be wrong. But a second, surreptitious glance confirmed his earlier instinct, he was not mistaken, her stare contained frank hostility. Somebody else didn't like him, apart from Lewisham.

He cleared his throat and opened with the uncontroversial statement, 'There has been another murder in the Edgbaston district of the city. The body of a young nurse, Rosemary Baring, was found yesterday afternoon.'

As he'd anticipated the red-headed girl was the first to pick up on it. 'Another murder, Inspector Forrest?' Her tone was unbelievably sarcastic.

'Just over a month ago, you may remember, the body of Colin Wilson was found on a patch of waste ground between Queen's Hospital and the old maternity block.'

Most of them looked up briefly and nodded. Yesterday's news and no imminent arrest. History to journalists. Only the red-headed girl's gaze remained sharp.

'You connect the two murders?' A male journalist in shirt and loosened tie was the questioner this time.

Forrest felt vague relief. 'Yes.'

'On what grounds?' Again the redhead's tone was icy.

'There were similarities between the two killings.'

'What?'

'Both victims had been knocked on the head from behind and strangled.'

'Yes?' It was as though only the two of them were in the room.

'Both bodies were dumped on the hospital site.'

She knew there was more.

'Both were found wrapped in hospital clinical waste bags.' He didn't know quite when he became convinced that this particular journalist knew something nearer the entire story. He felt cornered. 'Both had been mutilated, we believe with a scalpel. That's all I'm prepared to divulge at the moment.'

It was left to a plump woman, wearing too-tight jeans and an anorak to try to tease out the information. Pen poised, for a precise quote. 'Can you enlarge, Inspector?'

Everyone looked up then. No one was scribbling anything. They were waiting. Just waiting. You could have heard a pin drop.

Bloodhounds, Forrest thought nastily. Bloodhounds sniffing along the scent of a good story, taking delight in the horrid detail. They don't have to deal with the family or friends, the other victims of crime.

The plump woman spoke again. 'Can you enlarge, Inspector?' she repeated.

'We're not anxious for details to be made public at this time,' he said quietly. 'Let's just leave it at that, shall we? Out of respect for the relatives and the victim. At the moment I can't see what advantage there is in giving full details of the victim's injuries.'

He was tempted to add: apart from selling newspapers. But it didn't do to antagonize the press. He had made his plea for privacy for Colin Wilson's wife and child as well as for the cold man who had identified Rosemary Baring's butchered body.

The redhead gave him a challenging smile.

He felt he had to say something. 'As you know,' he continued quickly. 'Colin Wilson was a self-employed plumber. Last night's victim was a young nurse. She worked at the privately run Cater Clinic. She was twenty-seven years old and lived with a friend in the Edgbaston area of the city.'

'Was there any connection between the two victims?' The questions started to come thick and fast.

'We don't know yet.'

'Did they know each other?'

'We don't know that either.'

'Is there any possibility this is some sort of a grudge killing against the hospital?'

'It's one of the lines of enquiry we're currently working on.'

'Was the killer known to the victims?'

'We don't know that either.'

'Is there any possibility this was a personal grudge against the victims?'

Forrest shook his head and let them work out the rest.

It didn't take them long. 'You're suggesting we have a serial killer somewhere round here who might strike again?' Forrest could feel the redhead's eyes still mocking him. 'Someone who stalks the hospital complex looking for victims?'

Forrest tried to demur. The victims had been dumped on the hospital complex. Not picked up there. He didn't like the angle they were taking, dreaded scanning the headlines in the morning. But he couldn't deny it – not any of it. He tried to remember his training session last year on 'Dealing with the Media.' Give clear, unambiguous statements. Remember your objectives; in this case to solve the case, keep the public safe, prevent a further murder, shield the relatives, avoid spreading panic.

'We're suggesting that until this killer is caught people in the Edgbaston district of the city should take care not to walk alone, not to accept lifts from strangers particularly around the hospital area.' He added that extra police were being drafted in to protect the public. It was a thin whitewash. However many extra police were drafted in they couldn't prevent the 'surgeon' from performing again.

The plump woman in jeans was nibbling the top of her pencil. 'What exactly do you think the connection is with the hospital?'

Forrest hid behind a smokescreen. 'We are at present discussing this point with the forensic psychiatrist, Dr Lewisham.' He gave a supposedly reassuring smile as though the psychiatrist would solve everything.

But these were journalists. The redhead spoke again. 'And how exactly does your forensic psychiatrist connect these murders with the hospital?'

'He's working on several angles.'

A man in a black polo neck threw the next question at him. 'Do we have any sort of profile of the killer?'

Forrest thought for a moment before replying. After all. It could do no harm. And there were plenty of instances where press assistance had helped solve killings quicker than police legwork.

'An adult male. Socially isolated. With some interest in the workings of an operating theatre.' Immediately he said it he knew it had been a mistake. They all looked up.

Someone said, 'An operating theatre? Are you saying that – ' then stopped.

Another voice began the sentence again. 'Are you trying to tell us that the killer performed *operations* on his victims?'

He had no option. 'There were some similarities to surgery, that's all I'm prepared to divulge at the moment.'

There was a slow whistling of breath followed by frantic scribbling.

'Is there any suggestion that the killer is a doctor?'

'No.'

'Were the mutilations identical?'

'No.'

'Was surgical knowledge needed?'

'Some.'

They all looked up again. 'Can you enlarge?'

'No,' Forrest said bluntly.

The red-haired girl gave him a satisfied smile. 'You've already said a scalpel was used. What else?'

'I'm not prepared to say.'

Having flushed him out the girl gave a brief nod.

'Do you believe the killer is or was employed at the hospital?'

'It's a theory we're working on.'

He stood up. The press conference was over.

Not for the girl. Even as he shuffled his way along the table she shot a last question at him. 'Why does he do it?'

'What?'

'Perform surgery on his victims?'

At first he tried to argue that it was not his job to speculate, but finally he was forced to acknowledge the fact that he didn't know. Damn it. He simply didn't know.

Chapter Ten

27 December 1999

Forrest had always hated the first day back after the Christmas break, the endless identical question thrown at him: 'Had a nice Christmas?'

This year was easier than the previous one, his last shared with Maggie, a Maggie so hostile towards him she had been more a stranger than a wife. This year he had the perfect excuse to growl at the festive enquirers. The discovery of Rosemary Baring's body gave the morning briefing a sharp focus and dampened down any lingering Yuletide jubilation. The watching faces in the Incident Room quickly lost their sparkle to a wary tension. The investigation was mounting in size, expense and importance. Hours of work lay ahead. And what else?

Forrest called DS Shaw and DS Fielding over to him when the others had been dismissed.

'Have you got any ideas?' He would welcome anything – even Shaw's smart-arse thoughts – but both officers shook their heads. 'Well,' he said, 'if you do, don't hesitate to come and see me.'

Shaw gave him a fleeting smile as he went out behind Caroline Fielding.

Forrest eyed the phone. There was no excuse for not calling Lewisham. But for once his mobile phone was answered by a British Telecom voice who invited him to leave a message. Feeling satisfaction at discharging his duty without having to speak to the psychiatrist, he said briefly, 'Detective Inspector Forrest here.' A pause before adding. 'We've found another body.' Another pause. 'I'm afraid.'

Lewisham surfaced at lunchtime, appearing in Forrest's doorway just as the Inspector was about to take a bite out of a Big Mac. He eyed the psychiatrist, then the burger before taking a huge bite. Lewisham screwed up his fleshy nose in disgust.

'So, you've got another body, Inspector.'

Forrest chewed thoughtfully before nodding. 'A nurse,' he said between mouthfuls.

Lewisham sat down. 'Ah,' he said. 'And you *still* haven't found a connection between Wilson and the hospital?'

'No.'

Unwittingly Lewisham was echoing Karys's words. 'There will be a connection between the victims,' he said sharply. 'It's simply that you haven't found it yet. Might I suggest that you visit Wilson's wife yourself?' The words were heavy with implied criticism.

Forrest felt defensive, as though he had been accused of mishandling the case, of doing too little himself. 'I already have – she couldn't tell me anything.'

Lewisham ploughed on. 'Tell me about the nurse's injuries. I don't suppose the report's typed up yet?'

Forrest's hands shuffled through the papers on his desk. 'I don't think I've received it,' he said. 'It generally

155

takes a day or two. But I can remember the main points. The lethal injuries were the same as before,' Forrest said. 'But . . .'

Lewisham gave an impatient jerk. 'The "surgeon" won't make the same mutilations.'

Forrest was intrigued. 'How can you *know* that?'

Lewisham leant right back in his seat and steepled his fingers together in a condescending, smug attitude. 'Because,' he said, smiling, 'no surgeon wants to spend his entire working career operating on simple hernias.' He moved forward in his chair. 'Am I right?' he asked eagerly.

Forrest nodded.

The psychiatrist's eyes gleamed. 'So what was it this time?'

'He'd removed a breast.'

'Really? Right or left?"

'The left.'

'Chickens,' Lewisham said.

'Sorry?'

'He practised on something, don't you think? I wonder whether it was chickens. You know. Getting to know the anatomy. Essential, don't you think? Occurred to me while I was eating my Christmas dinner.'

Forrest felt too nauseated to point out the obvious fact that chickens and human beings possessed completely different anatomies. Maybe it didn't matter – to a surgeon. Carving was carving. Maybe he only needed the chance to saw bones, divide ligaments, cut meat. Forrest would never feel the same about Christmas dinner in the future.

Lewisham stood up. 'I think it's time I paid our pathologist a visit.'

Forrest watched him go with relief.

Karys crammed a couple of squares of chocolate into her mouth and read through her PM notes on Rosemary Baring. Forrest might be busy pursuing traditional police investigations but reluctantly she sided with Barney: the solution would lie in the killer's motive. That was what would eventually give him away. It would make a big difference if the victims had been unknown to him or if they had known each other. Her hand reached out to break off another square of chocolate as the thought struck her, how did the surgeon feel after he had killed? Was there a guilty satisfaction followed by deep revulsion? Why *did* he use hospital waste bags? Poetic justice? Expediency? Availability? There must be a reason. It was obviously deliberate. She was beginning to realize it was *all* deliberate. That was why he had to dump the bodies on the hospital site even though with extra police and heightened public vigilance it would have proved increasingly risky. Karys frowned and shoved her glasses up her nose, cupped her chin in her hand and thought – hard.

She had the uncomfortable feeling that she knew things about this killer that no one else did. Not just the forensic detail that told her the sequence of blows, of the element of surprise, the extent of the injuries. That was natural. They had shared the corpses, handled the same body. But there was something else, something that felt like privileged knowledge, something she was meant to know. He had deliberately planted *something* for her to find. The trouble was she didn't know what it was. But the feeling was enough to chill her because it felt as though the 'surgeon' was pushing her towards some preordained point. He was controlling her. She sat very still at her desk and allowed her mind to drift as *he* wanted it to, asking the same old questions. Back to the hospital. Why dump the bodies there? Was it because this was where the 'surgeon' felt they ultimately belonged? Or was the killer abandoning them on the doorstep of an institution in the same way as a woman might leave an unwanted newborn on the steps of a church? Was the hospital then – sanctuary? Her mind tussled with this without seeming to arrive anywhere.

Why make a surgical incision? Answer to suture it. Why murder then mutilate? Answer to further the whole charade. But *why* her mind screamed again. Why the whole bloody thing?

Brenda had taken another day off after Boxing Day. She couldn't have worked anyway. The pounding headache and nausea kept her in bed until lunchtime and when she tried to make some coffee she noticed her hands were shaking. She wouldn't have been much use to Pinky Sutcliffe today, she would have dropped the instruments, or thrown up over the patient. Feeling the cold she wrapped her pink towelling dressing gown round her, switched the gas fire on, pressed the remote control of the TV and lay back, eyes half closed.

She was woken by the doorbell and sat up with a start. It was dark outside. She must have been asleep for hours. All day. She had left her curtains wide open.

Anyone could have looked in and seen her lying on the settee. She stood up and wrapped her dressing gown round her. There was another ring followed by a sharp knock on the door. She staggered along the hall and turned the key before realizing she had forgotten to put the chain on.

It was only Terry. He looked her up and down, took in her dishevelled appearance in the dressing gown and lack of make-up and gave her a playful tap on her backside. 'Hungover are you, Ma? Not been to work?' He pecked her on her cheek. 'I rang. They said you were off sick. I guessed.'

She led the way back to the sitting room. 'You're right about the hangover. Anyway, there's no list today,' she said, tacking on a lie to avoid being reduced in his eyes.

Terry gave her a sharp look and flopped down on the sofa. 'So you're not neglecting your duties then?'

She squeezed next to him, longing to lay her still muzzy head on his lap. But she didn't quite dare.

He leant right back against the cushions. 'Shani's got nasty with me.'

Brenda closed her eyes.

'Said you was leading me on.'

'Little cow.'

Terry stared down at his mother-in-law's face. 'Don't like your Shani much, do you?'

Brenda didn't even bother to shake her head.

He pondered for a moment before changing the subject.

'Seen the papers, have you?'

'Lying here on the settee? Some chance.'

'There's been another murder. Some nurse.'

Brenda stretched her arms above her head and yawned.

'They found her on the new maternity site. Post-mortem was yesterday. They say it was the same bloke what did in the plumber. That Wilson.'

Brenda threw caution to the winds, obeyed her instincts and dropped her head onto her son-in-law's lap, her feet dangling over the armrest. Terry ran his fingers over her face. Without her make-up she looked saggy and old.

Brenda closed her eyes and enjoyed his cool stroking fingers. 'That's nice, Terry.'

'Girl called Rosemary.'

Brenda yawned again, feeling herself gradually dropping back to sleep.

'There's lots of Rosemarys,' she murmured.

'She worked at some clinic.'

'Oh.'

Terry wondered how much to tell her. The head-lines had been lurid. 'He'd cut her about. Bloke's a madman.'

'Mmm.' She was almost past caring. About anything.

'I wonder if it's someone from the hospital.'

The statement roused her. 'Never. We're all normal there, Terry. Boringly normal.'

'Brenda . . .'

'Mmm?'

The idea had come to him that morning, while he had been studying the morning news. 'They made out the bloke cut her with a scalpel.'

'Oh?'

'You know what? I reckon it's Malcolm. I mean – he

collects scalpel blades, doesn't he? And he's definitely weird.'

Brenda was shaken out of her daydream. She sat up. 'You what?'

'I reckon it's Malcolm,' Terry repeated. 'I mean, what does he want scalpel blades for?'

'He does marquetry.'

'Yeah? And I'm a Dutchman.'

Brenda laughed. 'You're more likely to be a Dutchman than Malcolm is to be a serial killer. He wouldn't hurt a fly.'

'Have you ever seen any marquetry he's done?'

Brenda stalled. 'He's promised me a picture.'

'But have you actually *seen* any of it?'

'No.'

'He wouldn't need all those blades just for marquetry even if he does do it. One or two would be enough.'

'Anyway. The plumber was strangled. I read it.'

'Yeah, but he was cut about with a scalpel. It was in the *Post*.' Terry put his face down close to hers. 'You should stop taking him blades, Brenda.'

'But he depends on me. No one else ever goes to see Malcolm. He hasn't got many friends.'

'I think we should tell the police about him.'

'No! I can't believe it of Malcolm. He's really gentle.'

Terry looked sceptical. 'How do you know such a creep anyway?'

'We used to work together. He was a theatre porter.'

'So why isn't he now?'

'He left.'

'Why?'

Brenda wrapped her dressing gown tightly around

161

her. Her desire for Terry had evaporated. 'It was really sad,' she said. 'His mum got ill. Cancer. She had to have a colostomy. She couldn't cope. Malcolm left to look after her. It wasn't long after that that she died. But they wouldn't give him his job back. Then he got more and more peculiar, lonely, I suppose.'

'What did she die of?'

'His mum?' She shot him a look of pure exasperation. 'Well, the cancer of course.'

Terry swivelled round in his seat. 'Sure of that, are you?'

'Yes. Of course I'm sure.' Brenda moved away towards the other end of the sofa. 'Look, Terry. I don't know what you're suggesting but there's no harm in Malcolm. He's a sweet, nice person. Just a bit strange. That's all.'

DS Caroline Fielding approached a pair of swing doors with trepidation. She hated hospitals. But most of all she loathed operating theatres. This was the fourth she had visited in as many days and she was getting hospital phobia.

She knocked on the door of Theatre Four.

It was opened ever so slightly by a plump, middle-aged woman wearing a green surgical gown and white clogs. A few dark hairs escaped from a hat that looked as if it had been made from a blue J-cloth. She looked enquiringly at Fielding as she flashed her ID card.

'Sister Watlow? I did ring earlier.'

The nurse nodded.

Caroline Fielding had been careful to ring earlier for three reasons: as a matter of courtesy, to check availability, and to quell a holy terror that she might barge into the wrong place at the wrong time and witness an operation in progress – yet another hacked body. Alive this time. Something to add to her nightmares. Nervously she peered past the nurse's shoulder.

Brenda Watlow sensed her concern. 'It's all right,' she said. 'Nothing going on at the moment. We've stopped for lunch. But if you're coming in you'll have to put some overshoes on. And a gown over your clothes.' Her manner was decisive, brisk, authoritative. 'And you'll have to finish your questioning by two thirty at the latest,' Brenda continued crisply. 'We get going again then.'

Brenda helped Fielding into a large cotton gown of the same shade of green as her own and tied the tapes at the back, then she handed her a pair of white, wooden-soled clogs. Catching sight of herself in the mirrored door of a locker, Fielding realized with a shock that she looked like one of them now. She eyed herself curiously, running her hands down the shapeless garment. The disguise was complete. No longer a forty-something copper, married to another copper for more than twenty years, but part of the theatre staff. She gave a hesitant smile at herself, shook her dark hair and followed the nurse into a small, square room, painted grey, with orange chairs. A coffee table stood in the centre set with plates of sandwiches and four blue mugs of steaming tea. Three other people, also dressed in green cotton, were at various stages of lunch.

Brenda sat down and helped herself to a sandwich. She spoke to the three occupants. 'This is DS Caroline Fielding. She is investigating that poor nurse's death.' Reaction rippled across the three faces. Concern, interest, but no grief, as Brenda Watlow continued with the introductions. She indicated the tall man on her left. 'This is Mr Sutcliffe, one of our senior surgeons.'

The tall man gave an elegant nod and took a neat bite out of his sandwich before replacing it on his plate. Caroline Fielding gained a swift impression of piercing, intelligent blue eyes before her glance moved on.

'Mr Raja, surgical registrar.' The Indian also inclined his head.

'And Staff Nurse Ellery.' A slim, pale girl with a disconcerting stare who fixed wide eyes on Caroline Fielding. 'I knew Rosemary Baring,' she said with difficulty. 'We trained together.'

It was a good starting point. Fielding took the last available chair to sit right next to the nurse.

'You knew her well?'

'I did then. I haven't seen much of her since she left to work at the Cater Clinic.' The nurse thought for a moment. 'And that was a couple of years ago – at least.'

'Why do you think she moved there?'

The staff nurse blinked rapidly. 'I don't know. I mean, the pay isn't wonderful at these private clinics, and you can't join the superannuation scheme. They're often understaffed. All the money goes on making the place look posh.'

There was resentment in the girl's words which Fielding picked up on.

'Have you ever worked there?'

The nurse looked sulky and glanced sideways at the theatre sister. 'A couple of times,' she confessed. 'When I'm a bit short of cash I do a couple of shifts there. I didn't bump into her though.'

The theatre sister tut-tutted. 'Moonlighting, Staff

Nurse?' But her eyebrows were pointed and her fleshy face was touched with humour.

'When did you last see Rosemary Baring?' Caroline Fielding continued.

The girl thought for a moment. 'Six months to a year ago,' she said finally. 'I bumped into her in Sainsbury's.'

Fielding felt a sudden irritation. 'Which was it – six months or a year?'

'I don't know.'

'What time of year was it?'

The girl looked blank.

Caroline Fielding tried a long shot. 'I don't suppose she said anything that might give us a clue?'

The girl gave a sad, twisted smile. 'What?' she challenged. 'That she was expecting to be knocked off by some madman some time over Christmas?'

'You think it was a madman?'

All four of the theatre staff present nodded their heads vigorously. Sutcliffe was the only one who made a verbal comment. 'Has to be. Stands to reason. The man is barking bloody mad.'

Caroline Fielding watched the surgeon speak. The one so sane, so well balanced. And the other? Mr Sutcliffe had to be right. The other made a grotesque masquerade of the medical profession.

The Staff Nurse gave a long sigh. 'It's awful,' she said. 'I mean – you don't expect someone you know to be murdered.'

Fielding muttered something about it being a rare occurrance. But she couldn't blame all four staff for expressing their concern. Two murders, both bodies left around the same teaching hospital. Not such a rare occurrence here. And no one knew better than she just how little they had to go on.

She tried another angle. 'Did any of you know Colin Wilson, the plumber, who died earlier on this month?'

This time all four managed to look uniformly blank.

Sutcliffe shifted in his seat.

Caroline Fielding moved her questions across to the theatre sister. 'Would you mind if I saw where you keep your stores?'

Brenda Watlow stared at her defensively. 'Why?' she asked bluntly.

Fielding didn't want to tell her but she had the feeling she would get much further with this woman if she took her into her confidence. Partially at least. She stood up. 'This is for your ears only, Sister,' she said and felt quite satisfied when Brenda followed her to the door and passed through it with a brisk and capitulating, 'Very well.'

Brenda led the way into a large windowless store cupboard, stocked from floor to ceiling with shelves full of surgical accessories. Even Fielding knew it would be impossible to keep a check on such quantities of surgeon's gloves, scalpel blades, suturing material, surgeon's masks, gowns and the other paraphernalia of surgery.

'We believe the killer used a scalpel blade to make an incision on his victims after he'd killed them. The blade has been identified as being a number 22?'

'Like this?' Brenda Watlow put her hand out to one of the cardboard boxes, drew out something sealed in foil. Caroline Fielding looked down. There was an outline of a scalpel blade inked on the pack along with the number 22.

'Yes,' she said. 'And then he sewed them up with some very fine suturing material. It's been suggested that this is an unusual combination, the materials possibly originating from a theatre specializing in abdominal or plastic surgery.'

Brenda Watlow was a calm woman ideally suited to her profession, able to listen to such horrors without displaying emotion. The only sign she gave that she had both heard and understood was rapid blinking and a slight tremor of the hand that reached inside a small, plastic box. 'Like this?' she asked.

Fielding's gaze dropped to another foil packet in her hand. It was suturing material, 5/0 silk.

'Just like that,' she said quietly. 'May I keep it?'

'By all means.'

Fielding put it carefully in her pocket and took a good look round at the stacked equipment, almost identical to the other theatre stores she had examined. 'This cupboard isn't kept locked?'

Brenda Watlow shook her head. 'There's no need.'

'So anyone could have access?'

'Only theatre staff,' Brenda said. 'We're the only ones who come in here.'

'And at night?'

'At night the theatre's kept locked. I lock it myself if I'm last out. Otherwise Staff Nurse Ellery does the honours. It's the responsibility of a trained member of staff and the keys are handed in at the front desk.'

Fielding took a cursory look around. 'You've never noticed stores going missing?'

'What sort of quantities are we talking about?'

Fielding frowned. 'A couple of scalpel blades. Two packets of sutures.'

The theatre sister raised her eyebrows, and Fielding agreed with her. How could such a minute quantity be missed? Again she ran her eyes up the stacks of equipment.

'Did you know Rosemary Baring, Shearer that was?'

Brenda frowned. 'I think,' she said slowly, 'she worked here as a student nurse. We've all been talking about it – naturally. But I can't say I remember her.'

'Could you check?'

Brenda Watlow hesitated. 'I'm pretty sure she did, but it would have been a few years ago. Is it important?'

'How many years ago?'

'Five or six. Maybe more. The student nurses come and work in the theatres in their second year of training. They only stay for a few weeks before moving on. Lots of nurses have worked here. I can't remember every single one.'

'But you think you remember her?'

Brenda Watlow's dark eyes flickered. 'Yes,' she said abruptly. 'When I saw her picture in the paper I thought I did.' She hesitated. 'I thought she looked familiar.'

'Can you remember anything about her? Anything at all?'

'No.' Irritation leaked into the nurse's voice making it sharp. 'As I said. Lots of student nurses pass through here. Look – have you finished? I've got work to do. Trolleys to set up.'

'Yes. At least I've finished in here. But before I go I'd better just have a word with the other three members of staff, if that's all right.'

Brenda Watlow didn't answer but led the way back to the sitting room. The staff nurse had left. Caroline Fielding decided to speak to Mr Sutcliffe first. She had already formed an opinion about him; proud, haughty, autocratic – all the things one might expect a surgeon to be. She wondered if the man they were hunting was like this too, pompous, slightly theatrical.

She watched Mr Sutcliffe take a bite from his sandwich, drink a sip of tea from his cup. His movements were all exact and controlled. Almost stage managed. But there was an advantage to his surgical precision. He answered her questions with the exactitude she would have expected from one of his profession.

'How long have you worked here?'

'Twenty-eight years next October the fifteenth.'

'Always as a senior surgeon, sir?' Instinctively, she felt the 'sir' was a necessary part of the interrogation.

'Of course. My registrar years were carried out at the City Infirmary.'

'I see. I don't suppose you knew either Rosemary Baring or Colin Wilson?'

'I believe not. Although.' He hesitated, weighing something up. 'Was Mr Wilson not a plumber?'

'Yes.'

'My wife and I have recently employed the services of a plumber.' He tightened his lips. 'But as for his name I really couldn't tell you.'

'And what did you have done, sir?'

'We had a rather large bedroom,' Mr Sutcliffe said. 'It was decided to fit an en suite bathroom at one end.'

'But you can't remember the name of the firm you employed.'

'No.' The implication was clear. Such domestic details were beneath a surgeon's notice.

'Cheque stubs, sir?' Fielding prompted.

The surgeon looked even more haughty. 'I don't see what . . .'

'It would help us,' she said, 'in our enquiries.'

The surgeon left the room, irritation in every staccato step.

Raja put his hands up. 'And it's no use you asking me,' he said pleasantly with a flash of bright teeth. 'I have only been working in this hospital for about three months.'

Caroline Fielding met his gaze with a bold one of her own. 'And that's just when the murders began.' She watched the pleasantness drain out of the Indian's face as though someone had pulled a plug.

'Excuse me?' he said.

Fielding smiled at him. 'It's all right, sir. We're not really entertaining the idea that the killer is one of the senior surgeons in this hospital.'

Raja folded his arms and smiled. 'Thank goodness for that.'

Mr Sutcliffe returned and read the cheque stub out to Caroline. 'Fourteen hundred pounds,' he said unnecessarily. 'That was the plumber's bill. But I'm afraid it wasn't paid to your friend Wilson but to another firm, Campbell de Morgan.'

Caroline held her hand out and the surgeon reluctantly passed the chequebook to her. Typically it was filled in: the payee, the date, the amount – pence as well. Thirteen hundred and forty pounds, eighty-nine pence. With a balance below. No money worries for Mr Sutcliffe then. They all watched as she handed the chequebook back.

There was something in this theatre that had not been present in the others. A certain guardedness. Or

was she imagining it, goaded on by the fact that Rosemary Baring had once worked here, that one of the
staff nurses had actually trained with her, that the
sutures and scalpel used on the surgeon's victims were
commonly used here, and lastly that the surgeon had
recently employed a plumber. Not Colin Wilson, but
the coincidence of the surgeon having an en suite
fitted? Like the job which Colin Wilson had been lured
away from. Lots of people were having their own
private bathrooms fitted.

She was clutching at straws.

Staff Nurse Ellery walked back in. 'The first patient
from the afternoon list is being anaesthetized,' she
announced.

Fielding stood to leave. As she passed through the
door she took a good look back at the two nurses and
the senior surgeon. She had the tiniest feeling that the
surgeon and theatre sister were uncomfortable about
something. That they were relieved to see her go. Why?
They should have been the allies of the law, confident
of their innocence. But looking round at the theatre
sister's dark eyes and the surgeon's thin, guarded
patrician exterior she knew they wanted her to leave.
The point was, was it relevant to the investigation?

Probably not. The likelihood was that the surgeon
had an expired tax disc on his car and the theatre sister
was in the habit of nicking the soap from the theatre
sinks. Or even that they were simply anxious to get on
with the afternoon's operations.

Lewisham reached the mortuary at four in the afternoon. It suited him that it was already dark. He had

deliberately waited. He rang the bell, glancing round the car park. He could guess which would be Karys's car, the black Mercedes. His lip curled. A bit flash.

She opened the door to him and stood very still. 'Barney,' she said.

'How are you, Karys?' he asked coldly.

She shrugged.

'I expect you're wondering what I'm doing here.'

'Not really. I'm just surprised you ended up doing psychiatry. I thought you had ambitions to be a surgeon.'

Barney closed the door behind him. 'Exams were too hard. Swines kept failing me. There were strong hints that were I to apply for the post of registrar in psychiatry and throw in a couple of theses for my FRC Psych. jobs would fall my way. And they have, Karys. There may even be a professorship in the offing.'

She stared at him, her thoughts flat. To think this – nothing – this nobody was responsible for all those years of heartsearching. She felt an enormous sense of anticlimax.

Barney touched her arm. 'On your own?'

'Yes.' She had no fear of him now, no apprehension. It was as though a great weight had dropped from her shoulders. The shrinks were right. To confront a fear was to watch it evaporate.

'Well then,' Barney said. 'You'd better lead me to your office and I'll take a look at your PM notes on this unfortunate nurse.' His eyes held hers for a second. 'Your inspector told me our surgical friend attempted a mastectomy.'

'He isn't my inspector.'

Barney smiled. 'No? No. Of course not. From what I

hear you're shacked up with a woman. A journalist so I've heard.'

Karys felt her face flame. 'It's none of your bloody business.'

'No. Of course it isn't. I just hope you're not still making such an appalling muddle of your personal life these days, Karys,' he said. 'You were such a mess.'

'You made me one.'

He didn't answer the accusation but strolled along the corridor, seeming to know instinctively which was her office. He switched on the light and sat in the armchair staring up at her. 'Your breakdown was nothing to do with me.'

Karys perched on the edge of her desk. 'The psychiatrist said it was.'

'But don't you know, Karys? Psychiatrists can deceive.' He peered at her over the rim of his glasses.

'Why would they?'

'Lots of reasons. For malice or sport or merely to manipulate a person. You know one person's weakness feeds another's strength.' Karys put her hand up as though to shield herself from his words. Idle, jesting words, meaning nothing. Yet doing his best to rob her of her confidence. But it was too late, he had lost his influence. He was now simply an unpleasant man. Even so her hand strayed towards the chocolate drawer. Barney seized on it. 'No use looking for props, Karys, dear. And my word – haven't you put on weight. Doesn't your, um, *friend* mind?'

As usual he was deliberately wrong-footing her. For the first time in years she needed to conjure up the psychiatrist's words. '*You* are in control now, Karys. Not him. Obey only your will. Not his.' It was a struggle. She

173

opened her eyes to see him staring at her. She had forgotten how repulsive he was. How squat, how short his legs were. How ugly his hands, like two shovels, spatulate fingers sprouting from broad palms. How pale his skin was. The nine o'clock shadow was black against it. Was he never exposed to sun, to the fresh air? But she knew the answer to that. Barney Lewisham spent all his time poring over books, swotting up medical facts. Always studying so he could be the smartest in the class, superior with his extra knowledge. It had always been important to him to know the most. About everything.

How the hell could she ever have fallen under his influence?

Barney Lewisham read all that was racing through her mind. He adjusted his gold-rimmed glasses and smiled.

Chapter Eleven

She was tired. Barney was still there after almost two hours, questioning her about the details of both post-mortems. And what could she tell him that was not already typed in the report? Nothing. It was all there. And he knew it.

So why was he still questioning her?

'There isn't any more to know,' she said, in an attempt to end the interview.

'There might be something,' he said. 'Some small detail that you've left out of your report.'

She was stung. 'I don't leave details out of my reports.'

He leaned right back in the chair. 'No. Of course it's of great significance that both bodies turned up back on the hospital complex. A surgeon always dumps his cases back on the hospital machinery – morticians, nurses, pathologists. It's what you do with them. It's what we did.'

Karys was shocked. 'Are you saying . . .' she hesitated ' . . . that this is the work of a genuine surgeon?'

Barney laughed.

She knew that laugh. There was something mad – uncontrolled – about it. Head thrown right back, mouth obscenely open so she could count every gold filling. He had always found things amusing that would repulse any normal human being. As abruptly as he had begun he stopped. 'No.' He waited to give his words full effect. 'It's all part of the mimicry. If it's what real surgeons do then it's what he does.' The words were spoken quietly but they made Karys feel strange and unreal. She closed her eyes, trying to blot him out, but his soft voice penetrated again . . . 'And Karys. If you have any bright ideas about this case do get in touch with me – directly.'

'I thought Detective Inspector Forrest – '

'No need to go through the police channels,' Barney said smoothly, 'when we are such old friends.' Again that laugh. 'Or should I say partners in crime?'

'Besides,' he continued smoothly, utterly sure now of his ascendancy. 'I can't see your *friendship* with Inspector Forrest really getting anywhere. Most red-blooded men have a holy terror of lesbians.'

'I'm not a—'

Barney leaned forward, his eyes glittering behind the half-moon lenses. 'Prove it.'

She felt sick.

Barney relaxed back in his chair. 'Exactly. Difficult isn't it, to prove a negative? Now listen to me. This case is my great opportunity. Don't spoil it for me. I intend to write it up in the journals. I wouldn't be surprised if the result is that they elect me one of the first ever professors in forensic psychiatry. I shall be world famous.' He puffed out his chest. 'They will invite me to speak all over the English-speaking world on this criminal's motives and methods. It will make the name of *Professor* Barney Lewisham synonymous with the unusual criminal psyche. And who better to illuminate them, Karys? Who better?'

There was no answer to this delusion of grandeur. He gave her one last smile before strutting to the door and pulling it open, pausing in the doorway. 'Don't forget, Karys. You owe me one.'

She was astounded by his conceit. 'I *owe* you?'

'Exactly.'

She was still sitting down when she heard him let himself out. He had been her ruination once, had very nearly dominated her mind to the point where it had threatened to destroy it. And she still sensed that desire for destruction.

Memories intruded.

Her first mistake had been to tell him about Sam. There had been no need other than a wish to share the knowledge and by sharing it gain absolution, from a friend. But Barney had not really been a friend. All her confession had achieved was to give him the perfect lever with which to push her towards the brink. He had used it with good effect. Looking back she could see how deliberate, how calculated it had all been. Beginning with another date when Barney was deliberately late. His timing had been perfect. Even the weather had co-operated with him. Hot, airless. Stifling. By the time he had turned up she had been more than annoyed. She had been furious.

As he had *meant* her to be.

When he had arrived she had given him a cold look. 'You think you can mess me around,' she began.

He played the penitent. 'Sorry, sorry. I forget the time.'

'Well, you could have rung.'

'Yeah, yeah. I could have rung. You're absolutely right. I apologize.'

She had made her mind up then. He had to go. He was, as her mother was constantly telling her, not good for her. She had followed him out to the car, anxious to say her piece away from the ears of her parents. She was twenty-two years old. She must handle her own affairs now.

'Look, I'm not coming with you, Barney. I've had enough.'

His eyes had glittered a devilish yellow in the summer light. 'What are you saying, Karys?'

His voice had been saturated with menace.

'Just that I'm sick of playing your stupid little games, Barney, I want out.'

'Are you saying that you don't want to see me again?'

Her anger had prevented her from seeing what he was up to. 'Yes, I bloody well am.'

Slowly he had climbed into the car and taken something from the back.

A shotgun.

'What on earth are you doing?'

He had smiled.

Instant alarm.

'Is that what you're saying?' Asked very slowly, very deliberately. 'That you don't want to see me again?'

'Yes,' she said. 'That is what I'm saying.'

He had released the safety catch.

Frightened she burst out. 'Is that thing loaded?'

He had smiled again and nodded. 'With two pellets.'

'You're mad.' She had pulled the passenger door open, just as he jammed the handle of the shotgun against the dashboard, through the steering wheel, the barrel end inside his mouth.

'No. Please! No! Sam, don't do it.'

And Barney had won.

It had been as simple as that.

Later he had assured her the gun had been loaded with live cartridges, and that he would have done it. She had believed him.

Now she knew she should have been stronger, walked away from him then. But she hadn't. The more time she had spent in Barney's company the wider the rift between them and the other students had become.

She despised the woman she had been. And the lasting result was that her confidence could not grow while she still held the memory of the pliable little thing she had once been and where that compliance had led her.

To be the cause of an innocent man's death.

Forrest dealt with the afternoon's briefing with a tired feeling. A second murder and still nothing had really been unearthed. In a way Rosemary Baring's circumstances had not been very dissimilar from Colin Wilson's. She had been a divorced woman who had shared a quiet life with another nurse in a flat less than a mile from where she had been murdered. In her personal life there had seemed little to indicate such a violent end. According to the team of officers who had already interviewed her flatmate, her family and her colleagues, Rosemary had expressed no concern over her safety. She had made no particular reference to Colin Wilson's murder beyond the usual comment, that it had been a tragedy. Forrest went over and over the transcripts of the interviews and felt at a loss. Why had she been selected for the surgeon's second killing? And why had he butchered her?

He would liked to have discussed the case with Karys but something held him back. But he badly needed to do something. So he planned for the early part of the evening a follow-up visit to Rosemary Baring's flatmate. And just to show no ill will he took DS Shaw with him.

Rosemary Baring had lived in a small block of purpose-built, red-brick maisonettes, three storeys high surrounded by a very public patch of grass tracked thin and brown by folk taking the direct route from the car park to the front door. Forrest kept to the path and rang the bell for the second-floor flat bearing the joint names, Baring and Stevens. A wavering voice asked who was there.

No one had told him Baring's flatmate was elderly. He glanced at his pad. Stevens. Cassie Stevens. It didn't sound like an old woman's name.

'Inspector Forrest. City police.'

A dull buzzing noise indicated the catch being released and Forrest climbed the steps until he faced a red painted door. There was the sound of bolts being drawn back. A chain rattled.

Cassie Stevens wasn't old, no more than thirty. She was just frightened. The face that peered round the rim of the door was white, her eyes darkly staring, on the edge of hysteria. Forrest felt terribly sorry for her. Grief, for a friend, was bad enough. To compound it with terror for your own safety must be a hundred times worse. He knew he should reassure her. But how?

Knowing nothing about the 'surgeon's' motives he couldn't say who was next in his sights. Whatever her perception, Cassie Stevens was probably in no more danger than anyone else. The point was that she felt vulnerable.

'Miss Cassie Stevens?'

The girl managed a faint, friendly smile.

Her skin was the palest Forrest had ever seen. Whether it was the shock of current events, some illness or her natural colouring he couldn't tell but it gave her a ghostly effect. A pale, insubstantial ghost. She frowned at them each in turn. 'I suppose you've come about Rosemary.'

As always with victims' loved ones he wondered how much to tell her. Full details could only compound her distress and serve no useful function. On the other hand there was a chance that Cassie Stevens might know something that would help them find her flat-mate's killer. But Forrest knew that in cases of violent death even tiny forensic details could cause immense suffering to the survivors. He was fully aware that the girl had already been subjected to an interrogation by a couple of WPCs that had exposed nothing helpful, but he did like to check things through. Besides, new evidence had been unearthed. Rosemary's bag had been found in the grounds of some derelict flats in Edgbaston. There had been other signs near the handbag, kicked earth, an earring, a dropped shoe, that had told the police this had been where the actual murder had been committed, but not the mutilation. There had been no blood. They had traced the nurse's movements from the pub. The block of flats was directly on her route home, well situated for the killer who must have anticipated her journey. He must have followed her on more than one occasion: this had been no chance encounter. The venue was far too convenient. Near the road home but safely hidden behind sheets of corrugated steel. Tailor-made.

Armed with these facts Forrest faced Rosemary Baring's closest friend, the only person who seemed to mourn her. Rosemary's mother had given a brief statement to the press that she had not seen her daughter for many years and had no information to offer them. Since Rosemary's father had identified his daughter's body Forrest had spoken to him twice and, like Colin Wilson's wife a month previously, he had assured the police that his daughter had had no enemies. How would he have known anyway? There had been little contact between father and daughter or mother and daughter. Casual questions had unearthed acrimony between Rosemary's parents, a second marriage for the father to a much younger wife, another couple of children. A new life. Rosemary, with her messy divorce and advancing years, must have been little more than excess baggage to the middle-aged Shearer. Out of a sense of duty he had taken her handbag home with him after it had failed to yield anything to the team of SOCOs. They had also called round to Rosemary's flat and searched through her personal belongings. This too had yielded nothing.

Forrest and Shaw followed Cassie into a small kitchen tastefully furnished with white units with bottle-green plastic handles and a green formica worktop. Spotlessly clean without ornament except for a set of graduated, matching storage jars with cork lids painted with bunches of herbs. Cassie Stevens settled herself in a hardbacked pine chair across the table from them, and rested her chin on her upturned palm. She looked tired, the smudgy rings beneath her eyes suggesting she had not slept since her flatmate had failed to return. She did not offer them coffee but stared into space and said nothing.

Out of politeness Forrest waited for a few moments before opening the interrogation with a couple of routine questions to which he already knew the answers. 'Can you tell me about Rosemary's movements last week?'

The girl's face tightened in spasm. 'She was on lates. All week. She used to call in the Irish pub on the way home.' A half smile, terribly, draggingly, sad. 'Said it helped her unwind. She'd have a half of lager – or two – and then carry on home.' As though she felt she needed to defend her dead flatmate she added quickly, 'I mean it wasn't a long walk – or particularly dangerous.' Then her expression became overcast with recent events. 'At least that was what we thought. It wasn't lonely or anything. There were usually plenty of people around.'

No one needed to add, Not on that night when poor weather had kept potential witnesses indoors or hurrying along with their heads down.

'She would have finished work at what time?' Forrest already knew. He couldn't even have said why he always did this – went over and over questions to which he already had the answers. He always hoped something new would be uncovered. Already knowing the answers meant he didn't need to concentrate so hard, giving him the opportunity to study the examinee intently.

'At ten.' The girl was incurious. Flat.

'Had she ever noticed anyone following her?'

Cassie shook her head. 'Not that she mentioned.'

There seemed to be nothing she could add to the already scanty facts they knew. Forrest tried again, patiently. 'Had she ever mentioned any unpleasant incident that happened to her as a nurse?'

Cassie Stevens's face jerked upwards. 'Sorry?'

'Trouble, maybe with a patient, a relative, perhaps a court case?' Did he have to spell it out? 'Someone who had a grudge against her?'

'Nothing recently.' The girl's face flushed. The two bright spots stood out against her pallor. 'I mean – I think there was a spot of bother when she was a student nurse. But that happens to us all.'

Maybe it was the first true clue. Forrest felt his interest quickening. 'What sort of bother?'

'I don't know. Probably somebody died or something.' The girl's eyes met his for the first time. 'People do die, you know, in hospital.'

'But that wouldn't be classed as a spot of bother, would it?'

'An unexpected death might.'

'So it was an *unexpected* death?'

'I don't know.' The girl was obviously harassed by the questions. 'I mean, I really don't. It was simply something she said to me once when I'd tried to resuscitate a patient and failed. I hadn't called the crash team quick enough. I was upset. She was cheering me up.'

'So what did she say?'

'Just something about a patient of hers once when she was a student who'd died.' Cassie Stevens stopped for a moment. 'Said something about resuscitation not always working anyway. There must have been something a bit peculiar about the incident for her to mention it at all. We see more deaths than we'd like. We don't really talk about them.' She shrugged. 'Occupational hazard.'

'When was this?'

'I don't know. Look, I said, it was when she was a student nurse.'

'And she qualified when?'

'About six years ago.'

That narrowed the field to between six and nine years ago. 'You don't remember anything more?'

The girl shook her head.

Forrest tried a different tack. 'Did she have a boyfriend?'

'No. She was divorced a few years ago. Her husband was a nasty piece of work. Brought his girlfriends home and all that. She was well rid of him.'

Had it not been for the murder of Colin Wilson Forrest might have pursued the ex-husband with a little more vigour. As it was he felt he could afford to discount him.

'Did she have any . . .' Forrest tried to choose his words with care . . . 'friends who were specially interested in operating theatres or hospitals. Perhaps a failed medical student, an ex-nurse. Something like that. A connection.'

Cassie thought about his question for a few seconds before answering. 'Not that I can think of. I mean we didn't go out that much. We were quite happy here, just the pair of us. And we don't know anybody weird.'

Nobody ever does.

After a few more questions that also led nowhere he stood up to leave but was briefly delayed by concern for the girl. 'You don't have another friend you could go and stay with?'

Cassie Stevens's eyes filled with tears. 'We lived quietly,' she said. 'There was just the two of us. We kept ourselves to ourselves. Both Rosemary and I had had bad experiences with the opposite sex. I was badly and humiliatingly let down once. It made us careful. Wary.'

Once in the car he invited Shaw for his observations. 'So what do you think?'

'I suppose it's back to the records department.'

'My thoughts precisely. I think, Shaw,' Forrest tried to make a joke of it, 'that you're going to be tied up at the hospital for a while.'

Shaw groaned.

Forrest drove on in silence, trying to conjure up some solid image of the killer. But he still appeared a shadowy figure. All they knew had been fed them by Lewisham. In fact Forrest was beginning to realize just how directed they were by the forensic psychiatrist. It was as though, having called in the professional, the police team had ceased to think for themselves.

But what if Barney Lewisham was misleading them? Surely not. Lewisham was a professional. Not some medical student wanting to play tricks. Or would it pander to his ego to watch the police flounder, and then to enlighten them. Forrest suddenly felt vulnerable. Lewisham was not the person he would have chosen to control the investigation.

The 'surgeon' was proud of his operating theatre. It had taken a great deal of careful planning. He had done it all himself, cleaned the place out, whitewashed the walls, fixed the lights up and put a board across an old bed to use as an operating table. He had draped the table with a white sheet for clinical effect, and hygiene. When one was soiled he would change it. He had his standards. And then he had to launder the soiled one. Himself of course. A proper laundry might have asked awkward questions. He moved his eyes from the operating table to the instrument trolley, a tea trolley adapted to provide a mobile surface. He had cut white formica to fit the tops which he scrubbed scrupulously after each operation ready for the next case.

He felt very pleased with his professionalism. His skill was still developing, of course, but there was no doubt his standards were high. He could have been a real surgeon. It was just a shame that his patients were unable to appreciate the effort made on their behalf. Such a shame. Especially when his next patient was in a prime position to realize the trouble he was taking for her. She would have appreciated both his skill and his commitment. He stopped still for a moment, the embryo of an idea beginning to take shape. The trouble was that anyone who had witnessed his skill, like those who had seen the face of God, could not live. Although he knew that what he was doing was right and proper the euphoria he had felt after Colin Wilson's surgery had not quite been repeated after Rosemary Shearer's death even though her operation had been much more major. He needed more. A greater challenge. His eyes drifted blankly round the white-painted room silently waiting his next patient. He sat down at his desk. And carefully spelt out another name.

Brenda.

He didn't need the surname.

Chapter Twelve

Rupert Shaw was sick of sitting in the hospital manager's office and reading through staff records. He felt right out of the investigation – sidelined – not out on the street as he liked to be, interviewing suspects, chasing up leads. Frustrated, he kicked the edge of the desk. He was too perceptive not to realize his senior officer didn't have much time for him. Unenthusiastically he flipped through the records, his mind only half on the job.

Deanfield stuck his head round the door. 'Getting on all right, are you?' There was a tinge of malice in his voice that didn't improve Shaw's mood.

He grunted and forced himself to concentrate.

He was surprised at how petty the records could be – odd reports from sisters towards junior nurses, especially. Complaints about lateness, too much make-up, 'attitude problems'. All logged down on file, ready to be drawn on when the nurse wanted a reference.

Three years ago Rosemary Baring had put in her request for a reference. It must have been about the time she had moved from Queen's to the Cater Clinic. Shaw scanned the letter. It told him nothing. Why had she moved? In a larger hospital she would have had a better chance of promotion and DS Fielding had reported that the move had not been for financial gain. Had there been a negative report on the nurse? Had she been unsatisfactory in some way? But glancing through the reference for a second time he picked up nothing. There seemed no reason for her move. And surely a private clinic that specialized in cosmetic surgery was a less rewarding and prestigious post than a staff nurse in a teaching hospital.

The ring of the phone interrupted his train of thought.

'Shaw?' It was Forrest. 'Found anything in Baring's records?'

'No, sir. She did apply for a reference when she left but there's no mention of a problem.'

So what was the incident Cassie Stevens had referred to? Whatever it was there was no mention of it here. Maybe it hadn't been important. Or, Shaw frowned, had the hospital covered the event up?

Forrest sighed. He had hoped for something. 'OK, Shaw,' he said wearily. 'Keep looking. There's a good chap.'

Rupert Shaw flicked the button off and returned to his task, wondering if he had imagined an overture of friendliness in his superior officer's voice.

At the Incident Centre Forrest was feeling fidgety. All morning he had sat and stared at the Police National Computer 2 screens in front of him as they flashed up case after case of serious assault or murder country-wide in the last two years. He knew it was a waste of time. The 'surgeon' had not struck before this. Had *never* struck before. Once heard, the details were too grisly ever to have been forgotten. The forensic details were headline grabbers. So why was he checking for the second time? Because he had so little to go on. Because a previous case might give him a valuable clue.

The two crimes had been planned, maybe months ahead of the attack on Wilson. The surgeon must work somewhere undisturbed. He must have time to make the incision, insert those stitches. In fact he must have light, quiet, and privacy. And cleanliness? Forrest rubbed the thinning patch on his head. Karys hadn't mentioned any debris in the wound. So did he work under sterile conditions? For one pulse-stopping moment Forrest held his breath. Surely he was not murdering his victims before taking them to a real operating theatre? That had to be impossible. How would he do it?

Back came the answer. On a mortuary trolley. The image was nightmarish. A serial killer calmly walking through the hospital, wheeling his victim on a mortuary trolley?

Forrest switched the computer off. He'd just sat for two whole hours in front of the screen and moved not one step forward. More time wasted in this frustrating investigation. Forrest knew he didn't have much time before the responsibility of another life lay at the door of his floundering investigations.

He stood up wearily. He had no option but to speak again to Lewisham. Round and round his head the facts spun: why Colin Wilson; and why Rosemary Baring? Neither of them worked at Queen's. Had they been randomly picked? His thoughts moved back an inch. While Baring had once worked at Queen's, Colin Wilson never had.

A glimmer of light shone through. According to his wife. But he had only been married for . . . Forrest searched frantically through the notes on Wilson. Three years. And Rosemary Baring had left the hospital three years ago. Coincidence?

Forrest sat very still. He didn't believe in coincidence – not in murder cases.

Three years ago, 1996, seemed a good time to start.

Maybe Shaw should be concentrating his efforts prior to three years ago when they knew little about Wilson and Rosemary had still been working at Queen's.

But if the incident which had triggered the murders had happened three or more years ago, why had the 'surgeon' waited until now to act? He had to speak to Lewisham himself.

Again Lewisham answered on the first ring, and managed to get his questions in first. 'So what have you unearthed for me so far, Inspector?'

Forrest stifled his dislike. 'Not a lot, Doctor.' He gained the impression that Lewisham was waiting for him to proceed. 'Nothing really except questions.'

'Ah.'

But even in the short reply he felt that Lewisham was not displeased at the lack of police progress, rather the opposite. The psychiatrist didn't mind that the police had no information to give him, that they were consulting him all the time. It gave him status, power, ascendancy. The realization didn't make it any easier for Forrest to eat humble pie.

'I've been wondering. What kind of event triggered off this man's crimes, sir?'

'Oh, I would say some sort of surgical accident.'

'To him or to a relative?'

'I think he was witness to it.' A pause. 'Have you any idea of the shocking events that can go on in an operating theatre?'

Forrest frowned. 'No. Are you suggesting that he is a doctor, a porter, a nurse who saw something happen and—'

'Decides to mimic it,' Lewisham finished the sentence for him.

'Well in that case all our investigating officers should be speaking to hospital staff.'

'Not necessarily at Queen's. Look for someone with a medical connection. That's all.'

Forrest felt chastened.

Lewisham was waiting for the next question.

'This event. Would it have taken place in the last few months?'

'About a year ago – unless – '

'Unless?'

'Unless our friend only learned of it six months to a year ago. Then he began his preparations.'

'What kind of surgical accident?'

'You should concentrate on cases in which botched surgery resulted either in death, serious brain damage, paralysis. That sort of thing.'

All Forrest could think was, like my father. Why hadn't Lewisham told him this before? He must have known how these facts would further the inquiry. Yet he had – deliberately it seemed to Forrest – held them back as though he was happy not to do the job he had been hired to do. Or had he been fearful of misdirecting the police enquiries? Recalling the psychiatrist's inflated ego he doubted it. Fear didn't seem part of Lewisham's makeup.

Forrest phrased his next question carefully. 'Were Wilson and Baring picked at random? Or deliberately?'

'Deliberately.' Lewisham sounded annoyed. 'I thought I had made myself quite clear. This man might to all intents and purposes be insane, Inspector, but he has, I can assure you, a reason for all he does. Selecting victims randomly, like the winning numbers of the lottery, is not quite in his line. Investigate Wilson's past life a little more thoroughly and you may unearth a few answers. Add to that a peep into your nurse's past *professional* life and you might actually get somewhere in your investigations.'

Forrest felt chastened. Maybe he should have paid more attention to Lewisham from the start.

He dialled another number and spoke to DC Shaw again.

'I want you to move along and concentrate on the last two years. Look for surgical accidents. Get hold of Rosemary Baring's personal file and scrutinize it. Again. And when you've done that you might as well wander along to the Cater Clinic and see if you can unearth anything there.'

Shaw mumbled his reply.

When he'd put the phone down Forrest thought for a moment. The Cater Clinic specialized in plastic surgery. What better feeding ground for complaints from embittered people who were still alive but scarred, not as beautiful as they had thought they would be.

The more he thought about this idea the better he liked it.

Then he picked up his coat and car keys. He had a perfectly legitimate excuse for calling on Karys.

Malcolm had cut himself. He had been lining up the scalpel blades, laying them out in order of size and one had got stuck in the box. He'd tried to pick it up. The next thing he knew his finger was bleeding – badly. Malcolm stuck it in his mouth and was too frightened to take it out. He knew that scalpel blades were sharp, the cut could be deep. And Malcolm didn't like the sight of blood, particularly his own. Brenda had warned him about playing with the blades, about how they were designed to cut through skin and flesh easily, like butter, she had said. That was why he collected them. Their very sharpness was the reason for his fascination. And now the blade had got its own back on him, taught him a lesson for using it as a plaything. After all, they were not toys but designed for serious work.

He ran to the bathroom and stood in front of the sink, looking into the mirror. His eyes were wide, staring and frightened, his finger still inside his mouth. He pulled it out. Immediately it started bleeding again. The blood dripped into the sink, pinking the bowl. Malcolm gave the whimper of a kicked dog. He would have to go to the hospital.

But he hated hospitals. They were dangerous places. He, of all people, knew that. That was where his mother had learned she had the cancer that had eaten her from the inside out. And then she had died. Hospitals were cruel places. He did not want to go there however much his finger bled. He looked at the wound again. Perhaps if he bound it really tightly it would be all right.

Everything would be all right.

Forrest took great comfort from the fact that Karys had looked pleased to see him. Even her friendship meant something to him.

'How are you, David?'

'Not good,' he admitted. 'We're nowhere near an arrest.' He rubbed the top of his head. 'I feel – ' He began again. 'I'm reduced to waiting. Simply waiting for him to murder again.'

She gave the ghost of a smile. 'Sometimes being a pathologist seems an easy task compared with . . .'

He put a hand on her arm. 'I'd never call your work easy,' he said. 'But I have to admit recently – since these killings began – I'm finding being a policeman a difficult option.'

'Stressful too.'

'Yes.' He hesitated. 'Time for a coffee?'

'Yes, of course. Come in.'

Once inside he began to apologize for being there at all. 'I'm sorry to offload on to you,' he began.

Swiftly she stopped him. 'It's all right, David.'

'It's just that—'

She stopped him. 'Hasn't Barney Lewisham helped at all?'

'A bit. Not much. It's all right getting an offender profile but the trouble is that we can't haul in all the adult males with a fetish for surgeon's gowns. He thinks it's an employee of Queen's.'

'I'm an employee of Queen's,' Karys said lightly.

Forrest grinned at her. 'I don't think we're seriously considering you as a prime suspect.'

'No?' Karys gave a short laugh. 'Has no one ever told you pathologists have dark pasts?'

'No.'

She looked as though she was about to say something, and then thought better of it. 'Was there something else you wanted to ask me?'

Forrest settled back in his chair. 'I wondered about debris in the wound,' he said slowly, 'what sort of conditions our kinky little "surgeon" is working under? How far does he go in his attempt at an authentic operating theatre.'

Karys leaned forward. 'There wasn't any debris. I think I mentioned it in my report. I mean, I wouldn't say he's working under sterile conditions though I didn't take swabs for culture.' She considered for a moment. 'Infection wouldn't have had a chance to progress anyway, but the place where he takes them to . . . It is, at the very least, clean.'

'He takes care then, our "surgeon".'

She nodded. 'He takes a good deal of care.'

Chapter Thirteen

4 January 2000

Brenda was in a panic. Tuesday's list had lasted almost an hour beyond the usual time. An appendectomy complicated by peritonitis followed by two emergency cases. It had been bad luck. Now she had at least an hour's work before she could go. She scrubbed the sets of instruments wishing she hadn't been quite so generous in letting Staff Nurse Ellery go off early. It left her alone in the darkened theatre, and she was nervous. Pinky Sutcliffe had vanished an hour ago in the direction of the ward to check on his cases. The anaesthetist had hurried back to his wife and family. The orderlies had finished their antiseptic dousing of the entire theatre and its contents. Alone, even in such familiar surroundings, she was uneasy.

She put the last batch of instruments into the steam autoclave and switched it on. Now she should wait for twenty minutes. She was not supposed to leave the sterilizer running unless someone was around to supervise it. There were frequent faults. The pressure of the steam had been known to build up to a dangerous point. She hesitated before flicking the switch. Once the cycle had begun she must stay.

She checked that everything was prepared for the following day's list, each piece of furniture cleaned and back in place, that the porter had done his job thoroughly. She peered at the thermometer in the door. The autoclave hadn't even reached its maximum temperature yet, then it had to hold for four minutes. She toyed with the idea of ringing Terry. He would come and meet her. Thinking of Terry calmed her. He was so strong, so – masculine. She felt warm at the thought of him. Shani, she banished from her mind. Silly little cow.

She thought about Rosemary who had been a nurse too.

Brenda caught sight of her distorted reflection in the stainless-steel autoclave door. Her eyes looked very dark against the paleness of her face.

She remembered perfectly well who Rosemary Shearer had been. She'd recognized the photograph as soon as Staff Nurse Ellery had brought the newspaper into the coffee room. It had turned her stomach because she had put two and two together. As far as she knew she was the only one who could connect Rosemary Shearer, nurse, with Colin Wilson, plumber.

He hadn't always been a plumber.

She continued staring at her reflection in the autoclave door, visions swimming in front of her eyes. Blood spurting. Panic, a sense of madness. A death that never should have happened. She had spent hours wondering what had really led to the sequence of events that day. So many years ago. And still so fresh in her mind.

Beneath her theatre hat her face looked even more strange. She wasn't used to seeing herself without a frame of thick, dark hair. It didn't look like her. She looked as pale as a corpse. Her face, distorted by the stainless steel, looked like that of an older, frightened woman. Years older than forty.

She should speak to the police.

Panicking now she glanced again at the autoclave. She had to get out of here. Theatre was not a good place to be alone, at night.

The autoclave had reached full heat. Hold for four minutes.

Almost in a dream she drifted back into the operating theatre, hesitating before flicking the lights on. The operating table lay stark black underneath the unblinking illumination. Empty. Without a patient and the huddle of green-gowned staff it looked naked and unfamiliar. Undramatic.

As though drawn by magnetic force her eyes turned upwards, checking. Immediately she was reassured. It was a perfectly clean ceiling. There was no splash of blood. It had been cleaned off. She dropped her eyes. The floor too. Perfectly clean. It had all been washed down properly.

But the image was still strong. Brenda closed her eyes and shivered. She was tired and cold. It had been a long day. The heating must have gone off. She switched the lights off and returned to check the sterilizer. The thermometer showed the temperature had been held for two minutes.

Still two more minutes before she could leave.

She wandered back into the coffee room. There were still a couple of mugs lying around, one cigarette butt in the ash tray. To kill time she took them into the kitchen and washed them up, smiling at the fact that Bill Amison, the anaesthetist, still smoked. At the same time she wished she could conjure him up to see her home – safely.

The sterilizer bleeped four times. Thank goodness, it had finished its cycle. She was free to go. She flicked the switch, took her coat from the hook and glanced through the window of the cloakroom. Pitch black. Nothing to be seen but a few orange lights. No flashing blue ones, ambulances or police. After the Christmas break the hospital was usually quiet: the drunks were sobering up. There had not been another murder – yet. She peered further out through the window and wished her mind did not keep clicking back to the past. Was he out there? Somewhere? Watching? If Rosemary Shearer and Colin Wilson – innocent, quiet Colin – if they had been his intended victims who would be next? Her?

In a panic now, she dialled Terry's mobile number. But he must be working, away somewhere. An impersonal voice announced that the Vodafone she had dialled may be switched off. She was invited to try again later.

He was out there, his eyes fixed on her silhouette. He was smiling because he could see his prey while she could not see him. He was camouflaged against the night.

Brenda moved away from the window. Terry was not available to pick her up and she did not want to ring his home number for fear of speaking to Shani.

Keenly aware of the time she hurried along the hospital corridor, wishing she had arranged a lift with her son-in-law earlier. It was past eight o'clock. Hours later than she usually went home.

He watched as the windows turned to black and he smiled, picturing Sister Brenda Watlow hurrying along the corridor. It had been a long wait tonight. She had worked late. But she would be worth it. Brenda would be a prize worth having. It was only a shame that she would not be in a position to appreciate all the attention she would soon be getting. After all, she was an allied professional. She would recognize his skill, his attention to detail, his dedication, the work and training that had gone into his achievements. Surely she would consider it a compliment that he had selected her for his most invasive procedure so far?

The hospital corridors were almost empty. Two nurses walked passed her, chattering too hard to take any notice of a weary off-duty, theatre sister. A doctor walked behind her until she reached the corner. Brenda hardly glanced at him, masked and gowned he must be on duty for one of the other theatres. He peeled off to the left. She carried on to the porter's window and hesitated. Should she call a taxi and wait here, in safety, until it arrived? Unusually indecisive she didn't know what to do.

She tried to work out a plan. It was too far to walk, so it must be either a taxi or the bus. An inherent meanness in her argued that catching the bus would save her two pounds.

She made her decision, smiled goodnight to the

porter and handed over the keys to the theatre before leaving the safety of Queen's, taking brisk strides outside to the freezing air and the soft quiet of a January night. She hurried towards the bus stop.

Two floors up Rupert Shaw was working late, earning himself a bit of overtime, idly scanning through the hospital files from the 1990s. So many irrelevant facts to be tossed away. So far he had turned up nothing. He must have gone through years of employment records. Six, seven, eight? And nothing had sprung out at him as having the slightest relevance to the case. He hadn't even found anything in Rosemary Baring's staff record. He yawned and took a huge bite out of a Mars bar and a swig of Coke straight from the can. It was much more relaxing without Deanfield spying on him from the room next door. He rested his feet up on the desk and leafed through another file. He wouldn't have admitted it to Forrest but he was convinced that he would recognize the connection between the 'surgeon' and his victims when he finally unearthed it. So he didn't mind working late into the night. He would be the one to crack the shell of this case. Shaw daydreamed: promotion, accolades. Maybe a few newspaper headlines: 'Bright young copper finds vital clue to serial killer.' A brilliant career would inevitably follow.

Deanfield had searched out the yearbook logs. They were confidential and Deanfield had assured him they would prove irrelevant. So far they had.

Shaw flipped open the next file, scanning through the events that had merited a mention in the log of 1991. He was halfway through, in July, when he found a familiar name. Immediately he sat up, giving a low, contented whistle.

This was it.

He picked up the telephone and dialled Forrest's mobile phone number. 'I've found Wilson,' he said. 'He used to work here, in the operating theatre.'

'When?'

'Eight years ago, sir. He worked in Theatre Four.'

'Theatre Four?' Forrest felt a prickling of satisfaction.

'Yes, sir.'

'Right.' Forrest was thinking quickly. 'We'll speak to all the staff of Theatre Four tomorrow morning. Some of them were there eight years ago.'

'Yes, sir.' Shaw felt unbelievably proud that he had been the one to make the first breakthrough.

'What exactly does it say?'

'I haven't read through it properly yet. I thought I'd better get straight in touch with you.'

'I'll want to read through everything.'

'The hospital manager isn't keen on anything going out of the building.'

'It doesn't have to. I'm on my way over. I'll be there before nine.'

Shaw glanced at his watch. Eight thirty-five.

It would be a late night.

Chapter Fourteen

It took Forrest forty-five frustrating minutes to reach the hospital. Traffic was heavy and there were road works with four-way traffic lights along the Hagley Road. He sat in his car and fumed. What he wouldn't have given for a squad car, a flashing blue light and a good, loud siren. He was still fuming by the time he pulled up outside the hospital.

Shaw had not been idle while waiting for his senior officer but had spent the time reading right through Colin Wilson's file – twice. The trouble was he could see no early clue to Wilson's violent death. The file was unremarkable. Wilson had worked at the hospital from the end of May 1991 to the middle of September of the same year. Just a few months. He had been employed as a theatre porter, his duties fetching and carrying the patients to and from the operating theatre and generally being a dogsbody for the rest of the staff. According to the file he had had a blameless work record and had left citing as his main reasons: 'I want to earn some more money', 'I'm not reelly suited to the work', and that he wanted to have a chance to run his own 'bisness.' The letter was in the file, badly spelt in spidery writing on blue writing paper, the address a flat in the northern part of the city and dated the fourth of August 1991.

Shaw held the letter in his hands. There was something poignant about sharing the man's aspirations when the only contact you had had with him was as a witness to his post-mortem. It wasn't even as though the monetary ambition had been fulfilled. Casting his mind back to the description DS Fielding had so graphically given of Wilson's home there had been no hint of wealth. DS Shaw folded the letter and returned it to the file. Still, Wilson had realized one of his ambitions. He had, at least, run his own 'bisness'.

So, Wilson had once worked here. It wasn't much help. Whatever connection there was with his murder it wasn't held here. So where? The answer must lie with Wilson's colleagues of the time. Shaw returned to the filing cabinet.

Forrest burst in noisily, apologizing for the time it had taken. Shaw grinned at him. 'It's all right, sir. You can't go breaking the speed limit, can you?'

Forrest grunted and Shaw handed him Wilson's file, waiting for him to read it before hitting his senior officer with his second breakthrough of the day.

Forrest finished scanning the file and turned a pair of puzzled eyes on Shaw. 'I can't see what you're looking so pleased about,' he said grumpily. 'There's nothing here.'

With a touch of triumph Shaw flipped a second manilla file onto the desk. 'This is Rosemary Shearer's,' he said. 'I fished it out as soon as I found Wilson had worked here. Just a hunch,' he added smugly. 'But it paid off. Guess where she was working during the summer of 1991?'

Forrest shrugged. But his eyes were alert.

'Theatre Four.'

Forrest sank into the chair. For a moment he said nothing but his heart was pounding with anticipation. This was the moment he had been waiting for. 'So what happened?' he asked quietly.

Rupert Shaw perched on the edge of the desk. 'That's the trouble,' he said, frowning. 'That's where the whole thing seems to melt into thin air. There isn't anything I can see. No awful accidents, no deaths on the table. Either they simply did their work without any trouble or . . .'

'Or,' Forrest picked up, 'there was a great big cover-up.' His eyes narrowed.

'What about her work record?'

Shaw shook his head. 'Not a thing. She was just an ordinary student nurse doing her couple of months' stint in the operating theatre. When that was over she moved back onto the wards. Her references were impeccable.' He hesitated before continuing quietly. 'And that seems a bit weird.'

Forrest glanced at him.

'Well, all the other student nurses seemed to have fallen foul of the sisters – particularly the theatre sisters. Compared to the others Shearer's file was a bit bland.'

'What are you thinking?'

'I just wondered,' Shaw said awkwardly. 'Well, what if there was some sympathy for the girl?'

'Over what?'

'That's the trouble. I just don't know. Just a thought, sir.'

Forrest bent back over the file, took a few minutes longer to read it and scratched his head.

'Theatre Four,' Shaw pointed out. 'That's where they both worked. As far as we can tell it's the only thing the two of them had in common. Don't tell me it's all coincidence. Would any of the staff be the same, after eight years?'

'Some of them will be. It's the only theatre Fielding singled out of all six. It's perfectly possible some of the staff have worked there for the whole eight years. The senior staff: the surgeon; maybe the theatre sister; the anaesthetist. It's worth talking to them all. In the meantime, we'd better look a bit more closely at the record of Theatre Four for the period that Wilson worked there. Find out if there was some incident. It's only a few months. It shouldn't take long. And there were only two months that both Shearer and Wilson worked there. It narrows the field considerably.' For the first time he seemed aware of the time. 'It's late. I expect you'd like to get off home. They'll have stopped operating by now. The place will be empty. Nothing much we can do until tomorrow.'

He liked a fresh corpse, still warm, it felt right. Cold corpses felt wrong. Told him he was not a surgeon operating on a live patient but a pathologist performing a post-mortem. That would not do. He was a surgeon.

Brenda was fatter than he had imagined. Working through her abdomen almost buried his hand up to the wrist. But he must work deep. Nothing too superficial today. He had a real job to do. A thorough job. No small cuts. The whole hog. He screwed up his face. How he

207

loved some phrases: the whole hog. As he worked he hummed, a silly tune, something sentimental and romantic. Only it wasn't really. 'If I said you had a beautiful body would you hold it against me?' Humming made his work quite soothing. He felt a huge, tidal wave of happiness. This was his purpose, his destiny. Playing nemesis.

A moment later he was scowling. The trouble with the song, the 'surgeon' decided, was that he only knew the one line and a bit more of the tune, and it wasn't enough. The sentiments were great. Suitable too. But he didn't know any more, and that was a pity. He liked music as he worked. Maybe he'd bring in a radio here to keep him company. Brenda had told him some surgeons operated to music, it helped their concentration. It might help his. But he couldn't risk being heard.

He continued his work without any accompaniment to his tuneless, repetitive humming. But at the back of his mind was a feeling of dissatisfaction. It was beginning to disturb him, this distinction between the work of a surgeon and the work of a pathologist. He had tried to pretend that he was a surgeon, a real surgeon, when really he was operating on dead people. They did not bleed properly. Their hearts did not beat. It was no good pretending. The dissatisfaction was beginning to spoil his pleasure in his work. It was being exposed as a sham, a pretence. There was only one thing to do.

He sewed Brenda up carefully before writing the next name in a neat, tall script.

Karys Harper.

Underneath he added, in brackets, Doctor.

Chapter Fifteen

5 January 2000

Forrest and Shaw were back at work at seven forty-five in the morning, neither having slept much. Shaw had fidgeted for half the night and slept only fitfully for the rest. Forrest had sat in a chair without bothering to go to bed.

They met at the Incident Room and drove silently to the hospital. Forrest watched the streams of people hurrying through the doors – nurses, doctors, porters, managers, ancillary staff – and was suddenly seized with anxiety that he was barking up the wrong tree, wasting time, risking lives by following a paper chase instead of the real scent. He frowned. This had to be the real scent. There was no other.

This first connection between the 'surgeon's' two victims could not all be coincidence. Feeling compelled to hurry he parked the car on double yellow lines and together they walked into the hospital. Forrest was glad to note a porter challenged them before allowing them to enter the lift and ascend to the fourth floor. The theatre was only a short distance away. Shaw knocked.

The door was flung open by a tall, green-gowned man, scowling at them, tension combing lines down his thin face. He glared at them both. 'And who the hell are you?'

'Detective Inspector Forrest, sir, City Police. And this is DS Shaw.' With his arrogant air of authority this had to be the surgeon. 'Mr Sutcliffe?'

The man nodded brusquely.

Shaw was eyeing him closely. 'You have a problem?'

'Only that the damned theatre sister's late.'

Forrest was aware that it was still only a minute or two passed eight o'clock.

'Surely, sir, it's early yet?'

'Early, yes,' the surgeon said impatiently. 'But I'm ready to discuss the morning's list with her.' He stared past them, along the empty corridor, before letting the door swing back. 'Bloody woman,' he said. 'She's got really unreliable lately. I don't know what's got into her.' He glowered at them both. 'And now you two arrive thinking I can spend my morning answering more stupid questions about plumbers. What are the police doing here again, anyway? We've already had a visitation from one of your lot over the murders. None of us could tell them a thing.' Maybe he realized how callous this sounded because he added quickly. 'Sorry. Didn't mean that. I really am sorry about the nurse. But I've a job to do and you lot get in the way. So what can I do for you?'

'Have you worked in this hospital long?' Forrest asked.

'Yes I have.'

'How long?'

'I've been a senior surgeon for nearly twenty-eight years.'

'In this theatre?'

'Oh, about ten years.'

Forrest was aware of a tingling in his toes, a feeling

that this man had information, something he badly needed to know. The problem would be winkling it out of him, especially here, in the anteroom of the operating theatre, a place too public for confidences. 'Is there somewhere a bit more private we can talk?'

Sutcliffe looked uncurious. 'You'll have to put protective gear on. And be quick. The minute that sister arrives I shall have to begin. I haven't got much time.'

'Neither have we, sir,' Forrest put in quietly.

Sutcliffe turned back. 'What the hell do you mean by that?'

'Only that every day we fail to catch our killer another life is in danger.'

Sutcliffe scowled. 'What has that got to do with me?'

'We don't know yet.' Forrest was aware that behind his right shoulder Rupert Shaw was staring fixedly at the surgeon. He would have given a fifty-pound note to know what the officer was thinking.

Sutcliffe silently handed them both some overshoes and green cotton gowns, waited for them to put them on and led the way to the empty staff room.

Once all three were seated he prompted, 'Well fire away, Inspector.'

'Were you working in this theatre eight years ago last summer?'

Sutcliffe nodded. 'As I have already assured you I have worked here, in this theatre – ' He allowed himself a quick, fond glance around the room – 'for the last ten years, so you will be able to deduce that I was. Although what connection that fact could possibly have with your current investigation I cannot even begin to guess at.'

'We're working blind here, sir. So far.'

Sutcliffe's eyes were sharp and intelligent. 'Then why pick on one specific period? Why eight years ago? Why this theatre. Why me?'

'Because we believe that both Colin Wilson and Rosemary Shearer, or Baring as she later became, also worked here then.'

Sutcliffe's eyes flickered. 'The two people who were murdered?'

'That's right.'

'I don't remember either of them.' The surgeon gave a dry cough.

'Well, you might not. Colin Wilson was only here for a total of four months, as a theatre porter.'

Sutcliffe interrupted. 'I thought the man was a plumber. That's what the papers – '

'After he left here he became a self-employed plumber.'

'And the nurse?'

'Rosemary Shearer was just one of the many student nurses who passed through here. There must be lots.'

'Oh, yes.' Sutcliffe nodded vigorously. 'Oh, yes. They change every couple of months. I never really get to know them. Unless she was unusual in some way.'

'She was perfectly ordinary.' Shaw said gravely. 'Unremarkable as far as we know.'

'Which makes it all the more strange that she was murdered, doesn't it, sir?'

Sutcliffe's eyes met those of Forrest. 'I suppose it does,' he said warily. 'I really don't know. Are ordinary people more or less likely to be murdered than unusual types? I'm sure it's a perfectly wonderful point to ponder, Inspector. The problem is – I don't have the time to ponder such things. I have operations to perform.' He flexed his long, bony fingers. 'Lives to save and all that.'

'So is there anything you can recall about either ex-members of staff?'

Sutcliffe took a little time to reflect before looking up. 'I do seem to recall a porter who came and went pretty quickly. Just learning the job, beginning to be useful and off he vanished. Quiet bloke. Skinny. I think he had ginger hair. It would have been round about eight years ago.' He cleared his throat. 'I can't be sure and I don't remember speaking to him much. I certainly didn't know his name.'

'That could have been Wilson.'

'Ah.' It was a sound of sympathy. 'Well, I don't see how my vague memories of two junior staff from a while ago is going to be of much interest to you, Inspector.'

Forrest wasn't disappointed. He hadn't really expected some dark secret to come tumbling out. There might not even be one. The murderer could merely have had some brief, brushing contact with two members of staff and for some, as yet unknown, reason had decided to kill them. Give them a taste of their own medicine. The thought transfixed him. Was that what the point of the murders was? A taste of their own medicine? And if that was what it was were other members of staff who had worked here during that period and might have had contact with the 'surgeon' in danger too? Like this surgeon?

The unpalatable fact was that it might take yet another murder to find out.

Forrest probed further. 'Can you name the other

members of staff who also worked here at the same time as Rosemary Baring?'

Sutcliffe shook his head dubiously. 'Not really. Oh, except Brenda, of course.'

Shaw was quick. 'You mean the theatre sister.'

'Yes.'

Forrest continued his questioning. 'Can you think of anything . . .' he hesitated ' . . . untoward that happened in that period?'

Sutcliffe chose to take offence. 'What sort of *happening* did you have in mind?'

'I don't know, sir. Anything unusual?'

'As far as I remember,' the piercing blue eyes stared coldly at Forrest, 'and we're talking about a very long time ago there was just the normal day-to-day work of a busy operating theatre. Nothing memorable, I assure you.'

He looked from one to the other, waiting for them to accept this version as the truth. For the two police officers there was little to go on, a tightening of the hands, a contraction of a few facial muscles, especially those around the eyes and the upper lip. Forrest reminded himself that this was a man well-schooled in the concealment of emotion, able to screen shocking diagnoses from grieving sufferers. He was suspicious enough of Sutcliffe to pursue his questions further.

'Some sort of accident,' he prompted. 'Maybe an unexpected death through – a mistake by one of the other staff.' Forrest was anxious to deflect the blame away from the surgeon. 'Maybe the anaesthetist?'

Sutcliffe gave a tight smile. 'Bill? You must be joking. If anything he . . .'

Forrest's interest quickened. 'He what, sir?'

But Sutcliffe had returned to normal. Not even his eyes betrayed the fact that for a split second he had allowed his guard to slip. 'The anaesthetist is there to keep the patient alive.'

'And eight years ago it was the same anaesthetist?'

'Yes.' Sutcliffe gave a showy stare at his watch, pulling his sleeve back and holding his wrist stiffly in front of his eyes. Forrest ignored the hint and Sutcliffe gave an irritated grunt. 'Look, I'd like to help but I don't know what you're looking for.'

'That's the trouble,' Shaw put in, 'neither do we.'

Sutcliffe held his pale hands out, palms uppermost. 'There's nothing, I can assure you. The fact that two ex-members of staff who just happened to work here during the same period many years ago have been murdered is pure coincidence. This is a normal operating theatre. Tragedies do happen. Patients do die. We can't help that. They are here because they are sick people.'

'And you can't think of any reason why someone might . . .' Forrest persisted.

'Pick us off like flies on a bloody cake? No, I can't, Inspector.' Another quick glance at his watch. 'Now where is that damned theatre sister?'

A nurse similarly dressed in theatre green popped her head round the door. 'Morning, sir. Coffee?' The words were out before she had registered the presence of the two police officers with faint surprise. 'Sorry. Didn't see anyone was here. Hello.'

Sutcliffe glared at the girl. 'I hope Sister Watlow is out there with you, getting the trolleys ready, Staff Nurse Ellery?'

The nurse looked flustered. 'No, sir. I thought she was in here with you. I heard voices. I just assumed . . .'

'Well, you'd better set the trolleys yourself. It's a straightforward enough list. Couple of hernias. Varicose veins. Nothing you can't cope with.'

The nurse flushed but she also looked taken aback. At a guess Sutcliffe wasn't usually so peremptory with his orders. Could it be that they had succeeded in rattling him? Or was it purely the lateness of the theatre sister?

'She hasn't rung in with another hangover?'

The nurse shook her head.

'Or left a message at the porter's office?'

'I'll go and check.' The girl left.

Forrest didn't make a connection.

Sutcliffe finally lost patience. 'Look, I don't want to be rude,' he unbent his tall, thin body and stood up, 'but I've got a list to get through this morning. With apparently only a staff nurse to assist me.'

Forrest and Shaw stood up too. They were both anxious to be out of here before the surgeon started his grisly work. They'd seen enough of it recently to last them a lifetime. Mr Sutcliffe was still grumbling as they followed him along the corridor towards the doors. 'My bloody registrar doesn't appear to know his Achilles tendon from his frenulum and . . .'

They reached the door and started divesting themselves of the theatre wraps and overshoes. 'OK, we're going. But we'll want to talk to you again, Mr Sutcliffe, as well as the theatre sister – when she turns up.'

'*If* she turns up, you mean.' It was Sutcliffe's final, bad-tempered shot that eventually pulled the tripwire.

The two policemen looked at one another. Forrest spoke first. 'We'd better call round and see this theatre sister at her house.' He shot out of the door, dropping gown and overshoes as he went.

It took Shaw a second to move. He caught his senior officer up halfway along the corridor. 'Sir,' he began.

Forrest appeared not to hear him.

Shaw tried again. 'Sir.'

'What?'

'Why did he say that?'

Forrest was in an evil temper. He hadn't liked Pinky Sutcliffe. He'd positively *hated* the way the man had condescended to answer his questions, and now he had concerns about a missing theatre sister.

He vented his anger on Shaw. 'What? Say what?'

'That bit about tragedies do happen. Patients do die. It seemed out of place. Why did he bring it up?'

'We'd been questioning him about two murders,' Forrest barked back. 'Or doesn't that qualify as tragedy or death?'

'I just wondered. That's all.'

Forrest walked a couple more steps before speaking again. 'What's in that clever little mind of yours, Shaw?'

'It's as though something *had* happened. Somebody *had* died. Maybe unexpectedly. I don't know, sir,' he was forced to confess, 'I just had a feeling.'

They strode back along the hospital corridor, scattering nurses, patients on trolleys, patients in wheelchairs, quickening their pace until they reached Deanfield's office. They barged straight in.

He was sitting at a computer. 'What the hell?'

Forrest strode right up to him. 'Where does the theatre sister live?'

'Who?' Deanfield looked furious.

'Watlow,' Shaw supplied. 'Sister Brenda Watlow. The sister who works on Theatre Four.'

'What do you want to know for?'

'She hasn't turned up to work today.'

Deanfield smirked. 'Checking up on all absenteeism, are you?'

Forrest shook his head slowly. 'No,' he said. 'Only the ones who worked in Theatre Four in the summer of 1991.'

Chapter Sixteen

He hated bagging up his bodies and finally abandoning them. He would like to have kept them but he was afraid of decay. It repulsed him. All the same it didn't seem quite the way to treat his patients after the care he'd lavished on their bodies. Brenda's in particular. He had made an almost perfect job of stitching her up. He really was quite proud of his mounting skill. But it was time to say goodbye. Reluctantly he wrapped Brenda's body inside the double plastic bag and secured it with tape.

Dumping the bodies was dangerous too.

He backed the van up and gave a fond glance round his theatre. Instruments at the ready for the next case.

Once Brenda's body was loaded he drove towards the hospital site. Not so near this time. There was a noticeable police presence there these days. He passed a few police cars. Going the other way. In a hurry. He averted his eyes and carried on driving along the leafy lanes of Edgbaston.

Near the bottom of the hill at the hospital site was the old incinerator, marked by a tall chimney, unused now because of pollution laws. One day it would be demolished. Not just yet. He drove to the tiny, empty car park, round the back, out of sight, opened his rear van doors and waited – feeling suddenly uncomfortable for a reason he could not initially pin down. It took him a few minutes before it registered; the distant wail of a police siren. He glanced quickly at the body to reassure himself all was well. If the police were looking for Brenda they had missed her early. Too early. Something was going wrong.

Even with Control directing them it took the two detectives more than twenty minutes to locate Brenda Watlow's home. A more ordinary residence couldn't have been imagined or anywhere further from intrigue or drama. Small, square, built in the late sixties, part of a long row of similar houses, each with their own stamp of individuality: a UPVC porch; a flowering cherry, bald now, in the front of the garden; a low brick wall; a plastic chain link fence. Some of the houses had cars in the drive. Not in the drive of number 69.

The curtains were drawn. Maybe Brenda Watlow really was sick. Or hungover. Forrest pulled the car over without a word and together he and Shaw marched up to the front door. Forrest banged. Twice. Tried the doorbell. He heard it ring inside. No answer.

He was considering walking round the back when a vehicle pulled up. The door was flung open. Forrest stared at a man in his thirties with a plump, ruddy face and curly dark hair. Handsome in a fleshy sort of way. Striding up the path.

The man looked at them suspiciously. 'Who are you?'

'Police.' Forrest flashed his ID card.

'What are you doing here?'

'We're looking for Sister Brenda Watlow.'

The man looked even more hostile. 'She'll be at work.'

Forrest shook his head. 'She didn't turn up.'

'What?'

'She didn't turn up at work today,' Forrest repeated.

The man jerked his head towards the house. 'Well, is she in?'

'She hasn't answered so far.'

'May I ask who you are?' Shaw spoke up.

'I'm her son-in-law, Terry Carling.' He looked at both of them. 'Why are the police here just because she didn't turn up at work today?'

Instead of answering the question Forrest motioned towards the door. 'Have you got a key?'

'Yeah, but . . .' Carling pressed his finger on the bell and called out, 'Ma. Ma. Are you in there?'

The three men stood on the doorstep. The door remained closed. And from behind it there was no sign of movement.

Carling banged a couple more times before pulling a bunch of keys from his pocket, and inserting one in the lock.

He was still shouting as they filed into a small hall. 'Ma. Ma.' He turned back to the police. 'She isn't here,' he said.

Shaw and Forrest followed him into a small lounge, watching as Carling hastily drew back the curtains and surveyed the empty room. 'She must have gone to work.'

'Maybe.' Forrest made a quick recce of the house. Two and a half bedrooms, tiny bathroom, kitchen-diner.

No sign of a struggle. All was neat. Organized. Exactly the way she must organize the operating theatre.

He returned to the lounge just as Shaw was walking back in through the front door holding a mobile phone. 'She still hasn't turned up, sir.'

Forrest addressed Carling. 'Is there anywhere else she might be?'

Carling shook his head. 'Not without letting us know.'

'Is she married?'

The question provoked a chuckle. 'No. Divorced years ago. More of a merry divorcee.'

'So she lives here alone?'

Carling nodded.

'When did you last see her?'

'Sunday. We came round for meal. She's a marvellous cook. I didn't see her Monday.'

'And yesterday?'

Carling grinned. 'I was up to my ears all day. I run my own business. She was working at the hospital. A long list. My guess is she'd have worked until the list was finished then have taken a taxi home. She sometimes calls me to ask for a lift but she didn't yesterday. Maybe someone else brought her home. Sutcliffe or the anaesthetist chap, Amison.'

'She doesn't have a car?'

'Doesn't need one. I give her lifts anywhere she wants to go. She can't drive anyway. Never learnt.'

'So how does she get to work?'

'By bus or taxi usually, unless I give her a lift.'

Shaw glanced around the room. No family photographs, plenty of nursing textbooks and four shelves of Mills & Boon. It told him a lot about the nurse: took her

222

work seriously; was a romantic; not much for the family. Shaw sneaked a glance at Brenda's son-in-law. Except for him. And what was he doing here, anyway?

He masked the cynical policeman's question by affecting a friendly tone. 'What brought you round here today, Mr Carling?'

The question didn't faze Carling. 'Doing a job round the corner.' He grinned. 'Often pop round. Know what I mean?' He gave a broad wink. 'Keep an eye on the place.'

'Close to her, are you?'

Again Carling grinned. 'She's everything to me, mother, sister, sweetheart.'

Forrest thought it was a funny choice of words. 'So where do you think she is?'

Carling shrugged. 'Don't know,' he said. 'She takes her work too seriously to skive off.'

Forrest remembered something Sutcliffe had said. 'Except when she's got a hangover?'

Carling stared back at him, unblinking.

Forrest moved first. 'Let's take a look out the back, shall we?'

There was nothing there, either. A garden deadened by winter, mossy patio, a plastic dustbin, a rotary washing drier, twirling in the wind. Nothing on it. Forrest pulled the glazed kitchen door shut. 'Nothing here, Mr Carling. I don't suppose you've any other ideas where she might be?'

Terry shook his head. 'No. Unless there isn't a list and she's gone shopping.'

'Mr Sutcliffe is operating today,' Shaw said, 'he was wondering where she was.'

'There may be a perfectly rational explanation.'

'Like?'

'She could have missed her bus.'

'Yeah? Got there late. Maybe.'

This time it was Carling who dialled the hospital, covering the mouthpiece as he waited for the other end to be picked up. 'Direct number,' he said, 'theatre.'

Briefly he rapped a few questions down the receiver and slammed it down before speaking to Forrest. 'She isn't there,' he said, 'and it's eleven o clock now. They've practically finished the list. And they said the list had finished late last night. It must have been nearly eight when she left.' He flopped down on the settee. 'Why didn't she ring me and ask me to pick her up?'

There was no answer.

Forrest persisted with his questions. 'Is there no one she might have called round to see?'

'No,' Carling said tersely, 'there isn't.'

The three of them were thinking the same thing. Silently. Privately. No one wanted to be the first to voice it.

It was Carling who blurted it out. 'You don't think . . .?' He looked from one to the other. Swallowed. 'This geezer. The one who's sticking round the hospital. You don't think . . .?'

'No.' But the words stuck in Forrest's throat.

It was Shaw who had to make the feeble attempt to placate Brenda Watlow's son-in-law. 'I'm sure nothing's happened to her.'

Carling's dark eyes were almost pleading with him.

Shaw touched his shoulder. 'There's bound to be a perfectly rational explanation.'

Carling suddenly groaned, sank onto the sofa and

buried his face in his hands. The two officers waited for him to speak.

He seemed to have aged five years by the time he lifted his head up. 'There's something you ought to know,' he said.

The 'surgeon' had meant Brenda's body to be found quickly. He wanted Dr Harper to explore his work before any decay had set in, and the weather was going through a warm spell, it wouldn't take long. He knew that from the books. Twenty-four, forty-eight hours. Someone was usually around to find them. He never made any attempt to conceal his patients. That wasn't part of the plan. Part of the point of the yellow plastic was that it was easy to spot. Conspicuous anywhere. Particularly on a patch of open concrete. In this case it was an elderly woman out walking her dog who made the discovery and so, unwittingly assisted him.

The contents of the woman's call was relayed to Forrest less than ten minutes after the police had received it. It came in just as he was preparing to leave Brenda's house. He took the information with a tired acceptance of the inevitable. But hidden far behind the depression, that he had not been able to save this victim, was some elation that this time he had anticipated the killer's next move. If he had not been able to save Brenda Watlow's life he had, at least, known it would be her. Terry was eyeing him all the time he was speaking and Forrest knew he owed him some sort of an explanation.

'I'm sorry,' he said. 'I'm very sorry. A body's been found.' Like Shaw before him he put his hand on

Carling's shoulder and watched the look of disbelief turn to one of denial.

'You don't know it's her,' Carling blurted out. 'It might not be. She could still be shopping. Brenda's a terrible one for clothes.'

Forrest recognized the babble as a symptom of shock. He put his hand on Terry Carling's shoulder a second time. Carling twitched and Forrest felt swamped by sympathy for the man.

Carling swallowed. 'I don't suppose you'd like me to . . . If it is her, someone'll have to . . .'

'No,' Forrest said. 'Better we go on our own.'

But Terry turned difficult. 'You must be bloody joking! If it is her, I want to be the one to know first.' He blinked. 'It'll help, won't it, if you get identification quickly. I want to help – do something.'

Forrest nodded. But both Forrest and Shaw knew this was not a good idea. Relatives did not belong anywhere near the scene of a crime. 'You've already helped,' he said kindly. 'A lot. You've given us a name. A person. Now just tell me about this Malcolm Forning again. Where does he live?'

Chapter Seventeen

Terry Carling's white face was watching him in his rear-view mirror and it made Forrest uncomfortable. He preferred as little as possible to do with murder victim's relatives. It upset him. But Carling had been determined to go to the scene of the crime.

Forrest covered the distance between Brenda's house and the hospital in less than ten minutes. She had not had far to travel. She should have been safe.

The worst thing about serial killing was the feeling of déjà vu, the flashing blue lights, the familiar white body-tent, the journalists, the voyeurs. Forrest drove right through them, hating them with the fervour he usually reserved for football fans. 'Ghouls,' he muttered as he drew to a halt as near as possible to the police tape. Two or three had camera cases slung over their shoulders. One was accompanied by the red-head and he didn't want to fend off her questions. Not here. Not now.

He swivelled round to speak to Terry. 'Look,' he said awkwardly. 'She . . . umm . . . she might have been . . .'

Terry's unblinking eyes met his.

Forrest felt suddenly out of his depth. Almost angrily he added. 'Are you sure you want to go through with this?'

'Yes.' Terry spoke dully.

'OK, then,' he said, with real misgiving and opened the car door. It was in all their interests to get Brenda Watlow identified as soon as possible. Carling was practically her next of kin. And if Brenda Watlow had been carved up Forrest didn't want her daughter to see it.

The cold seemed to intensify as he stood and watched Detective Sergeant Steven Long slit open the plastic sack. Pale limbs were exposed. Brenda was still wearing her nurse's uniform but it had been pulled up. Forrest glanced quickly at Carling. He was as white as the skin of the corpse. Forrest's gaze moved downwards. All the way here, in the car, he had steeled himself to expect something. Something awful. He had half expected the 'surgeon's' work to escalate. Lewisham had prepared him for that. But even he was not prepared for the blood that stiffened the woman's dress. Forrest held back the nausea and fixed his attention on Terry, who was staring at Brenda's face.

'It is her,' he said hoarsely. 'It's Ma all right.' He clenched his fists together. 'What has the bastard done to her? What the . . .?'

'I did warn you.' Forrest was too appalled himself to spare much sympathy on this man.

Carling was here by choice. He was here in the course of his duty. But he recovered himself in time to add, 'I'm sorry, Mr Carling. I'm really sorry. I wish you hadn't seen this. I didn't know it would be so so . . .' Words were inadequate. 'So bad.'

'Just get him,' Carling said through clenched teeth. 'Get the bastard – before I do.' He lifted the flap of the tent and strode away just as Karys Harper's black Mercedes slid into view.

Forrest felt a sudden warmth towards her as he watched her pick her way through the waiting press and approach him. She gave him a swift, tentative smile and held his eyes for a moment longer than normal.

'What have you got for me this time, David?'

'Another corpse, I'm afraid.' He put his hand on her arm. 'But we're hauling someone in for questioning. We think we have him.'

'Thank God,' Karys said. 'Who?'

'An ex-theatre porter, with a special interest in scalpel blades.'

'And what does our forensic psychiatrist friend say to that?' Karys asked the question lightly, but she was aware of an uncomfortable tightening of her chest. And not for anything would she have uttered Barney Lewisham's name.

Forrest grimaced. 'He doesn't know yet. I'll have to ring him.'

'So – back to work, eh?' She took a quick look at Brenda Watlow's plump form and slid her hands into a pair of examination gloves. 'Do you know who she is?'

'Yes. We've had a positive identification from her son-in-law.'

'Oh?'

'He was at her house. We'd gone round to find out why she wasn't at work.'

'Really? It sounds to me as though you had an instinct about her.' She dropped her eyes to the pale shape still half cased in the yellow plastic bag.

'Her name's Brenda Watlow. She's a theatre sister at Queen's.'

229

Karys started. 'I know her,' she said. 'Theatre Four, isn't it?'

'That's right. She . . .' But Forrest was beyond curiosity, lulled into a sense of security by the prospect of an imminent arrest.

Karys volunteered the explanation. 'She was the theatre sister when we were all medical students.'

She seemed about to say more but changed her mind, returning instead to the corpse. 'Abdominal surgery this time,' she said drily.

'Don't you ever—?'

She pre-empted his question. 'I know what you're going to say, David,' she said, her eyes behind the glasses, wide and hurt. 'And the answer is yes. I do. I feel horrible thinking what one human being is capable of doing to another. And I daren't dwell on the amount of pain they must have suffered immediately before death. But that isn't my job. Sympathizing with the victims doesn't help anybody. It wastes time and clouds my judgement. I can't afford too many human feelings.' She smiled. 'I wouldn't sleep at night. And I'm not the best of sleepers anyway.'

The insight into her privacy would have encouraged him to speak but they were not alone. Whatever he said to her, however quietly, would be heard by at least four other police officers.

As usual her examination of the body was cursory but methodical. It took less than ten minutes before she straightened up. 'Almost the same modus operandi,' she said with a sigh, 'but not quite. I can't see any sign of contusion. No blow to the head,' she explained. 'As far as I can see she was simply strangled with a ligature. In this case it looks as though he used her own nurse's

belt. I'll take it off in the mortuary and see if her relatives can identify it. She hasn't been dead that long,'
she said. 'Probably less than twenty-four hours. We've
found her quickly. As to that.' Her eyes dropped to the
horizontal groin wound and the ugly black sutures. 'I
can only guess what grisly tricks our friend has been up
to. I'll be able to tell you more at post-mortem. I don't
want to open her up here.'

'Can we move her now?'

Karys nodded, and a couple of officers helped her
zip the corpse into a black body bag.

Forrest waited until the removal was complete
before picking up on something Karys had said earlier.
'Did you say you knew her?'

'Yes.'

'Bit of a coincidence isn't it?'

'Not really,' Karys answered, her eyes following the
sombre procession of police officers loading the bag
into the back of the mortuary van. 'When you think
about it almost all the medics round here trained at
Queen's Medical School. Sister Watlow was a theatre
sister. We all do a turn in the theatres, we cover most of
them by the time we're qualified. I didn't know her
well. I mean, she wasn't a friend or anything but we'd
all know her.' There was a touch of defiance in her
voice. The van doors were slammed shut. 'Believe it or
not,' she said, her voice shaking only slightly, 'she was a
bit of a flirt. Had eyes for anything in trousers. And she
drank. She was a good theatre sister though. Always
ready for the unexpected. At least,' her voice shook,
'almost always ready.' She took her glasses off and pol-
ished them with a cloth. 'It was a bit of a joke. She
and Pinky – the surgeon – had such a good working

relationship that he hated working without her. They even arranged their holidays at the same time. Same weeks every year. Two weeks in the summer, ten days at Easter, a week in October. Christmas and Boxing Day.' She put her glasses back on, pushed them roughly towards the bridge of her nose. 'He'll be terribly upset. Devastated. They must have worked together for ten years. Maybe more.' And in a gesture unusual for her she brushed Forrest's arm with her hand as though seeking human contact. 'I don't mind doing PMs, David,' she confessed. 'But on someone you know. Particularly when they've . . .' She didn't need to say another word.

Forrest badly wanted to put his arm around her, draw her to him. Instead he gave a dry 'Hmm' before turning, embarrassed, away from her.

'I tried not to look, but what about the . . .?' Forrest asked.

'The surgery? This time I suspect a deeper, more professional job. Maybe,' she added in the same weary voice, 'in deference to Brenda's status. I don't know. I don't understand this "surgeon". I don't *want* to understand him. Let Lewisham ponder the wretched man's warped mind. He'll *delight* in such things. When I did the PM on Colin Wilson I felt a revulsion for such a character. Then the Baring girl. And now this. That revulsion is increasing with every case. I'm almost frightened to open Brenda Watlow up. I don't know what I might find.'

Chapter Eighteen

They broke Malcolm's door down at three o'clock in the afternoon, without giving him the opportunity of opening it himself. It was a measure of their repugnance for his crimes. He had stood behind the door, like a frightened rabbit, listening to the heavy steps clomping up the stairs, the loud, aggressive voices. He knew they wanted him. He knew why. It was because he was different. Unusual. He always had been different from a child, ailing, lonely, mother-smothered. He moved back as the door finally splintered and burst open. Malcolm shrank back into the corner and put his hands over his mouth to stifle his screams. People didn't like the sound of screaming.

What terrified him were the suits they wore. White paper, like disposable space suits which crackled as they walked. It made him feel – contaminated. They wore gloves as though they were frightened to touch him, surgeon's gloves, pale rubber. They reminded him of the nightmare days when he had worked in the theatre. In the worst possible place for someone with his dark, half-buried phobias. But the Social Security had told him he must take the job. Otherwise they were in a position to withhold his money. Now he was beginning to understand a little of where the terrors had directed him. Here. To men in paper suits and surgeon's gloves. At night his sleep was infected with his own screams as he descended into the underworld of anaesthesia. And now, he was still able to hear the groans of the newly recovered, sore, unable to move, in pain. It still upset him, brought back memories.

He dropped to the floor in a paralysis of fright. Unable to speak one word.

The police weren't friendly either. A huge hunk of a man built like a rugby player flashed a card in front of his eyes.

'Malcolm Forning, we are arresting you on suspicion of the murders of Colin Wilson, Rosemary Baring and Brenda Watlow. You do not have to say anything. But it may harm your defence . . .'

Malcolm didn't hear any more. Brenda. The words *Brenda* and *murder* punctured his brain. 'B-b-b-renda,' he managed.

The police officer leered down at him. 'Yeah,' he said. 'Friend of yours, wasn't she?'

Malcolm nodded eagerly. Brenda was his friend. She would help him, speak up for him. Brenda liked him. 'Brenda,' he said again. 'Can I telephone her?'

The police officer made a face to the uniformed men standing behind him. 'Get the bloody cuffs on,' he said. 'This bloke's out of his tiny brain.'

They clipped some handcuffs on him and chivvied him down the stairs. Roughly.

Mrs Stanton, his landlady, was waiting at the bottom, wearing her slippers and a blue towelling dressing gown. She gave him a distasteful look as he stopped in front of her. She didn't speak to him, only to the policeman. 'I always knew there was something funny about him,' she said.

'Yeah, well, ma'am,' the policeman said politely. 'We'll have him out of your way now. I don't think he'll be back.'

Her look changed. 'Goodbye,' she said to Malcolm. 'And good riddance.'

She kicked him then, right on the leg but no one seemed to care. No one smiled at him or apologized for the kick or told Mrs Stanton off for being so nasty. Maybe they hadn't noticed. They pushed him towards the door. Some people were standing outside. Watching. Malcolm tried to smile at a couple of them but their faces didn't change. They simply carried on staring. Someone opened the door of a police car. Someone else pushed his head down so he didn't bump it. They shoved him inside. The big police officer unlocked one of the handcuffs and clipped it to his own wrist. The policeman muttered something under his breath.

He risked talking to the policeman. 'My stuff,' he managed.

The policeman gave an incredulous stare. 'They'll give you an inventory,' he said.

And, by pressing his finger to his mouth, Malcolm managed to say nothing until they reached the police station. But his mind was picturing the men, searching his flat. They would find his box with the blades in it. His beautiful collection that had taken him so long to acquire. Malcolm blinked back the tears.

It frightened him that they left him alone for a long time after they'd emptied his pockets and taken his fingerprints with some mucky black ink. The room he was in was empty with no windows except a tiny one in the door, which was smothered with bars, and an even tinier one too high up for him to see out. That had bars too. They had locked the door behind him.

There was a toilet in the corner, without a seat. Malcolm's bladder was full. Overfull. But he dared not use it. The policeman, or even worse one of the women like the one who had taken his fingerprints, might peep in and see him urinate.

Malcolm was terrified now. He sat, huddled in the corner.

Forrest eyed the dishevelled, shrinking creature in front of him. It was always like this when you came face to face with a killer. You wondered whether they really could have done it. This insignificant person surely could not be the one with the ego he had always connected with the 'surgeon'. He had pictured someone confident, someone strutting around. Conceited. Someone more like Pinky Sutcliffe. Someone with character and a presence. Maybe Forning changed when he became the 'surgeon'.

He whisked through the evidence against Forning. The collection of scalpel blades. Mentally he drew a big tick against that. It fitted. He had actually worked at the operating theatre, Theatre Four, though not at the same time as either Rosemary Baring or Colin Wilson.

He sat down opposite Malcolm at the table and stared at him for a moment before switching on the tape recorder. Shaw sat by his side. A uniformed policeman stood at the door. Forrest looked deep into

Malcolm Forning's pale eyes and hunted for the killer within them. But he just couldn't see it, or was this man clever enough to conceal that side of him?

He began.

'Your name is Malcolm Forning?'

Malcolm nodded.

'You have to speak, Malcolm. The tape recorder doesn't hear nods of the head.'

'Yes.' His voice sounded like a frightened little mouse.

Forrest stared at him. What metamorphosis happened to turn this timid being into a scalpel-wielding killer?

'First of all I have to ask you whether you would like a solicitor present?'

'No.'

'We have to advise you that at some point, because of the serious nature of the charges levelled against you, it would be advisable for you to have legal representation, Malcolm.'

Malcolm nodded and the tall police officer with the bald patch described the action into the tape recording. Malcolm risked a swift peep at all three of the officers. None of them looked at him. He tried to listen hard to what the policeman was saying.

'You used to work at Queen's Hospital, as a theatre porter. Is that right?'

'Yes.'

'When was this?'

'Five years ago.'

'You didn't stay very long.'

'No. My mum was ill. I had to look after her.'

'Did you enjoy the work?'

Malcolm didn't know how to answer this one. All he knew was that the detective who had only been nice and polite to him up until now was frowning. Something was wrong.

He answered politely, as though he'd been offered scones for tea. 'Yes. I did like it, thank you.'

The police officer looked a bit more pleased at that.

'So you enjoyed working in the operating theatre.'

Malcolm shuddered inwardly. Like? No. He had not liked. Fearfully, he glanced at the policeman. He gave him an encouraging nod. 'Yes,' he said formally. 'I thought it was extremely interesting work.'

The other one spoke then. Not the uniformed officer blocking the doorway but the tall one with the dark hair. 'Is that why you collected scalpel blades?'

Malcolm sensed a trap. 'No.' He stammered. 'I d-d-do m-m-marquetry.'

Immediately he knew he shouldn't have said that. The white-suited men would search his flat and expose the lie. There was no marquetry. Only the blades.

The dark-haired detective put his face close and smiled as though he knew everything.

'How well did you know Colin Wilson?'

'I don't know him at all.' Malcolm swallowed. 'Who is he?'

'Your first victim.'

They fiddled with the tape recorder then and had a quick word among themselves. The detective with the bald patch looked kindly at him. 'The men who are searching inside your flat haven't found any marquetry, Malcolm. Now, what do you really use the blades for?'

There was a horrible silence.

It took him ages to work out what to say. 'P-p-p-play with them.'

The pale policeman's face turned red, as though he was angry with him. Very very angry.

Lewisham was ominously quiet when Forrest informed him by telephone that he'd hauled someone in for questioning. He sensed the psychiatrist would have much preferred it if *he* had been the one to produce Forning, like a rabbit out of a conjuror's hat.

'I'm surprised,' Lewisham finally responded petulantly, 'that you've gone so far as this when you knew I had an interest in the case. You could have consulted me at any time.' He paused long enough for Forrest to draw breath. Not long enough for him to reply. 'I only hope you haven't made a ghastly mistake. I mean, in the case of a serial killer, the general public are unlikely to be amused at the investigating task force getting sidetracked by questioning a completely innocent man, Inspector Forrest, while the real killer goes free.'

Forrest swallowed. Certainty was shrinking to a hope and a prayer.

'You'd better give me the main details.' Lewisham was at last giving him a chance to parade his suspect. Forrest gave him all he'd got, the collection of scalpel blades, the short-lived employment in the hospital, his acquaintance with the latest victim, most of all the strange character of Malcolm Forning.

But to his chagrin the psychiatrist seemed unimpressed and intent on demolishing his case. 'All this is flimsy, circumstantial evidence, Inspector.'

Forrest knew he was being punished.

'Have you found any forensic evidence to link him with even one of the crimes?'

'Not yet, Doctor. We haven't located the place where he . . .'

'Performed.' Lewisham's voice mocked his squeamishness. 'Well, I think I'd better come down to the station and join you for the questioning of your suspect.' And again he repeated the ominous phrase. 'I only hope you aren't wasting your time with a completely innocent man, Inspector.'

Then the line went dead.

Left to himself Forrest found himself reflecting that he probably did need the psychiatrist's expertise. Forning was a strange guy. All police officers these days were well trained in the interviewing of suspects but he didn't know how to get the truth out of him. The brief contact he had had suggested the man was not normal, that was a gross understatement. Forrest could swear that Forning was unaware of the crimes he had committed. According to the arresting officers, he apparently believed that Brenda Watlow was still alive. He'd actually asked for her to be contacted to vouch for his innocence. Surely this was proof that he was insane? When the officers had informed him that Brenda was dead it had appeared to be a shock to him. Both police officers had said that.

How could it be a shock when he'd killed her?

Did Forning have a split personality? Two personalities so far apart that one side seemed unaware what the other side had done?

*

Lewisham joined him within half an hour, sauntering into the interview room as Forrest was preparing to talk to Forning for a second time. He interrupted the flow, entering just as they were trying to persuade Forning to accept the services of a solicitor. Forrest scowled and spoke into the tape recorder.

'Suspect joined by Doctor Barney Lewisham at twenty-one thirty hours.' Straightaway Lewisham sat down opposite Forning and took a long, penetrating look at him. Then he smiled and turned to Forrest. 'So this is your suspect.'

It was all he said but it needled Forrest. Formally and in a taut voice he confirmed, for the benefit of the tape recorder, that Forning was indeed the suspect for the murders of Colin Wilson, Rosemary Baring and Brenda Watlow. At the same time he wished that Lewisham would switch off that irritating, supercilious smile that made him think the psychiatrist knew something he did not.

He introduced them formally. 'This is Malcolm Forning, Doctor,' he said. 'And Malcolm, this is Doctor Lewisham.' He had intended adding a phrase or two explaining Lewisham's role but Forning immediately protested. 'I don't need a doctor. I don't want a doctor. I'm not ill. Please. Take him away. Why have you brought a doctor here? What are you going to do to me?'

Forrest was startled. He didn't like Lewisham himself but this was a bit of an overreaction. People were frequently intimidated by the police, and some, he knew, felt the same about doctors. Yet Forning's panic at being faced with Lewisham was much greater than his reaction had been to any one of the police officers. It was strange. Or was it? Was it maybe the reaction of a fake doctor being confronted with the real thing? Because he knew a real doctor would soon expose him as a sham when a police officer might be hoodwinked?

'Tell me, Malcolm,' Forrest said, 'where were you on the night of the twenty-third of November last year?'

Forning stared back at him blankly.

'It was a Tuesday,' Forrest added.

He hated Forning's pale eyes. They looked as though he was not quite human. His face lacked colour too. Not simply pale with sallow cheeks but a greenish white, as though he never saw the light of day. The colour reminded Forrest of his father's face that too was never exposed to fresh air but was constantly stifled in a stuffy atmosphere. He was also repelled by Forning's hair. Lank and dull, falling to his shoulders, untidily and unevenly.

It took a while but Forning finally stammered out an answer to Forrest's question. 'I – I – d – don't know.'

Lewisham took over then, leaning right across the table and peering over his glasses.

'Tell me, Malcolm,' he said, in a falsely friendly tone. 'Do you have many troublesome dreams?' Forning shrank from the stare but Lewisham refused to drop his eyes. 'Do you?'

Forning nodded.

'Tell me about them.'

Forrest groaned inwardly. This sort of open-ended question would lead them nowhere – slowly. What he wanted were firm answers, ones he could use in court. Not dreams.

Forning was still mesmerized by the psychiatrist's stare. 'Too many to tell,' he muttered.

Barney was unabashed. 'I expect some of them are about the hospital, aren't they?'

Forning's pale eyes widened as he nodded again.

Lewisham gave him an encouraging smile. 'Did you *like* working in the hospital, Malcolm?'

Forning shook his head.

'What didn't you like about it?'

'The people.'

Forning was beginning to lose his terror of the psychiatrist. Lewisham was winning him over. Forrest watched the proceedings and couldn't help being impressed.

'Do you mean the nurses, the doctors?'

Vigorously Forning shook his head.

'The patients, Malcolm, was it the patients who made you dislike the job?'

Forning nodded.

And Forrest could tell the answer surprised Lewisham as much as it surprised him.

Lewisham had to think about the next question. 'What didn't you like about the patients?'

'Their hurt.'

Forrest shifted his feet round under the desk. It was not the answer he would have wanted. It was the wrong answer.

He took a surreptitious glance at Lewisham. That confident, superior look was there, painted all over his face. Forrest studied it for a moment and didn't like what he was reading. Lewisham didn't believe Malcolm Forning was the killer. Not for a moment. And the psychiatrist was pleased.

Were he and the doctor working on different sides of the law? Did Lewisham have an interest in a delay in catching the 'surgeon'? Did he dislike the investigating officers so much he *wanted* them to fail? It seemed too incredible to be true. And yet –

Another explanation struck Forrest. The psychiatrist had made no secret of his delight in being consulted over such a bizarre case. Openly he had spoken of writing it up in the medical journals, of the fame and status the resolution of such a case would afford. The more murders there were the more notable the case would become. Did Lewisham then *want* delay in the capture of the 'surgeon' to elevate his status? Forrest shook his head. That was not human.

Lewisham's soft voice addressed Malcolm Forning again. 'Is it that you *share* their hurt, Malcolm?'

Again Forning nodded vigorously.

'So you were glad when the time came to leave?'

'Yes.'

The vocal answer was a measure of how Forning was beginning to trust the psychiatrist. His pale eyes looked confidently across the table.

'You looked after your mother.'

'Like a nurse,' Forning said, smiling. Forrest found himself staring at Forning's teeth, irregular, yellow-stained. Two at the front eroded with decay, one into a sharp point.

'Like a nurse,' Forning had said. Only a short step from 'Like a nurse' to 'Like a surgeon'.

Feeling they were moving towards something, Forrest allowed Lewisham to continue his questioning, Lewisham leant even farther forward to invite confidences, or maybe to exclude the detective from the questioning.

'I expect you knew Colin Wilson?'

Forning's gaze didn't waver. 'No.'

'He was a theatre porter too. Like you.'

Forning thought for a moment, his pale eyes scanning the room. Inevitably they returned to Lewisham's powerful stare. 'No,' he repeated abruptly.

For the first time Lewisham's eyes slipped away from the suspect and scanned Forrest's face as though underlining the fact that this again was *not* the anticipated answer. He should have known Colin Wilson.

'And Rosemary Shearer? Did you know her, Malcolm?' Forrest knew Lewisham was deliberately using the nurse's maiden name, the name Wilson would be more likely to know.

Forning thought for a long, long time, making absolutely certain, before he answered. 'No,' he said finally.

Forrest rapidly did some arithmetic.

Colin Wilson and Rosemary Baring had worked together in Theatre Four for a couple of months during the summer of 1991. Brenda Watlow had worked there for years, certainly the entire time they were interested in. Malcolm Forning had worked there five years ago, for a short period, in 1995. The dates didn't tally, he wished they did.

He listened, without intervening, for a further half hour while Lewisham gently chatted to the suspect about his mother, his friends – it transpired he only really had one friend.

'And you remained friendly with the theatre sister.'

For the first time Malcolm looked quite happy. He nodded vigorously. 'Brenda was kind to me,' he said. 'She'll tell you I wouldn't hurt anyone.'

Lewisham and Forrest exchanged swift glances. Forning had been told many times that Brenda Watlow was dead, that he was charged with her murder, yet he still spoke about her as though she was alive. What was going on?

'Brenda is my best friend,' he said, smiling at them all.

'She brings you presents, doesn't she?' Lewisham prompted.

And suddenly Forning's manner changed completely. No longer open, naive, stupid; he became furtive, cunning, paranoid. He peered around the room as though expecting someone to jump out at him.

'No,' he said. 'No presents.'

Was it guilt that made him deny Brenda's gifts?

To Forrest's irritation Lewisham stood up. 'OK, Malcolm,' he said. 'I think that's enough for now.'

As Forning was led, shuffling, out of the room Lewisham turned to him. 'The minute they start lying to you,' he said cheerfully, 'its time to stop. You see they enjoy the company, having someone to talk to, tell their story to. It's a withdrawal of privileges to leave them alone again. In the end they'll say yes to anything – purely to keep you in the room.'

Forrest nodded.

'Are you still sure you've got the right man, Inspector?'

'Never a hundred per cent,' he admitted. 'Not until we've got some hard evidence, or a confession. Preferably both.'

Lewisham smiled but kept his thoughts to himself.

Forrest's curiosity got the better of him. 'What I don't understand is, why does he seem to think Brenda Watlow's still alive?'

Lewisham's smile grew even wider. 'It could be

denial,' he said. 'A powerful force of nature, denial. Protector of our sanity.' He waved his hands around. 'This incident will topple us into depression, anxiety, mania, therefore it did not happen. Usually we come to terms with unpleasant happenings bit by bit, our subconscious guarding the sluice gates so our sanity is not flooded. Understand?'

Forrest nodded and moved towards the door. He hated Lewisham a little less today, because he knew pomposity had grown out of real cleverness.

'Do you think Forning's our man?'

Lewisham turned towards him staring over the top of those half-moon glasses. 'I couldn't possibly say – yet,' the psychiatrist said. 'Now what time's the post-mortem tomorrow?'

Chapter Nineteen

6 January 2000

Forrest felt he should explain or apologize for Lewisham's presence as they filed passed Karys into the PM room. Looking at her he knew she hated the psychiatrist being there with him. For her it was the ultimate test. She grimaced at Lewisham. 'Hello there, Barney. Nice to see you. Going to watch, are you?'

It was a battle of two personalities.

Lewisham followed Karys into the sluiceroom and Forrest heard Lewisham's huge, uncontrolled laugh. 'You don't even want me to hold the retractors?'

And Karys's answer. 'Oh, bugger off, Barney.'

She sounded confident. Forrest caught sight of himself grinning in the mirror.

So, once again, Karys stood at the foot of the mortuary slab among a ring of police officers. But this time there was something intangibly different. She could sense relief in their manner. They had the 'surgeon' safely in custody. No longer an unknown. Just a mere mortal. Karys slipped her gloves on and read swiftly through Paget's preliminary notes. Brenda Watlow had been five feet five inches tall and, whatever she might have liked to think, had been slightly plump, weighing in at eleven and a half stones.

Karys moved towards the slab.

248

This time the 'surgeon' had made his incision right across the victim's abdomen, a few inches below the umbilicus. Karys stared at it for a few moments before speaking. 'They call this a bikini-line incision,' she explained. 'It's a common enough cut.'

'A common enough cut for what?' asked Forrest.

She didn't answer.

It was Lewisham who stepped forward to take charge, barely recognizable in a long green, surgeon's gown. The only one of them wearing a mask. 'Hysterectomy,' he said. 'What on earth's the matter, Karys? Squeamish?'

'Sometimes,' she said.

'Well you've a job to do.'

'I know.' A small flame of anger lit her eyes. When she spoke it was to address Forrest, not Lewisham.

'I'm reluctant to look beneath the sutures,' she admitted.

'Why?'

'Because I think that's what he's done to her,' she said. 'He's been working up to the removal of a major organ. Wilson's was minor surgery, just a hernia. Superficial. Baring's was cosmetic stuff, the removal of a breast. Ugly but not deep. I had the feeling that next time he would go for one of the major abdominal organs.' She half closed her eyes. 'Get in right up to his elbows.'

Two rookies were attending their first post-mortem. Forrest had deliberately subjected them to this. No point being soft on new officers. Their job would not ultimately be kind to them. They would see many such ugly sights. Few worse. Both of them had turned green.

Lewisham's voice echoed round the room. 'I do

believe you're getting to know this "surgeon", Karys,' he taunted, 'almost as well as I am.'

'Not quite,' Karys said through gritted teeth. She shot him an angry glance before bending over her work again.

Forrest was confused. There was something going on here, some distinct rapport between the two doctors from which he was excluded. He looked from one to the other for explanation. There was none.

Karys started the post-mortem as though she was oblivious to everyone else in the room, as usual beginning with the head and neck. Removal of the cranium, cross-sections of the brain. It didn't take long. It was ten minutes before she looked up.

'He broke form,' she said. 'This one wasn't coshed. Just strangled. He got near enough for that. It was a face-to-face assault rather than from behind. The marks clearly show no ligature this time. He used his hands. There are clear thumb prints on either side of the trachea.'

'You're sure it was the same killer?' David Forrest asked.

Karys allowed her eyes to drop to Brenda Watlow's torso. 'Oh, yes,' she said quietly. 'And his suturing skills are improving every time.'

'So why vary his method of killing?'

Karys shrugged. 'Maybe he got more satisfaction from the actual contact. Or maybe she knew him, and that meant he could get that close. Perhaps he's simply gained confidence.' She looked up. 'That fits your suspect, David, doesn't it? They did know each other.'

Forrest nodded.

Lewisham's loud voice chipped in again. 'Since

when have you been doing psychological analyses as part of your post-mortems, Karys?'

She flushed, but stood her ground. 'Ever since I've been a Home Office Pathologist, Barney.'

Lewisham peered at her over the top of his glasses. 'I'm most impressed,' he murmured.

The thorax didn't pose much of a challenge either. Rib cage intact. Normal, healthy heart and lungs.

It was twenty minutes later that she tackled the abdomen, first of all cutting through the stitches with deft skill. They were all placed in a specimen bag and handed to the Scene of Crime Officer.

The subcutaneous fat had not been sutured but it had been cut right through too, the thick, yellow layer of adipose parting easily under Karys's probing fingers. She exposed the severed ends of blood vessels and worked deeper. Beneath the fat was the omentum, a double sheet of fibrous peritoneum which lined the abdominal cavity and connected the stomach to the other abdominal organs. The line of the surgeon's cut was easy to trace. Karys located and removed the stomach for further examination.

'There's always a possibility that she was sedated,' she explained to the rookies who were looking at her with horrid fascination. She followed the line of the incision even deeper, beneath the bifurcation of the aorta, underneath the loop of large bowel. Her hands were searching for the uterus. But without much difficulty she could see where the 'surgeon' had incised it. A finger inserted into the vagina made it obvious what was missing. He had used the traditional bikini-line incision, the route taken by surgeons for women who wished to preserve their attractiveness. Had Brenda

Watlow been a living patient the surgeon would have chosen this exact same route. The thought chilled Karys. The cuts had not been absolutely precise, there was damage around the area. It had taken him a little searching to identify his target organ. In some areas his knife had slipped and he had severed another blood vessel. But of course, as with his other 'patients', she had not bled to death.

Karys was suddenly struck by a thought. She had always called Colin Wilson and Rosemary Baring the 'surgeon's' victims. But this time she had, without thinking, referred to Brenda Watlow as his patient.

She was starting to think the way he wanted her to think. He was ordering her thoughts. By his work. By his presentation.

Look, she told herself sternly. Look for yourself. Stop seeing what he wants you to see.

'You're a bit quiet.' Only Barney would interrupt her deepest thoughts. Without flinching she faced him across the table. 'Yes,' she said. 'I find thinking, quietly, invaluable to my work.'

'So what inspiration are you coming up with, my dear?'

'I do wish you'd be quiet.'

She forced herself back to a study of Brenda Watlow's body. Something was missing. A mark. She knew what it was. That hint of humour that had been evident in the two previous murders. No funny tie around the throat, stockings ligating the neck, plastic surgery for a nurse who worked in a private, surgical clinic, a hernia repair for a plumber. Brenda Watlow's injury had been more brutal. This time the 'surgeon' had not been smiling. Karys knew he had been angry?

252

Unless . . . The idea was grim. A few months ago she could not have thought of it. Her mind would have rejected such an idea as being beyond the depths of human depravity. But doggedly Karys searched the entire abdominal cavity. Had the 'surgeon' played a trick, removed the womb only to hide it behind the bowel, knowing that the pathologist would be forced to join in this terrible game of hide and seek? To her relief it seemed not. Even thorough searching failed to find it. The organ had been removed.

'Well, there's a turn up for the books.' It was Lewisham who made the comment. 'I wonder what he's done with it.'

Karys glared at him. 'Satisfied?' she demanded. 'Seen enough, have you? Enjoyed yourself?'

The psychiatrist seemed unmoved. 'Oh yes,' he said.

She didn't hear the knock on her office door. The next thing she knew, David Forrest was sitting opposite her.

'Nasty business,' she said, breaking off from writing her notes.

Forrest nodded, hesitated. 'I've got rid of Lewisham for you.'

Karys pressed her hand to her forehead. 'Thanks.'

'Knew him well, did you?'

She nodded. 'Look – I don't want to talk – '

Forrest smiled at her. 'It's OK.'

Then she really studied him. For the first time in weeks, no months, he was grinning. His eyes were crinkling round the corners. He looked . . . happy?

She broached the subject tentatively. 'You must feel much better now you've made an arrest.'

Forrest nodded. But her trained eye noted some reservation. Perhaps until a suspect was convicted and behind bars there always was some doubt. 'We've had a further report from the SOCOs. The bloke's flat was stashed full of scalpel blades. He kept them in a box. Velvet-lined, would you believe.' Forrest didn't care that he was babbling. 'Black velvet.'

Karys lifted her eyebrows. 'Really?'

'Yeah. An ex-theatre porter. A really strange guy. And yet, Karys,' he felt compelled to share a confidence with her, 'there wasn't much of the killer about him.'

'From what you've told me they aren't usually any different from the rest of us.'

'I thought,' he was conscious he was rubbing his bald patch again, 'I just thought – with the crimes being so – so – macabre. I thought he'd be different. I thought this time I would notice something. I don't know what. Maybe staring eyes, or peculiar habits. And all he was, was a guy who missed his job because he had to leave and nurse his mother. It was nothing more than that.'

'And what does Doctor Lewisham say?' Karys asked cautiously.

Forrest gave an embarrassed laugh. 'I don't think he's as convinced as I am.'

'And how convinced are you?'

'Not quite a hundred per cent.'

'I see.'

Maybe if Forrest had been less distracted he might have noted her anxiety. As it was, he was wondering when to ask her out for dinner.

'Why do you think he took her womb out?'

'You're not going to draw me on that one,' she said. 'You'll have to ask Lewisham. And now you have your suspect you can ask him. Only he really knows the answer.'

An awkward silence developed between them until Forrest blurted out clumsily. 'Look. We've both had a bit of a grim time lately. Have dinner with me.'

She looked startled. 'When?'

Forrest did a quick calculation. Most of today he would be questioning Forning. 'Tomorrow night,' he suggested. 'I'll pick you up.'

Karys flinched at the familiar phrase. If only Barney's ghost would lie down and die. 'No. I'd rather meet you there – wherever.'

Forrest felt a vague disappointment, as though her answer had firmly put him in his place. She was telling him she did not want him to know where she lived or who she shared a flat with, if anyone. She might live alone for all he knew. But not for all he cared. The next moment he was telling himself off for being adolescent, puerile, stupid.

Karys was looking at him strangely. 'So where shall we go?'

Forrest found himself embarrassingly mumbling something about 'having to book' and 'letting her know', and all the time he had the feeling that behind those thick glasses the intelligent eyes were laughing at him. *At* him or *with* him?

Forning had another twenty minutes to go before yet another official meal break. A hot one this time.

Lewisham took over the questioning. 'Tell me about the games you play with your blades, Malcolm.'

Malcolm stared beyond the psychiatrist. 'Not games,' he said. 'Marquetry.'

Lewisham gave a small, irritated cough. 'Now then, Malcolm,' he said sternly. 'The policemen haven't found any evidence that you do marquetry. There are no wooden pictures.'

'I did try,' Malcolm said. 'The therapist at the hospital – after my mother died – she suggested I do marquetry.' He paused. 'But the wood kept splintering,' he said politely. 'That was why Brenda got me the blades.'

Lewisham leaned right across the desk. 'Tell me about the blades.'

Malcolm's mind began to wander. His fingers twitched, as though he was lining up the blades in a military display. He would put them in order. He would polish them until they sparkled. He would put all the curved ones together. All the pointed ones together. All the tiny ones in order of size, left to right until he got to the very biggest and fattest one. He put his hand over his mouth to suppress his giggle. The one that cut through fat people's tummies.

He started. The policeman was speaking to him. Not the psychiatrist. And he wasn't talking about games. He was asking him where he'd cut the bodies.

Pleadingly he stared back at Forrest. 'What bodies?' he managed to say. 'I don't know anything about any body. I'm sorry.' He had thought the apology would placate the policeman. But it didn't seem to.

The policeman scowled at Malcolm. 'Look,' he said. 'You're tired. You're hungry. Why don't you tell us where you do your operations. We'll go and clean the place up for you.'

Malcolm felt his mouth drop open. Operations? He didn't do operations. He had just been a theatre porter. Not a surgeon like Mr Sutcliffe. Malcolm recalled the surgeon's brisk, condescending manner and shuddered. It had been his frantic worry every day he had worked in the operating theatre that he would do something to displease Mr Sutcliffe. In fact, he had lived in permanent terror of annoying the man, dropping something, making the tea too weak, too strong, touching an instrument or a surface that was meant to be sterile. There were so many things one could do wrong in an operating theatre. He dropped his head into his hands and remembered only the misery of the job. The failure.

Forrest watched him despairing. 'We must get him a solicitor,' he said to Lewisham.

'That would seem prudent.'

Forrest ignored Forning and said, 'How much of what we're saying to him is getting through? Does he understand the seriousness of the charges against him?'

'Oh no.'

The psychiatrist's answer was not the one Forrest wanted to hear. He spoke to the uniformed officer at the door. 'Take him away,' he said. 'Feed him.'

'Sir?'

'Yes?'

'There was a telephone call for you.' The way Forrest was feeling it had better be good news. 'They've found a packet of sutures in the suspect's flat. 5/0, they said.'

Forrest grinned. That was good news.

He found Shaw in the canteen, stuffing a sandwich into his mouth. 'I want to go to Forning's flat. Have a look round. You know they've found a packet of sutures there – the right size.'

Shaw stood up, abandoning his meal.

Flat B, Varsovia House, proved to be a large, double-fronted Victorian semi, four storeys high with bay windows, halfway along a long road of similar houses. Judging by the rundown appearance most were used as student accommodation.

They were met at the door by Sergeant Armstrong, a stocky, overweight man. He looked stolid enough. But he lacked the excitement of an officer who has unearthed some clinching evidence. 'We haven't found as much as we'd like,' he began, 'besides the scalpel blades and this one, unopened, packet of sutures. For a start this can't have been the base for his "operations". There's precious little blood around except in the bathroom sink and we've covered most of the flat. Besides,' he glanced through the window. 'Look around. This is hardly a quiet street nor a quiet house. Eight people live here using one staircase. There's always someone walking up and down the street and the stairs. How'd he get the body up here without anyone seeing or hearing?' He answered his own question. 'Impossible. The guy on the top floor's a taxi driver. He keeps mighty peculiar hours. I can't believe Forning could have worked here.' He looked almost ashamed to be saying the next sentence. 'In fact, sir, if I was his defence I'd use that line. He'd have to be bloody lucky.'

'Some nights it must be quiet.'

For answer the Sergeant gave him a poke in the shoulder. It didn't improve Forrest's temper. 'It might be quiet,' Armstrong said, 'if no one in the entire city of Birmingham doesn't have a yen for a lady of the night. Second floor. Know what I mean?' He winked and Forrest's temper further deteriorated. 'Besides. Does your little theatre porter have a car? Because if he doesn't there's no way he could have transported the bodies. It's a few miles from where they were abducted to here.' He tested a joke. 'I'd lay a bet he didn't use a wheelbarrow. And no one would know what fare to charge on the bus.'

It got no response except another glare from Forrest. Armstrong scratched his head and paused before adding. 'There's other problems too. We've tested the scalpel blades for blood. Only one of them was contaminated. The rest were clean. We've thought all along that the blunt instrument was probably a baseball bat. There isn't one here or anything else that could have been the stun weapon.'

'Make my day,' Forrest said irritably. 'Come across one of the mutilated corpses.'

'Talk to him about it.'

'How can I,' Karys demanded. 'He's a policeman.'

'He can give you some advice.'

'Impartial?'

Tonya thought about it for a moment. 'He *is* a friend.'

'A friend who doesn't need to know anything about my past. It's nothing to do with him anyway. We're colleagues. Not even really close ones.'

'He can advise you whether there's anything you should be doing – now. I'm sure he'll tell you to put it all behind you, to let the past remain undisturbed. Maybe you'll listen to him,' she added with a note of sourness.

'But is it undisturbed? The past? These killings . . .?'

'Surely,' Tonya answered uneasily. 'They can't be anything to do with you. They've got someone in for questioning.'

Karys was quiet for a moment, frowning. 'I know they've got someone. I don't know who. But this whole thing, it just can't be coincidence. Colin Wilson, Rosemary Baring, Brenda Watlow. It turns out they all worked in the theatre. I just didn't recognize the nurse's name because she'd got married. And as for Wilson – I don't think I ever did know his name. He was just a porter. Practically anonymous. It's only now that Brenda's been killed too, it's starting to click into place. We were *all* there. At the same time.' Karys turned to stare at her friend. 'So who's next, Tonya? Me?'

Tonya frowned. 'How can that – incident – be anything to do with these murders after so long? It doesn't make sense.'

'I don't know.' Karys turned away from her friend and stared instead deep into the flames of their gas fire. 'I don't know. But . . .'

'But,' mocked her friend. 'Take my suggestion, Karys. Talk to your policeman friend about it. It'll make you feel better.'

They were sitting alone in their flat, sharing a bottle of Australian red wine, warmed almost to blood heat. They'd lit candles and were chatting, Karys in a loose, long kaftan, Tonya in her 'uniform' of jeans and a silk shirt.

Tonya leaned across and refilled their glasses. 'So romance strikes you at long last.'

Karys flushed. 'It's just dinner. Nothing more. He's not even picking me up from here.'

'Why not?' Tonya asked curiously. 'Why don't you want him to know where you live?'

'I don't know.'

'Is it me?' With precision Tonya had touched a nerve. She narrowed her mocking green eyes, raised her glass to her lips. 'That bloody Lewisham and his damned insinuations.'

'Barney will say anything to discredit me.'

'I couldn't give a shit about sodding Lewisham.' Tonya was invariably foul-mouthed when half drunk. 'After what he got up to.'

Maybe it was the influence of the wine but Karys smiled and seemed at last to relax. 'Maybe you're right and none of that has any bearing on the case. After all – David is questioning someone. And he seems to think –' She stopped. What did David Forrest really think? How convinced was he of his suspect's guilt? Or was it her transferring her own doubt onto him? She took a deep draft of the wine and tried to stop thinking at all.

But Tonya was making it difficult. 'OK. All I'm trying to say is that Lewisham with his evil nature, thoroughly nasty personality,' she waved her glass around, 'not forgetting a medical degree that would make him at the very least equal to all this complicated surgery fits the bloody bill a bit too snugly for my tastes. Besides which he's clever. And as I've covered the story I've come to the conclusion that our "surgeon" is a clever man. Very clever indeed.'

Karys leant across and gave her friend a hug. 'You're

pissed,' she said. 'Remember. I've studied the work of this "surgeon" bloke. He is an unqualified person who has seen an operation or two. Malcolm Forning, whoever he is, will be charged and you'll be recovering from a lousy hangover and miss the best story of your entire career.'

'You're bloody kidding,' Tonya retorted. 'Story's dead now. The minute they charge him I'll have to hunt out something, or someone, else. The whole thing'll be sub judice. Slam.' She dropped her wine glass on to the hearth. Miraculously it did not smash. 'Stone dead. And anyway. I still think you should come clean with Forrest.' She gave a sly, sideways look at her friend. 'It'll do you good. He'll be wonderfully sympathetic, put his arms around you and fall truly, deeply, madly in love.'

'You are nuts.' Karys crossed to the window and stood, staring out at the city lights shining on wet pavements.

The 'surgeon' watched the silhouette illuminated by flickering candles.

People should draw their curtains if they didn't want an audience. He saw her half turn back into the room to speak to someone and caught something of her happiness. Something in the tilt of her head, in a quick flick of the hair. He smiled with her. She would almost be the prize. After her – his anticipation reached a crescendo. She was the one to most appreciate his skills. She could watch and know each instrument for what it was, know its purpose. He would have to restrain her, but he knew how to render people helpless. He would simply delay the dying stage until afterwards.

He needed appreciation.

The blood lust was welling up inside him. He knew now why surgeons found it so hard to retire: they lost their status, their *raison d'être*, their intimacy with the human body. He too would find it difficult to retire when the time came.

But he was nearly there.

In the bitter cold the 'surgeon' shivered. But he was not tired, yet.

He watched until the candles gave their last flicker and the window turned black.

Chapter Twenty

7 January 2000

Afterwards Forrest would criticize his actions, see only too clearly where each misconception had led to mistakes and invited tragedy. By three o'clock in the afternoon they had had to charge Malcolm Forning, but still the questioning had never really progressed beyond the, 'Do you own a car?' stage, even with the prompting of the duty solicitor, an earnest young woman named Samantha, pale-faced and still yawning from an on-call the night before. Forning remained bemused, too terrified either to confirm or deny anything except his name and address. It was little help. Forrest had met criminals who denied because they genuinely were innocent and criminals who, outraged, denied just as vehemently when they and everyone else in the interview room knew they were guilty. But in whichever category Forning belonged, Forrest knew that Sergeant Armstrong was right. There were some pretty big holes in this case that had to be filled before they had a case that had any real chance of sticking.

So he turned back to Lewisham. The psychiatrist was subtle, his questions masquerading as innocent enquiries after Forning's lifestyle. 'I suppose you have few friends.'

Malcolm turned a pair of trusting eyes on him and nodded. 'There's only really Brenda,' he said.

'And do you get out much, Malcolm?'

'No. I collect my Giro cheque,' he said politely. 'That comes on a Tuesday. I usually go out then, unless Brenda's coming over.'

Lewisham contrived to look interested. 'Where do you collect the money from?'

'From the post office.'

'I suppose you walk down.'

'I do sometimes. But if it's raining . . .'

'You take your car?' Forrest couldn't resist trying to direct the questioning.

It was a mistake.

Malcolm Forning's pale eyes changed expression as they turned on the police officer, from bland innocence to defensive suspicion. 'I haven't got a car,' he said. 'I couldn't afford a car. Why do you think I have got one?'

Inwardly Forrest groaned. He tried again. 'Haven't you got a friend who does have a car?'

Forning shook his head. 'I can't drive,' he said simply. 'And as I've already said. I haven't got a lot of friends.'

Lewisham shot him an irritated look before moving on to his next batch of questions. 'Tell me about having to nurse your mother, Malcolm.'

'She was ever so ill. Sometimes she was sick. I had to wash her, dress her . . .'

In frustration Forrest left the table and approached Shaw, rolling his eyes. 'Where's this going to get us?' he muttered. 'Bloody nowhere.' He studied his wristwatch. Almost four o'clock. 'And time's running out. We're going to have to charge him or . . .'

Shaw's eyes glittered. He didn't dare say out loud what he was thinking as he watched Malcolm Forning being subjected to the questions: they'd hauled in an innocent man and were questioning him about a string of murders it was plainly obvious he hadn't committed. Someone else had done it. And they didn't have a clue who that someone else was. So he was free to kill again. While they subjected this miserable, inadequate specimen to the attentions of a forensic psychiatrist and the senior investigating officer.

No one was out there looking. The 'surgeon' must have heard the bulletin – that a man was helping the police with their enquiries – and he must realize the heat was off him.

Apart from breaks, questioning of Malcolm Forning had continued right through the afternoon, while the press gathered like a pack of hungry wolves outside the police station, howling for a charge to be made to catch the late editions of the evening papers.

Lewisham stayed right the way through, apparently tireless, asking his soft, pointless questions.

'Rosemary Baring was a nice girl, wasn't she?'

Forrest ground his teeth together in frustration. Rosemary Baring had been a mutilated corpse when he had seen her. How the hell could Lewisham possibly know whether she had been a nice girl or not? And how was it going to help convict Forning if she was? They wanted *facts*. How? When? Where? Why? Not all these bloody opinions, attitudes, memories, dreams. Psychiatric gunk, Forrest called it to himself. Forensic psychiatry was meant to be the future, the way to reduce crime by gaining insight into the minds of killers to prevent reoffending, to understand murderers.

Forrest didn't want to understand them. He wanted to convict them. He wanted to punish them. In fact if he couldn't see the bastards hang he wanted to see them locked away for life. Life. As in marriage. Until death.

He was tired. He wanted to go home, have a shower. Now he was not sure he wanted to meet Karys. He had lost his sense of confidence, of adventure, of any aspiration to romance. He simply wanted to have dinner. And sleep. Sleep without dreaming.

He glanced at his watch. Six o'clock. Another half hour and they should clock off anyway.

But it was a little past seven thirty when Forrest finally left the station and he barely had time for a swift shower and a change of clothes before heading to the small, private hotel along the Hagley Road which had been favoured with his custom. Shaw had recommended it.

Karys arrived a fashionable five minutes late, looking nice in a dark, understated dress – plain, with a scoop neckline, the hem a little above her knees, and a gold chain around her neck. She looked flushed. Flushed and happy. Forrest watched her thread her way through the tables of drinkers to the bar and thought how very smart she looked. Comfortable, relaxed. Most women would find those adjectives an insult, aspiring to look beautiful, glamorous, attractive, sexy. Certainly Maggie had done. But he had the feeling Karys was different, that she would be pleased to know how he thought of her. As she drew closer Forrest picked up the touch of lipstick and the gloss of freshly washed hair. Maggie had turned heads. Not one person gave Karys more than a swift glance, there was no appreciation, no appraisal. Somehow Forrest knew that this was what she was used to: little attention. He stood up and gave her a chaste kiss on the cheek and caught a faint waft, not of perfume, but of flower-scented soap. She grinned at him. 'I'm starving,' she said.

They discussed the food from behind their menus with great relish and spent ages choosing their starters, equally as long on their main course and twice as long selecting the wine, eventually plumping for an Australian Shiraz which was described as having a bouquet 'subtle enough to tempt the most educated palate'. Laughing over the wine blurb broke the ice and then inevitably they began to discuss the case.

'How are you getting on with your suspect?'

Forrest stopped munching his way through a Russian side salad. 'I'd get on a damned sight faster if Lewisham didn't keep him from answering our questions.'

'How's that?'

Forrest forked another heap of salad in before answering. 'It might be old-fashioned,' he said, 'but in the force we tend to want the answers to direct questions. You know the sort of thing. Where were you at nine o'clock on the night of the murder? We *need* the answers to those questions if we're going to proceed with a prosecution. We don't want to know what he thought of having to nurse his mother when she was dying.'

'Don't you think you want to know the answers to both questions?'

It was always this that threw him about her. This sense of calm, of proportion, of balance, of logic.

He felt chastened. 'I suppose so.'

She seemed to understand exactly what one of his problems must be. 'But I suppose it wastes time so you can't decide whether you have enough evidence to charge him.'

'That's right.' Her comprehension encouraged him to open up further. 'If we can't tie him up with a place where he did the operations as well as find how he transported his victims from the scene to there and back to the point of discovery of the bodies we don't have a case. It would only take the Crown Prosecution Service a minute to throw it out.'

She felt a tightening concern. 'But you do have the right man, don't you?'

Lines of worry deepened between his brows. 'What do you think? He fits the bill a bit too well to be innocent. He's strange, I mean really weird. Dysfunctional. He used to work in an operating theatre. He's obsessed with his collection of scalpel blades. They're the only thing he's shown any interest in since we brought him in. No family. No friends. And the SOCOs found some 5/0 silk at the flat. Besides, there's his frequent contact with Sister Brenda Watlow.'

'But not Colin Wilson or Rosemary Shearer?'

'Not as far as we know,' Lewisham said testily. 'He *says* he didn't know them. But we can hardly ask them, can we?'

'But he admitted to knowing Brenda Watlow.'

'Only, I think, because her son-in-law used to drive her round there.'

'Have you questioned Rosemary's flatmate? Or Colin Wilson's wife?'

'Ye-es,' Forrest said, 'and neither seemed to have heard anything about a Malcolm Forning but . . .'

'You're not convinced.'

He used the phrase for a second time. 'He just fits the bill a little bit too well.'

'I see.'

'And it's just as Lewisham described. He has an unhealthy interest in operating theatres.'

'One up to forensic psychiatry,' Karys said lightly.

They both laughed then.

'If you'd seen the way those blades were lined up. The velvet lined box,' Forrest continued. 'It was sick.' He paused long enough to fork some more salad into his mouth and ate thoughtfully. 'It was almost as though he worshipped the things.'

Karys waited until they were halfway through their main course. Breast of chicken oozing with a filling of Shropshire Blue cheese and wrapped in local, smoked bacon. 'You don't think you're putting too much faith in Barney Lewisham?'

Forrest stopped chewing for a moment. 'You don't like him, do you?'

'No.'

He poured them each a glass of wine. She gave a self-conscious laugh. 'No more wine,' she said. 'Having dinner with a policeman, makes me very conscious of the law. And I'm driving.'

He smiled with her and watched while she chose her dessert, catching her gaze over the top of the menu.

'Maybe I'll skip the Death By Chocolate,' she said, 'somehow, tonight I fancy fruit salad just a bit more.'

It was at times like this that Forrest wanted to pull her towards him, to quash her attempt at levity, knowing it was usually done to veil embarrassment. Instinctively he knew she was plucking up every ounce of courage she had to try to say something important. But Karys was like a roe deer. Approach too near and she'd shy away.

He could only watch and wait.

Until coffee.

'David,' she said tentatively, there was no going back now, 'I – I wouldn't have said anything, I really wouldn't, if I thought your guy was the one I would have kept all this to myself.'

He gave her a sharp look.

'Don't look at me like that,' she begged. 'I haven't done anything terrible. Not really.' But her eyes were fixed beyond him, fluttering round the other tables and the other diners as though she could not bear to watch his face while she spoke. 'At least . . .' She took a deep breath in, then covered her mouth with her hand. 'I don't know where to begin,' she said, agitated. 'I really don't. It's so long ago. And I shall never be quite sure exactly what role I played. I always feel I could – I should – have done more. And then your mind plays tricks so you remember only what you want to remember. Only what you dare remember.' She laughed into her wine glass but it was a nervous laugh. There was nothing easy or relaxed about it. Her face was pale, even by candlelight. 'I wish I could forget the whole incident', she said. 'I wish I could put it right behind me. I'm so sick of waking in the night and wondering.' Her face looked almost haggard. 'And even then . . .'

Forrest waited patiently, politely. But he had a sick

feeling in the pit of his stomach. He felt he didn't want this particular confidence. Depressed, he reflected, how often there was more to people than one realized. He had thought her uncomplicated. One of the few. Obviously he had been wrong. Very wrong. But years of watching suspects unburden their heavy consciences had taught him one thing. When the urge to confess was on, the best thing a copper could do was to listen, and say nothing until all had been revealed.

As though she knew that in his eyes she would never appear the same again Karys stopped scanning the restaurant and stared miserably back at him, unsmiling. 'You'll think less of me, David,' she warned. 'But without honesty we have no relationship. Not even friendship. I have to tell you.'

He wanted both to reassure and to encourage her but until she had told him what was preying on her mind he could not without being false. So he covered her hand with his own. 'At least I'll know you then, Karys,' he said. 'Warts and all. But before you download be absolutely certain that you really do want to tell me. Once I know I know.' It was the assurance of a policeman.

'I have to tell someone. And you feel as though you're the right person.' She gave a thin smile, but behind her glasses her eyes were like huge brown moths, their gaze fluttering around the room as though they didn't dare land for too long.

Forrest waited.

'I don't know whether Malcolm Forning is your killer,' she said slowly. 'I know there are things that point to him being the one. But there are other facts that point away from him. Some of the reasons you've

272

homed in on him have been fed to you by Barney Lewisham. You've trusted him too much, as I did once. But I
know him. I know him well. He is,' she faltered, 'not
what he seems.' Slowly she began to unburden herself
and tell Forrest about herself and about Barney. 'He is a
strange, malicious man,' she said. 'One who likes to
dominate. To a pathological degree. It's what he did
with me.'

'Hey, come on,' Forrest protested, 'I don't like the
guy myself. But this is a bit strong. He's a doctor.'

'He wasn't always a doctor,' she countered. 'People
aren't born doctors, you know. And anyway, not all
doctors are such saints. They are only human beings
with human failings. They just have more power, and
status. And in a way this is what it's all about – status.'
Her eyes had never looked more appealing. They drew
him in to her anguish. 'He has a malicious streak that
enjoys wielding that power,' she said, 'and I can prove
it. I had a breakdown when I was a medical student.
Barney precipitated it.'

Forrest squirmed. This was more than he had
expected. Worse.

Karys poured herself a glass of water. 'When I was
an A level student I sort of "went out" with a guy called
Sam. Sam Packard. We both wanted to do medicine.' She
took another sip of water. 'We had this stupid conversation one day about what we'd do if we didn't get the
grades to get into medical school. I said I'd shoot
myself. It was a joke, David. Something said in jest, not
meant to be taken seriously. The conversation progressed to where I'd get a gun from. You know – things
like that and I told him my uncle had a gun. Anyway, to
cut a long story short, Sam didn't get his grades. I did.

Sam shot himself. Exactly as we'd said. He broke into my uncle's house, stole the gun and shot himself. David . . .' she looked earnestly at him ' . . . it was a joke. I wouldn't really have shot myself. I'd just have studied something else. But Sam took me seriously. I made the mistake of confiding the story to Barney. I thought I could trust him. He used it. And one night when he'd pushed me a bit too far and knew I'd probably dump him he turned up with a shotgun on the back seat of the car and threatened to shoot himself if I didn't go out with him. He repulsed me.' She swallowed. 'I hated him. But I couldn't be responsible for another death. Things rambled on in a very half-hearted manner. And this is where your story comes in. Another joke. I never meant for Barney to take it seriously. It was just – fun. But I realized when I saw Brenda's body that there's a link between these murders. Only I don't know how. You see, there was an incident in the operating theatre in the summer eight years ago, it was on July the 23rd 1991. I can't see that it has anything to with Forning. He wasn't there. The rest of us were. Three are dead.'

Forrest hardly dared speak, except to encourage her. 'Go on.'

'It was this one single incident for which I have always believed myself responsible that pushed me into the hands of the psychiatrists. Can you believe that? It was so awful I lost my reason. I was paralysed. I didn't do anything I should have done. I couldn't be a doctor then. I wasn't fit. It took treatment and psychotherapy, all the psychiatric mumbo jumbo to rebuild me because he had destroyed me.' She stared at her plate. 'Maybe that's not strictly true. I destroyed myself, with careless statements. But all the psychiatrists said the same thing.' They *all* said, put him behind you. Put *it* behind you. Forget it. Don't let it ruin your career.' Abruptly she changed subjects. 'Why do you think I work with the dead, David?'

He stared at her. How could he know the answer?

She supplied it. Unflinching. 'Because I don't trust myself to take responsibility for the living. Not after what happened.'

'But you must have taken responsibility for the living once,' he objected.

'As a junior doctor, with a full team of senior staff right behind me to correct my mistakes. As soon as I could, I unloaded the responsibility. Responsibility for the living gave me sleepless nights.'

'I can't believe . . .'

She leant forward, lowering her voice so none of the other diners could possibly hear what she was about to say. 'Try this then.' Her mouth was dry. 'I was a third-year medical student. Twenty-one years old. Barney Lewisham and I had had an on-off relationship all the time I had been a medical student, from sharing the same anatomy corpse to three years later when we were allocated to the same operating theatre. Theatre Four. That's right,' she said. 'See how it all fits? Pinky Sutcliffe's patch. Still there, isn't he? Senior Surgeon. Stuffy old croaker. If it hadn't been for his over-stuffed character it's possible nothing would have happened, but right from the start Barney hated Sutcliffe. He thought he was pompous – which he was, – conceited – , which he was. Of course Sutcliffe had something to be conceited about. He was clever and possessed of the most extraordinary manual skill – a brilliant surgeon. I've seen him performing the most delicate work, saving the lives of people who would have died under a less dextrously wielded scalpel.' Her stare challenged David Forrest. 'See how everything links together. Barney was fond of strutting round the place mimicking Sutcliffe. He didn't care if Pinky saw him. Sutcliffe took his revenge, of course. In the way that he would, he made a fool of Barney on a ward round. Barney was clever but not quite clever enough. Sutcliffe made him look an absolute idiot, asked him some complicated questions and when Barney gave the wrong answer, quite coolly replied that he had just murdered his patient and that even first-year medical students knew better. It wasn't true, of course. The questions were far too advanced but it so happened that a group of nurses had joined the teaching round that day and their tittering made Barney's mortification complete.

'David,' she said earnestly. 'I saw Barney's face when Sutcliffe carried on asking the questions and I feared for him. I didn't know what would happen or when, but I did know that Barney would not forget, that he would get his revenge eventually. That was why he did it.'

'Did what?' Forrest was intrigued by the story. But even peering towards the end he did not see where the 'surgeon' fitted in. This was a tale of long ago. What could this have to do with the recent murders? Surely she could not really be telling him that Lewisham was the 'surgeon'?

'Barney put haloperidol in Sutcliffe's morning coffee,' Karys said simply, as though she was talking about sugar.

'I'm sorry, Karys. I don't follow you. I don't know anything about drugs.'

'Then listen,' she said. 'Haloperidol is an anti-psychotic drug, classed as a major tranquillizer. Colourless, odourless, tasteless. Just a few drops in a cup of coffee would be enough.'

'To put a surgeon to sleep?'

'One would think so, wouldn't one? I mean – haloperidol is generally used to treat schizophrenic psychoses. But putting a surgeon to sleep isn't the worst thing you can do. It certainly wouldn't have supplied Barney Lewisham with a fitting revenge. He wanted more than that.'

'I would have thought a surgeon going to sleep on the job would have been enough to destroy his reputation.'

Karys shook her head. 'No. What Barney was after was one of the side effects of the drug. Haloperidol gives you a tremor. Can you imagine a surgeon with a tremor, David?' When he said nothing she continued. 'I've known surgeons who don't drink caffeinated coffee because one cup makes their hand shake enough to cause major damage, to blood vessels, surrounding tissues, major organs.'

'Is that what happened then? Clumsy surgery?'

'Who knows,' she said, smiling abstractedly, 'what was in Barney Lewisham's mind when he added haloperidol to Sutcliffe's drink that morning? I've often wondered. But it was so easy. Sutcliffe was the only member of staff in the theatre to drink his coffee black, with plenty of sugar. Barney was perfectly safe lacing his drink. No one could possibly get them muddled up.'

'What happened?' Forrest repeated impatiently.

'I'll get there,' she said calmly. 'Don't worry. I shan't bottle out now. I will tell you. But in my own time.

277

Please. It's taken a lot of courage just to get this far. I've only ever told one other friend.' She took a minute sip of water before continuing. 'I can never *know* how much Barney anticipated the effect. Drugs are strange, unpredictable things, they affect different people in different ways. If I am kind I would say that Barney simply wanted Sutcliffe to lose control over his hands during the operations and have to call in the registrar to continue. He would look foolish.' She moistened her lips. 'That's if I'm being kind. Maybe he did just think Sutcliffe would nod off while operating and the staff would assume he'd had a drink too many the night before, or wasn't well – or something. The effects might not have been so disastrous. Sister Brenda Watlow,' again she stared at David Forrest to make sure he had noted the name, 'was very capable and the registrar could have taken over. But the registrar was new, a Greek, and quite incompetent. He couldn't have finished the operation himself. And Barney knew that. Besides, only that week we'd had a lecture underlining the unpredictable effects of the major tranquillizers. The case used to illustrate the lecture was that of a twenty-four year old junior doctor who took a swig of haloperidol to prove to a patient that it didn't have a nasty taste. The result was that the unfortunate doctor suffered from akathisia – motor restlessness, extreme agitation. He actually ran four times round the hospital before anyone could catch him and give him a shot of Valium. He was ready to throw himself out of a window to put an end to the agitation. That's how severe it can be.'

'Go on.' Forrest was stunned.

'After coffee we started again. Sutcliffe scrubbed up. Barney was watching him with one of those amused looks that I knew only too well. There was always a certain amount of malice mixed up in it. Spite, an anticipation of another person's suffering.' Again she looked hard at Forrest. 'A dangerous characteristic in a doctor. Anyway. The first patient was wheeled in, a middle-aged man. Nothing more wrong with him than a simple, inguinal hernia. Sutcliffe made the usual incision. And then everything went mad. He was fumbling for instruments, lost his concentration, started giggling, sweated. We all knew something was terribly wrong but we were powerless to stop it. You see,' she said calmly, 'he was armed. With a scalpel. And the patient lay beneath that scalpel, anaesthetized. Before we knew what was happening Sutcliffe had sliced through the femoral artery. There was blood everywhere. Ceiling, floor, the staff were soaked. That's how much blood the man lost. The nurse – yes – Rosemary Shearer led Sutcliffe into the coffee room. Everyone else thought he must be ill.' She licked her lips. 'Only we two knew.'

'You and Barney?'

'I looked at him. Barney was enjoying it. Like sitting on the front row of a really good play. There was such an expression on his face. He didn't give a damn. He just winked at me and murmured something like, "Good idea of yours, Karys, using haloperidol." Then I knew.'

'And the patient?'

'The patient had a cardiac arrest,' she explained. 'Naturally we resuscitated him but he died a week later in the Intensive Care Unit, never having come round from the anaesthetic. Cause of death, renal failure caused by shock caused by haemorrhage.' Her mouth twisted. 'Doesn't even sound like murder, does it?'

'I don't remember the case,' Forrest said curiously. 'I would have thought it would have hit the headlines. Such a drama in a hospital. How come Lewisham was allowed to qualify? What happened?'

'What do you think?' she asked dully. 'There was a whitewash. Unfortunate happening during a routine operation, Mrs Whateveryour name is. Shame about your husband, your father, your son, but you do understand. All operations carry a risk. That was the official line. The hospital express their regrets. And here are his pyjamas.' A spasm crossed her face. 'They even paid out a token compensation to the family. He was a divorced man. Sutcliffe was suspended pending investigation. They took some blood samples and did scans. Found nothing wrong and put the whole incident down to a "viral illness". He was reinstated a month later. Barney and I finished our spell in the theatre. He carried on. There was no inquiry. The staff may all have had their own private thoughts but we didn't talk about it. Sutcliffe was more anxious than the rest of us to put the incident behind him. Brenda might have had her suspicions but she was far too wise to risk her career. So the hospital got away with it. He got away with it. I got away with it.'

'I don't see why . . .'

'You don't see why I reacted as I did? Why I felt I shared the guilt? I'll tell you, David. It was my idea.' She shrank from his look. 'It was a joke. I make good jokes, don't I? I laugh and people die. At the lecture we'd had when they'd spelt out every single side-effect of haloperidol, I'd listened and whispered to Barney what fun it'd be to lace Sutcliffe's coffee with some. And he did it.'

'You didn't see him do it, though.'

'He told me,' she said dully. 'Afterwards. At the time I didn't connect. I was as shocked as everyone else when Sutcliffe went mad. But afterwards Barney told me. Then I realized I'd been responsible for an innocent man's death. I said nothing while it was smoothed over.'

'But surely you were under the psychiatrists by then.'

'Yes. I was.'

Forrest opened and closed his mouth like a fish. Karys stood up. 'It's all right,' she said. 'You don't have to say anything. And what action you take now is up to you. After all, you're a policeman. But I'm glad I told you. I'm glad I came clean. Maybe now I can face up to what's happened, what I did and what role I played. I do feel better.' She bent and brushed his cheek with her lips. 'I'm going home now.' She held out her hand. 'Thank you for listening, David. And now for God's sake stop him. Please.'

He stared at her.

'Malcolm Forning is not the killer,' she said. 'He's just a theatre porter. An innocuous little man I don't know. He has nothing to do with that hideous incident all those years ago. The people who have died all worked the theatre at that particular time. They were all part of the incident. It is not coincidence: Colin Wilson, theatre porter during the summer of 1991, dead; Rosemary Baring, student nurse during that summer, dead; and Brenda Watlow,' Karys finished quietly, 'Theatre Sister, also dead. I know this, David. What other explanation can there be?'

Forrest had no answer.

She didn't speak again but picked up her handbag and left the restaurant. Half an hour later Forrest walked out too without noticing that her black Mercedes was still standing in the car park.

Chapter Twenty-one

8 January 2000

Forrest was woken at some unearthly hour of the night by the incessant ringing of the telephone. It took him a few minutes to identify the sound, process it through a weary brain, pick the receiver up and mumble his name. A junior officer, apologetic, 'I'm sorry, sir. But I have an angry female on the other end of the telephone demanding to speak to you.'

'What does she want?'

'She says she wants to know where her flatmate is.'

Forrest was tempted to put the receiver down, and go back to sleep. Something stopped him. 'She asked for me – by name?'

'Yes, sir. Otherwise I wouldn't have bothered you. She really is angry, sir.'

'Who is she?'

'A Miss Tonya Farthing.'

The name meant nothing to Forrest. 'And her flatmate?'

'Dr Harper, sir.'

Forrest sat bolt upright. 'What do you mean? Karys Harper?'

'That's right, sir.'

'Then put this . . .' the name eluded him.

'Miss Farthing, sir.'

'Put her through.'

A click.

'Is that Detective Inspector David Forrest?' Karys's flatmate had a cold, angry voice.

'Speaking.'

'Karys had a dinner date with you last night.'

'Yes.'

'Is she with you?'

'What do you mean?'

'Is she there – with you?'

Had it not struck Forrest already that something was wrong he would have laughed out loud. He had not considered himself such a Romeo. But now he simply answered curtly, 'No.'

'Then where is she, Inspector?'

'I don't know.' A creeping fear made Forrest cold. 'Didn't she come back last night?'

'Of course not, you stupid bastard. If she was here I'd hardly be ringing you, would I?'

'Well she isn't here either. The last I last saw of her . . .' Forrest pictured her threading her way through the tables of diners ' . . . was when she left me at the restaurant at about eleven.' The alarm clock showed four a.m. 'Is there anywhere else she might be?'

'No.'

'Nowhere?'

'No. She doesn't get on with her parents. There is no one else.'

'Her car couldn't have . . .?'

'She'd have caught a taxi – or rung.'

Silence.

Then, Tonya said, 'He has her.'

'Who?'

'Who do you bloody well think?'

She was in a neat, clean room. Walls, ceiling, painted dazzling white. Her head ached and she couldn't move. Why couldn't she move? Straps were binding her arms and ankles. She tried to wriggle, but they were strong straps, tied tightly.

A light shone in her face, blinding her. She stared up at a green-gowned figure.

'Who are you?'

No answer.

'Why have you brought me here?'

'Don't you know?' A rough, coarse voice.

Karys looked around the room. Her nightmares realized.

The 'surgeon' turned his back on her, selected an instrument and held it up in front of her face. It was a scalpel.

Tonya Farthing was waiting for him outside her block of flats, a muffled figure in jeans and a bomber jacket, standing beneath the porch light. Forrest recognized her at once, by the bright hair. The red-headed journalist. Immediately things began to fall into place. No wonder she had worn that knowing smile, sharing a flat with the pathologist in charge of the case, she had been so much better informed than the others. If he hadn't been so taut with worry he would have made a note to chide Karys for her careless talk.

As it was he stopped beside Tonya and threw open the passenger door.

'She hasn't turned up?'

Tonya shook her head. 'He's got her. I know it. She did tell you about him, didn't she? She was going to.'

'Yes.' Some of her panic was transmitting itself to him.

'Then you should have realized she was in danger if you'd have had an ounce of sense. Ah, but,' she added, 'you're a detective, aren't you? What's the point in expecting sense from them?' She got into the car.

Forrest bit back a comment. He hadn't liked her when she had sat in the front row during press conferences now, sitting right beside him in his car he felt a strong urge to punch her. But that wouldn't help Karys.

'What's his telephone number?'

'You mean Lewisham?'

'Who else?'

Forrest pulled it slowly from his pocket. 'It's only a mobile. I don't know where he lives.'

'Dial it!'

Forrest pressed the keypad.

He won't answer it. No surgeon comes to the phone in the middle of . . . in the middle of what? He felt sick.

'Hello.'

Sheer amazement kept him silent for a moment.

'Hello?'

'It's Detective Inspector David Forrest here.'

'And what the hell do you want? It's the middle of the night.'

'Dr Harper's missing.'

'And you thought she might be having a quick . . .' A prolonged silence. 'A quick what?'

Tonya grabbed the phone. 'Where do you live?'

Frustratingly Forrest could only hear one side of the conversation, Tonya's sharp, 'Never mind who I am.' But Lewisham must have told her something. She started scribbling. One hand fished out the *A-Z* of Birmingham. 'That had better be the right answer because I've got enough on you, Barney Lewisham to put you behind bars for the rest of your natural. Don't touch her. I know the bloody lot. And we're on our way.'

Next she barked at Forrest. 'Start the ruddy engine.'

Forrest did exactly as she asked.

Karys felt sick. She wished her head would clear, so this was what concussion felt like this dreamy, sleepy quality. Real and yet unreal. She tried to open her eyes again but the light was too strong.

'Turn the light off.'

'I need it. For my work.'

'You can't – '

The surgeon's mask ruckled. He was smiling.

She struggled to move.

Forrest was shocked when Lewisham opened the door, fully dressed, alert, smiling even.

'Now what's all this about?'

Tonya got her words out first. 'Where's Karys?'

'I haven't the foggiest idea.'

As though she didn't exist he looked past her to Forrest. 'And to what do I owe the pleasure of this visit?'

'I told you Dr Harper's missing.'

Lewisham grinned. 'And you think she might be

287

bedding down with me?' He stood back. 'Feel free to search my premises. Don't forget to look underneath the bed. I won't even ask you for your warrant,' he called after them.

Karys was conscious of two overwhelming emotions: terror, a blinding, paralysing terror; and curiosity.

A childish instinct told her to shut her eyes tightly, squeeze out the horrors, as though not to see them could make them vanish.

And like a child she whimpered. 'Please. Help me. Let me go.'

But the 'surgeon' was waiting. Karys opened her eyes to look at him. A tall man, dressed in green cotton. Masked, so his nose and mouth were invisible. But she could see his eyes. Brown, cold. She tried to move her arms. She must escape.

Then anger flooded through her. She was not a child anymore. She was a woman, a doctor. And this surgeon was an imposter. He had no right.

'Who are you?'

Her voice sounded cracked and strange.

In answer the 'surgeon' lowered his mask.

Chapter Twenty-two

They had searched the house. Karys was not there.

Lewisham was sitting in the lounge, smoking a cigar. He treated them both to an amused smile as they came back in.

'Well?'

'Where is she, you bastard?'

Forrest knew Tonya's fury was a waste of time. They had to enlist the psychiatrist's help, not antagonize him. And there was only one way to do that: appeal to his vanity. There was no time to lose.

'I need your assistance, Doctor.'

Already he could sense it was working. Lewisham's face softened. He puffed out a cloud of smoke. 'Then tell me exactly what's going on.'

'Doctor Harper and I had dinner last night. She never arrived home.'

'And what on earth do you think this has to do with me?'

'Where is she?'

Lewisham shrugged. 'I don't know.' He hesitated. 'Her car?'

Forrest cursed himself. How could he have forgotten the bloody car. He turned to Tonya.

'What's the number?'

'CWA 95.'

In as long as it had taken to say it Forrest had repeated it down the phone and the name of the previous night's hotel, with a curt request to let him know immediately they found it.

Lewisham was watching them, still with that same condescending smile on his face. Forrest knew that Tonya shared his feelings: they would both have liked to throttle the man. But they dared not. If anyone could help them he could.

Forrest struggled to keep his voice calm. 'I know about the incident you were involved in in the operating theatre in July 1991. Karys told me. Everything. And there's a connection between that incident and these murders.'

Lewisham's eyebrows shot up. But he said nothing.

Forrest pressed further. 'I know you laced Pinky Sutcliffe's morning coffee with haloperidol with fatal consequences for his patient.'

Something did change then, Lewisham frowned at him. He took another big puff from the cigar and let the ash fall unchecked.

'These murders – '

Lewisham's mouth curved upwards in a demonic smile. 'You can't have thought I was your "surgeon"?'

Forrest held back.

'I would have had *much* more skill than that – hacker. And as for Forning . . .'

Forrest realized with a shock, that he had discounted Forning. He had not assumed Karys safe even though Forning was in custody.

Why not? Because he had never really believed Forning was the killer. He had *wanted* to believe it, had tried to convince himself he did believe it. But it had failed.

'Please, Doctor Lewisham. Help us find Karys.'

He had lowered his mask, still hooked round the ears, and tucked it under his chin. It could have looked comic.

Karys squinted up at him. The lights were blinding her. She could see nothing but a huge silhouette.

'I don't know you.'

'Yes, you do.'

'But I don't!'

'Think, Doctor Harper. Think.'

Karys closed her eyes. Had she heard the voice before. She must get away. Her feet. She might be able to slip . . .

He turned towards her again.

She knew instinctively that help would not come. She had to do this herself, or die.

They were still in Lewisham's sitting room when the call came through. 'They've found the car.' Forrest was swamped by a sense of hopelessness. 'It never left the hotel.'

Tonya was deathly pale, her face against the garish red hair making her look like a gaudy rag doll. She took a couple of steps towards Lewisham. 'Think, you bastard,' she said. 'What is the connection between the murders and what you did all those years ago?'

Lewisham puffed away at his cigar, mesmerized by the smoke. 'Intriguing, isn't it? I've recently spent quite a few happy hours pondering that very point. It came to me slowly – the connection. I'd forgotten the porter's name – if I'd ever known it – and the nurse had a different name then. It wasn't until he got to Brenda that I was sure.'

'And what conclusion have you come to?' Forrest knew he had to play this Lewisham's way.

'I decided,' Lewisham said slowly, 'to concentrate on the personae at the theatre that day.' He smiled. 'Perhaps I should say the dramatis personae as it was a theatre.' Another puff on the cigar. 'Some, of course, we can discount.' He peered at Forrest, ignoring Tonya. 'They're already dead.' He gave a short, braying laugh.

Forrest hated him for the delay. It might be costing Karys her life. But a knife held to Lewisham's throat wouldn't force him to speak, because he knew the power he wielded and was enjoying the omniscience. He knew they could do nothing to him while there was a chance that Karys was still alive.

Lewisham smiled to himself. Not much of a chance if what he had learned about the 'surgeon' was correct. He liked his corpses fresh. He lit a second cigar from the butt of the first, fugging the air, adding to the theatrical atmosphere of the room. He cleared his throat and spoke.

'Think of it this way.' He settled back in his chair. 'We were all in a costume drama that day. The surgeon, Pinky Sutcliffe, no longer a serious actor, more a ham actor. An object of fun. Tumbled from grace by my trick. And I was the director and Karys my puppet. The others mere bit actors. But there was to be a sacrificial lamb, if you'll pardon my mixing the metaphors. You all forgot about the sacrifice. A necessary part. One can't have a tragedy without death.' He smiled at them both.

Forrest knew they must hide their impatience.

'But you see. When someone dies it sets off a chain reaction. This has been your error all the way through. You should have looked with much more intelligence at past events. Why should *I* want to kill? If it had any connection with the slaughter of innocents you should have looked elsewhere.' He paused. 'Who would want to kill? Revenge was the right answer. But whose revenge?' He stubbed the cigar out on an ashtray and smiled. 'You don't know do you? When it's so glaringly obvious. Are the police such dolts? And journalists too?' He gave them both a withering stare.

The 'surgeon' had not tied the straps tight enough. Karys had wriggled her feet almost free.

'Who are you?' she asked again.

'You should remember, Doctor Harper. You met me. Once. Briefly.'

'Did I?'

The 'surgeon' held up his scalpel. 'Do you know there are more than twenty different types of scalpel blade?'

'Yes.' Only by remaining calm could she hope to survive. She desperately wanted to live. Start again. Work with the living. She had had enough of surrounding herself with the dead.

The 'surgeon' continued. 'I identified my mother-in-law just a few days ago. Now do you remember?'

The image swam into her mind. A burly man, a

fleshy face, thick dark curly hair. Very dark eyes. Almost black. She had met him. And forgotten him.

'I don't recall your name.'

'No? It's Terry. Terry Carling. Now do you remember me?'

Forrest was trying to cut short the theatricals.

'Look, Doctor Lewisham. Karys is in danger. Please. Help us. Quickly. If we waste time she might—' He could not continue.

Lewisham was eyeing them narrowly. 'You can't have thought,' he said. 'You can't really have thought I was him. The "surgeon" is a monster. A moron. Dysfunctional. Mad.' He drew himself up to his full, inadequate height. 'You can't really have believed.' He stopped speaking and closed his mouth, breathing fast through his nostrils.

Tonya spoke again, savagely. 'Well, if what Karys told me about you is true you're pretty weird yourself. Not exactly the average boyfriend.'

They glared at each other.

'Please.' Forrest spoke wearily. 'None of this – sparring – is getting us any closer to Karys.' He was remembering the earnest, pleading expression in her eyes as she had told her story. Begging him not to be too harsh a judge of her. He blinked fast to blot it out. Her vulnerability had touched him too closely. He was terrified she would be the next body to be discovered.

'Please, Doctor Lewisham,' he pleaded. 'Carry on.'

Lewisham smiled. 'As I said. You have to consider the point. Who would want revenge for the events of that day? Let's first of all consider Sutcliffe. He might

have wanted the silence of the staff who witnessed his
fall from grace, but not eight years later. It would have
to have been immediately. They had probably all forgotten it. Events do fade after a number of years. The
victim's family too should have wanted their revenge
still warm. But here I have done some investigating of
my own.'

Her mouth was almost too dry to speak. But she
managed the one word. 'Why?'

The 'surgeon' hooked his mask back up over his
nose.

'Time to scrub up,' he said cheerfully.

'Why?' she shouted.

Terry Carling was washing his hands.

Karys wriggled her feet free. He didn't turn around.

'Because you could have stopped it.'

'Stopped what?'

'You all had the power. None more than you, Lewisham, Sutcliffe, the nurses, the theatre porter.' There
was anger in his voice. 'None less than my father.'

'Who is your father?'

'Was my father, Dr Harper, was, He's *dead*. He was
your victim. Yours – and the others.' He had fitted elbow
taps to the sink, and was making a thorough job of
sluicing his hands and drying them on paper towels.
Karys began to shiver uncontrollably.

'Why don't you tell me how he died?' It was her
only hope – bluff. 'I don't know what you're talking
about.'

But she did. She knew exactly what he was talking

about. The old sin had returned to haunt her. As she had always known it would.

Carling smiled. 'It's all fate, you know. I would never have known his death was anything out of the ordinary but for fate. He and my mother were divorced. His death meant nothing to her. And I hardly knew him. When my mother said he'd died in hospital I thought nothing of it. But for my dear mother-in-law and her habit of recounting tales from the theatre I would never have known. But how she loved to prattle! And so I heard of the drama that was really a murder. A nicely smoothed over murder. I heard about the surgeon who had acted strangely during a routine operation. I heard how he had sliced through a major artery. How the patient had bled. Everyone thought Sutcliffe must have been ill. But he wasn't, was he? What did happen? It was Brenda who supplied the answer. She heard Lewisham say to you what a good idea it had been. But she didn't know my connection. You see my mother had married again, we didn't share the same name.'

Karys felt cold. Terribly cold. And tired too. She could hardly manage to open her eyes. The light was too bright.

'So why did my father die, Karys? Answer, because Lewisham gave him something to affect the surgeon's skill. It was your idea, wasn't it? And like bad Samaritans not one of you challenged the surgeon's authority and stopped him from killing my father. You all did nothing. And so my father died. And I was paid four hundred and fifty pounds for my loss. That was the final insult: that the hospital thought they could pay me off. So, I thought, I too shall play at this game, the game of surgery. I too can be a surgeon if the title awards its bearer the ability to murder – legally. All it took was a detailed study of a textbook on surgery and a few bits and pieces filched from the theatre when picking up my dear mother-in-law.'

'Please,' she begged, her arms straining feebly at the straps.

'*You* didn't care. Why should I? Afterwards not one of you told the truth. You let my father die without demanding justice. For that I hold you all responsible, to varying degrees, which in turn dictated my order of events. Colin Wilson, Rosemary Shearer, my mother-in-law. You, the innocent dupe, Lewisham, the diabolist and finally Sutcliffe too, the murdering surgeon. He deserves his final placing because it was his hand that killed my father. The Greek doctor admittedly has temporarily wriggled through the net by vanishing back to his own country but I'll find him. That only leaves Amison, the anaesthetist, out of all of you he was the one who did most for my father. My mother-in-law told me how hard he tried to save him. Retribution is not for him. It wouldn't be appropriate. Now then, Doctor. Breathe slowly. Through the mask.'

Forrest bit back his impatience again, he was beginning to realize that Lewisham had been ahead of the police investigation, had pieced together the whole story. He had concealed every single relevant fact from the investigations. Forrest watched him curiously. Why? The answer fitted his original assessment of the psychiatrist: because he loved the power such knowledge afforded him. He had enjoyed watching the police investigation flounder as he might have watched white mice scuttle blindly around a maze. Now he was reaping in the full harvest. Forrest realized just how much Lewisham was enjoying himself. Karys's life was unimportant compared to his enjoyment.

Lewisham continued. 'And here we have an interesting turn of events. The man who was so savaged by Pinky Sutcliffe that day was a man aged forty-three – a divorced man with no near relatives. No one to concern themselves too much with his fate. Of course when he died a few days later the spotlight was turned back on Sutcliffe. Complications arising from surgery are one thing, a death quite another. Various diagnoses were tossed around to explain Sutcliffe's condition that day: cerebral haemorrhage, various forms of epilepsy, that sort of thing. When they all turned out negative and the patient had died they started to search for some other explanation. But they never found one.' Lewisham gave his loud, slightly unbalanced laugh. 'A claim was made against the hospital. It spoilt the audit figures for the year. But one death resulting from a relatively minor operation is not dreadful enough to upset even the most rigid of auditors. Sutcliffe got away with it. But the young man had a son whose name I've learnt was Terry. And somehow,' he stopped smiling, 'even I do not know the full sequence of events, the dead man's son met the theatre sister's daughter and married her.' He made a face. 'Sister Brenda Watlow was a garrulous woman who loved to gossip about the dramatic events of an operating theatre. At some point, who knows when, this young man, quite cleverly, must have put two and two together.'

'Where can we find him?' Forrest asked.

Lewisham leant back. 'I can't spoonfeed you completely,' he said wearily. 'Some things you'll have to find out for yourself. And no doubt,' he finished, 'at some point the "surgeon" intends to attempt to exact his revenge on me. Which could be interesting.'

He was pushing the facemask towards her when she kicked out at him.

He hadn't been expecting that but her arms were still pinioned by the straps. It gave her only a small advantage.

The mask came closer.

She must escape. Or breathe. And if she breathed the gas she would die. Terror turned to panic.

Forrest was back in the car, radioing in for Brenda's daughter's address when, uninvited, Lewisham climbed in to the police car.

He leant forward from the back to speak to Forrest. 'By the way, Forrest, Karys has been wrong all these years. She should have listened harder to the lectures. Haloperidol only gives the side-effects of akathisia in a young man. Sutcliffe was in his forties. Far too old. In actual fact I put nothing into his drink. When I realized he was ill, I simply pretended I had. It's been fun getting Karys to believe she was responsible, but she wasn't.'

Forrest was accelerating towards the Hagley Road. 'You bastard.' He did not have to be polite to Lewisham any longer. He owed him nothing.

Lewisham pursued the point with less of his

preening confidence. 'It was an unfortunate incident.' He spread his hands. 'But I couldn't possibly have predicted the outcome of such an innocuous little joke. Just a joke.'

Tonya glared at him. 'People have died because of your "little joke". This entire incident . . . has been sparked off by your "little joke". Karys has blamed herself all these years, you didn't do a bloody thing about it. It's all because of you.'

Lewisham fixed the journalist with a stare. 'And what are you going to do about it? Expose me?'

'I won't need to,' Tonya said sweetly. 'When all this comes out people will ask why four people died. It'll all come out. The whole story. I'd be surprised if your career survives it. Or you for that matter. They're not too keen on doctors in prison.'

They glared at each other.

'I think you're forgetting something. I understand the way this maniac's mind works. I'm the only one who can anticipate his actions. If anyone can help Karys, I'm the one. The only one.'

Chapter Twenty-three

They say that when you believe you are about to die your life flashes in front of you. Small cameo shots of significant events. The bits that have made you what you are today.

The day when her mother had left her at the hospital, with chocolate and confused explanations. The day when the surgeon had peered down at her, when the nurse had clamped the mask over her nose and mouth, forcing her to breathe. The pain on waking.

But this time she would not wake, or have her parents coccooning her.

Barney. His devious mockery. The demolition of her character which had led in turn to her own self-deprecation. Self-doubt.

The surgeon would kill her, as he had killed others. She shuddered as she recalled the three most recent post-mortems. She would soon be among them. Another wasted life. One that had never really begun. Not properly.

She had never been herself. Only some timid mirrored version of how others had seen her. Her parents, Barney. Her fury was suddenly so strong that her terror was overcome. It had vanished. Lying down with death grinning at her from above she burnt with hatred and a feeling of frustration for having caved in to all the oppression.

As he bent towards her she fixed her eyes on him in a dumb appeal. She was not dead yet. 'Please,' she whispered.

For a second, no longer, he hesitated.

She was getting through. Karys clawed her way back to calm. 'I've been doing the post-mortems on your victims.'

I am still alive, she wanted to scream. I will stay alive.

The 'surgeon' could not resist seeking accolade. 'What do you think of my work?'

'I think it's very . . .'

'Professional?' he asked eagerly.

'You've got better.' It was surely safer to agree with this mad man?

'I was just short of practice.'

She said nothing. Fright was creeping back again, paralysing her legs, making her cold, tired.

'How did you learn?' she managed to ask.

'Through books,' he said. 'Textbooks. She had plenty.'

'Your mother-in-law?'

He nodded. 'Because of your status you all got clean away with it, Doctor. With murder I mean. It will be the same for me.'

'No,' she said.

He got angry then. 'You say that to save your own skin.'

'No,' she said again. 'The police – '

'Think it's Forning.'

She looked up to meet his eyes. 'But Forning's in custody now. They can't blame him any more.'

'Then they'll find someone else to blame.'

'They'll find you. Barney Lewisham will lead them to you in the end. He's clever.'

'I'm clever. And I shall find him too. Then my work will be complete.' He fixed Karys with a stare. 'What did you use to drug Sutcliffe?'

'Haloperidol,' she said without even having to think. The name of the drug had never left her.

Terry smiled. 'That was the only thing I didn't know.'

She sensed he was growing bored. 'Breathe,' he said. 'I want to see how successful my anaesthetics are.'

There was no way out. He was forcing the mask too tightly against her face. Karys took a long, spluttering breath.

Knocking Shani Carling up was like waking the dead. She'd mixed sleeping tablets prescribed by the doctor with the alcohol he had recommended she leave well alone and the combination had left her bleary eyed and groggy. She opened the door, leaning against the frame for support.

Forrest spoke first. 'Where's your husband?'

She was instantly on the defensive. 'Whadda you wanna know for?'

Tonya was less polite. 'Where the hell is he?'

'Not here.'

It took a few more precious moments to convince Shani that they were serious, deadly serious. She yawned, rubbed her eyes and finally addressed Forrest.

'He's got a lockup,' she said. 'On an industrial estate. It's where he runs his business from. He's an electrician.'

'Take us there,' Forrest ordered.

'What, *now*? I don't *know* he's there.'

Tonya gripped the woman by the throat. Instinctively she knew time was running out for her friend. She tried not to think. None of the victims had been alive half an hour after they had been taken. Not one. She might be dead already.

Forrest went through the motions of alerting the force, instructing them to surround the building while Tonya helped Shani dress, trying all the time to focus his mind away from Karys's face as it had been when he had last seen her. Appealing to be understood. To be liked.

If she was alive he vowed he would get closer to her. Never mind what else happened. He would be, at the very least, her friend. Her true friend.

Time was running out.

Chapter Twenty-four

Forrest bundled Tonya, Lewisham, and the still pro-
testing Shani into the car, and they sped off, directions
coming both from Shani and an over-excited switch-
board operator. 'Right, right right. First left, left, left
then right . . .'

Shani's help was less precise. 'I think it's along here
a bit.'

The police presence was obvious as they drew off
the main road onto a small industrial estate full of
soulless square lockups lit with orange streetlamps.
Possibly busy in the day, but deserted through the
night. Maybe by day Terry Carling did run his business
from here, but at night he had another purpose for it.
Shani directed them towards one of the lockups at the
end of the back row where most of the police cars were
concentrated. Stout roller doors guarded the entrance.
To the side was a second small door. The windows
were high rectangles which threw out pools of light:
the 'surgeon' was inside. The road had been blocked
off to all but the police. Forrest stopped briefly and
was waved on by a uniformed officer. The place was
crawling with them, their cars were everywhere, some
marked, others discreet and anonymous. In front of the

roller shutters men crouched, all in black, their bodies thickened by padded jackets, their faces concealed by balaclavas, with guns trained on the two exits.

The 'surgeon' was a multiple killer. He warranted such attention.

Forrest and the others got out of the car, noiselessly closing the doors. Outside it was quiet. Not a sound was coming from inside the lock up. It was eerily still. Nothing but distant, innocent, unaware sounds: traffic; dogs barking; unidentified screeches. No screams.

It could mean she was already dead. Or . . . Forrest found he couldn't think of an alternative.

He located the Chief Superintendent talking to one of the men in black. 'I believe he's got Doctor Harper in there, sir.'

Waterman nodded. 'We've run him to ground, at last.'

There was a trace of criticism in his voice.

Shani came into view. 'This is his wife, sir.'

'Mmm.'

'That's his van,' she said, pointing. 'The white one, parked round the front.' Shani's eyes were widening by the minute. The dope must be wearing off.

Waterman spoke to Forrest. 'You know Doctor Harper fairly well don't you?'

Forrest nodded miserably. 'I was with her last night, sir. Dinner,' he added.

Waterman made no comment. 'Normally, in cases like this, we would play the waiting game,' he said, 'speak to the hostage-taker and let him know we're here, try and reason with him.' Another pause. 'In this case the situation's a bit different. The man's a serial killer. We have a choice.' A wry smile. 'We either burst in, guns blazing, or we enter by stealth.'

Barney Lewisham cleared his throat. 'I think that stealth is preferable,' he said importantly, 'and the obvious choice is, of course, me.' The small group standing round the car were left in no doubt. Lewisham's moment had finally arrived.

Only Waterman objected. 'It should, if anything, be one of the armed officers,' he said. 'They're trained to deal with such situations.'

Lewisham smiled. 'I don't think so. You see, Karys Harper just might be alive. If she is, there will be some reasoning to be done with her abductor. Out of all of us, I am the only one trained in such matters. I *understand* this man. His motives. His weaknesses. Only I have the reasoning ability to convince him he should spare her. I am the one he wants next. For me to approach him will give me the advantage.' He shot a swift, meaningful glance at Forrest. 'It will shock him. If, on the other hand, she is already dead our man will be armed with a scalpel which he will have absolutely no hesitation in using randomly. I am prepared to go in, unarmed and unattended and speak to him. This is my *professional* advice and I don't think you're prepared to go against it, are you, Chief Superintendent Waterman? May I remind you we don't have much time if we have any at all.'

Waterman and the man in black withdrew for a couple of seconds, before Waterman turned back to Lewisham. 'OK,' he said reluctantly. 'But at least wear protective gear. A knifeproof vest.'

Lewisham had his answer ready. 'That will defeat

the object,' he said. 'It will reduce me to one of you, attempting to overcome by force and physical means, powerless to deflect an attack except by a mechanical device. That will not impress our friend. I must reason with him. Persuade him, if I am to gain any advantage at all.'

It was Forrest who spoke up then, grudgingly respectful. 'I don't see we've any option,' he pointed out. 'And I agree with Doctor Lewisham, if Doctor Harper is still alive we can't take the risk. And if he's prepared to go in . . .'

Shani, further roused by events, said, 'You're best using the side door. That's how he gets in. It'll be open. I only came here the once. On my own. Thought he was having it away with someone.' Her plump, doughy face crumpled. 'I never guessed he was up to this.'

Forrest took the key from her. He wanted to say something to the psychiatrist, to ask him to make every effort to preserve Karys's life. To use all his bargaining skills to keep her alive. Unhurt. Unmutilated. He screwed his eyes up in agony. But his resentment for the man prevented him saying anything. He handed the key to Lewisham without a word.

Lewisham walked briskly towards the door at the side of the lockup.

They all watched as he turned the handle, pushed the door open and vanished inside.

'Keep him covered.' Waterman gave the order softly to the waiting officers. 'Give him three minutes. No longer. And then we'll have to . . .' He didn't need to finish the sentence. They all knew they must use whatever force was necessary.

Moments ticked away slowly.

The watchers were motionless, straining for sound.

It took a few moments for Lewisham's eyes to adjust to the light.

It was bright in here. Clean too. White walls, neatly stocked shelves, white covering on the floor. Fluorescent tubes.

He blinked rapidly. It was a scene straight from *Casualty*, *ER*, any of the medical soaps. A patient, lying on the table, a green-gowned, masked figure bending over her, pressing a mask to her face. The patient was fully conscious. Not instantly recognizable as Karys. Her clothes were rumpled, two straps binding her.

The 'surgeon' looked up.

In slow motion Barney moved forwards.

Something flickered across the 'surgeon's' eyes. He didn't like being disturbed. He straightened, scalpel in hand.

Barney spoke quietly. 'Do you know who I am?' It was the voice he used to reassure disturbed patients. Sometimes it worked. This time he wasn't sure. 'My name is Doctor Barney Lewisham.'

Something registered. 'So you've come to me.' There was surprise in his voice.

Lewisham nodded. 'I've come,' he said, 'because I know about you. I know why you're doing this.' Not once did he look at Karys. It would have broken the bond that was forming between him and the 'surgeon'. He didn't want it to snap. He wanted to know the man.

Without even glancing at Karys, he knew how she would look. Pale, motionless, almost dead. But her eyes would be fixed open. Staring, pleading with him. Just the image was enough to intoxicate him.

'Why is your patient still conscious?'

Terry Carling gave Karys a brief squint. 'I don't seem to have got my anaesthetics quite right.'

So he had been right. The 'surgeon' was progressing. No longer happy to butcher the dead. He wanted to work with the living. Barney congratulated himself.

'What are you using?'

'Gas. Nitrous Oxide. I thought it would work. It *should* work – shouldn't it?'

Barney knew he was succeeding. The 'surgeon' had consulted him as a fellow professional. That meant he would, soon, accept advice. He answered casually, as though discussing a surgical technique with a colleague. Instinctively he knew this was the line to take. 'Yes, it should work OK, although my experience in anaesthetics is limited. Maybe you haven't got the mix quite right.'

It gave him the perfect opportunity to move closer. Perhaps it was a bit soon.

For a couple of seconds the two men stared at each other, hatred welled up inside Terry Carling's eyes.

It was long enough.

Karys took a deep breath in and kicked out hard. Terry fell backwards. The spell was broken.

'You bloody idiot.' Barney was furious.

'Set me free. Please.'

'I wanted to talk to him.' He raged. 'I wanted to tell him he was on the right track, that it was all your wonderful idea.'

She bit back her comment.

Reluctantly, Barney loosened the straps.

The 'surgeon' lunged.

When Forrest finally entered he found Terry Carling lying on the floor, two police officers restraining him. Karys was cowering in the corner and another couple of officers were desperately trying to staunch the blood that was still pouring from Barney Lewisham's back.

Chapter Twenty-five

February 2000

It was a month later. The first glimpse of snowdrops had arrived. It felt as though spring was round the corner. Or maybe the nights only seemed brighter because the threat was gone.

A rumour had reached Forrest, so he knew it was Karys's last day in the mortuary and he wanted to see her even if only to say goodbye. What her plans were he didn't yet know.

He was glad when she opened the door instead of Paget. He hadn't known how he would explain his presence to the mortuary attendant. The old chap would have seen right through it.

They went into Karys's office. It immediately struck him how much better she was looking. Slimmer, more confident, glowing. Recalled to Life.

'You know I'm leaving?'

Forrest nodded.

'I didn't want to do any more post-mortems,' she said, smiling. 'I've decided to do some re-training and go into general practice.' Her smile grew even wider. 'I feel I can do some real good, make something of my life. Of my profession.'

'And relationships?'

'Those too.'

The words hung between them.

'David,' she said tentatively. 'I've thought a lot about the night in Carling's lockup. I don't really mean flash-backs, they're natural, and anyway, I know they fade in time. No. It's another aspect.'

He sat down as though invited.

'It was Barney loosening the straps on me that turned Terry Carling against him. Up until then,' she smiled thoughtfully, 'I think Barney had the advantage. Carling was so shocked to see him, they were dis-cussing anaesthetics like a pair of medical colleagues.' She shivered at the memory.

'So?'

'It was my fault. Again.'

He went to her and wrapped his arms round her. 'I don't know how you can say that,' he said. 'It was all to do with Barney. If it hadn't been for his preening bloody confidence we'd have got to our bloodthirsty murdering friend a lot more quickly. Besides, if it hadn't been for Lewisham none of this would ever have happened.'

'You mean Terry Carling wouldn't have killed anyone?'

Forrest chuckled. 'Well, maybe his seducing mother-in-law. No one else, Karys. It was a sort of un-controlled fury that turned him into the monster he became. He must have spent hours pumping his mother-in-law about the event, and she accidentally fed him misinformation. Lewisham put *nothing* into Sutcliffe's coffee.'

She stared at him. 'You're lying. Trying to – '

'No. He told me that night. He merely milked your

guilt. That's all. Let you think it was all your fault. It wasn't your fault, Karys. It was his.'

Karys laughed softly. 'I've carried this around with me for years, David. I think I feel better already.'

'So do I, now we've got him. Carling had spent months planning everything right down to the last detail, collecting blades, surgical equipment, sutures, even green towels. All from the theatre. Every time he picked his mother-in-law up from work he must have filled his pockets. He'd drawn up a list of victims, all written just like a surgeon's whiteboard in the theatre. Got the names of the operations right too.'

He dropped his eyes as he recalled Karys's name and the procedure that had been selected for her. He never wanted her to know.

'Enough of this,' he said quickly. 'How about dinner? Again?'

'If I can choose the restaurant this time.'

'No, at my place.'

He'd buy a new picture before she came. Throw out the memory of men in bowler hats raining depressingly on identical roofs. It was time to find something prettier, more comfortable. 'And I'll do the cooking,' he finished triumphantly.

Karys didn't argue.

Author's Note

For those of you frustrated by the omission of the name of the Magritte painting which had once adorned the wall of Detective Inspector Forrest's sitting room the missing title is *Golconda*.